The
Bridges at
Union Point

The
Bridges at
Union Point

Les Pendleton

Essie Press

Palm Coast Services, Inc. dba **Essie Press**
901 Sawgrass Court, New Bern, NC 28560
www.LesPendleton.com
EMAIL: essiepress@gmail.com

ISBN for Print: 978-0-9754740-6-8
eBook: 978-0-9754740-7-5
First printing
Cover by Damonza
Published in the United States of America
September 2020

This book is dedicated to my family, who have added so much joy and inspiration to my time on the planet.

My Wife
Susanne Harrison Pendleton

Our parents
Howard Leslie Pendleton Sr.
Annie Laurie Moore Pendleton
James Robert "Jim" Harrison, Sr.
Mary Catherine "Kay" Burwell Harrison

A special 'Thank You' to the city of New Bern, North Carolina and its residents. New Bern is a unique place to live and is the inspiration for this novel. Also, there are a number of 'real' individuals in this work who were gracious enough to lend it their names and personas. The willingness to be a part of this tale is another indication of your gracious nature and generous spirits.

ACKNOWLEDGMENTS

Thank you to Jim and Kay Harrison, my in-laws. They lived what they believed and set an example for all who followed. They were married for 64 years and placed their family, marriage and religion above everything else in their lives.

Also
Steve & Elaine Steinbeck
Bobby & Sue Prather
Becky & Tommy Pollard
Alan Gleeson
Rich Cipolla
The Santiago Family

Bill & Roberta Flynn
Buddy Jewell
Phil Hewett
Chuck Hutaff
Ted Clark
Don Knight
Rick McRae

Reverend H. Paul Canady – Christ Episcopal Church

Merchants
Athens Theatre
Morgan's Tavern and Grill
Kim Glenn / The Boathouse
Les Still / WCTI Channel 12
Mitchell Hardware - Family of Greg Smith –
    Lindsay Sims & **Winnie Smith** & Staff / David Bloodgood
Tom McIlhenny / Oriental Marina and Inn
Tom Ballance – Captain Ratty's
Mark Mangum – Galley Stores and Marina
Ed McGovern – Stingray Café

1

1986 – New Bern, North Carolina

HURRICANE CHARLEY MADE landfall on the North Carolina coast. It was a minimal strength storm with winds of only eighty miles per hour when it came ashore. However, it brought significant flooding along coastal areas. Hurricanes were nothing new to New Bern and a category one storm was of little concern to most residents. They removed the umbrellas from their patio furniture, secured the trash cans and that was about it. When the strongest part of the storm began to affect the city, some of the more adventurous kids put on their wading boots and made their way down to the edge of the Neuse River to see how big the waves would get. Jimmy Harrison and his best friend Alan Gleeson had the well-earned reputation of being two of the most daring of the group. Jimmy had an idea.

"Alan, let's walk out on the bridge and check out how big the waves are. I guarantee you it'll be closed to traffic during the storm so we can walk out on it and get a great view of the Trent and the Neuse."

"You know the bridgetender isn't about to let us walk out on the bridge."

"Get real! With zero traffic, you know he'll be sleeping. Look, the crossbars are down across the road. No cars on the span. Trust me, he's asleep. We'll be quiet and won't stay long. No harm, no foul. Follow me."

The two young boys, both thirteen, eased along the paved traffic lanes on the old and rusted turnstile bridge. Occasionally they took a quick look at the bridgetender's small office located near their end of the bridge and saw no one moving about. They continued toward the center of the bridge.

Alan was the first to notice a small rowboat which had broken free from its lines and was being pushed downriver toward them. Once it cleared the structure, it would be on a straight course to the middle of the Neuse River. The river at that point was over a mile wide. If it made its way under the bridge, the little boat wouldn't last long in the whitecaps that covered the river. The forty mile an hour winds were kicking up a severe chop.

"Jimmy, it'll sink if it makes it through the bridge. Let's try and grab it."

"You're crazy, we'll have to crawl down the side of the bridge to even get close to it. What if there's no rope inside? How can we hold on to it?"

"If there's no line, we'll just let it keep moving. We won't touch it."

"I don't know, Alan. I don't think it's very smart to try and do this."

"What? Jim Bob Harrison afraid of a little excitement? That's not the Jim Bob I know."

"My name is Jim, not Jim Bob. I've told you that a thousand times."

"There's no other way to shorten the name James Robert. I'm not calling you James Robert. That's the name of somebody who wins spelling bees."

"You're pushing my buttons, Alan."

"Alright, grab these support girders and let's climb down as far as we can. I think the bottom one is low enough to grab the boat."

The two boys climbed over the metal guard rail on the side of the bridge and started to scale down the rusted steel girders that supported the structure. Large patches of rust broke off as their feet touched the surface of the beams. The entire bridge was ancient and scheduled to be replaced in the next couple of years. It was long overdue.

"Don't cut yourself on this piece of junk. You'll get lock-jaw for sure. Have you had a tetanus shot?"

"Relax, this is nothing compared to climbing the water tower and painting 'Go Bears' on it last year. You haven't suddenly developed a fear of heights, have you?"

"No. I'm just afraid of doing something stupid. If we fall in, they'll never find our bodies. We'll be swept out to sea as fast as this dinghy is moving. Besides, what'll we do with it if we can grab hold of it?"

"One step at a time, Jim Bob. Maritime law gives us salvage rights to it. We just claim it. Then we'd have our own boat. You know that's what we've been trying to figure out for years. How to get a ship of our own."

Jimmy looked down at the water below his friend. The dark water had swift moving swirls on its surface indicating a strong current. Once the river waters cleared the bridge, they became covered with a boiling froth of whitecaps, their tops being blown off by the wind. If it was winter, it could have passed for snow blowing across the water's surface. No one in their right mind would be out on the Neuse right now.

Alan climbed down to the lowest part of the bridge lining himself up with the drifting skiff. Jimmy remained about five feet above him straddling the next lowest girder. The waves directly under them were being stirred up by the wind and even as high above as he was, he was getting soaked. As the small boat approached them, Alan laid down on the beam as flat as he could. He kept one arm tightly wrapped around the hard, steel frame and reached out with his other arm as far down as he was able.

"I think I can reach it. And look! There's a line right on top of the seat. I've got this nailed."

As the small boat passed straight under him, Alan stretched his arm as far toward it as he dared. When the boat's seat came under his outstretched hand, the rope's wet braids touched the tips of his fingers. It was that close. He felt a strong adrenalin rush.

"Careful, Alan. It's not worth falling in. The current is screaming down there. You won't be able to swim to shore. Stop, it's just too dangerous. Please, stop now. We don't need a boat this bad."

Without replying, Alan gave his arm the extra four inches of reach he still needed to grab the rope. That move put his body just on the edge of what his other arm could hold. The rust covered piece of steel he was counting on broke free. His hand came off the rail along with it and he dropped instantly. Jimmy heard a loud crack as Alan's head hit the wooden rail on the side of the boat. His body dropped off the flat-bottomed fishing skiff as it quickly spun around and away from him. He saw no movement from Alan. He was floating on the surface but he knew that wouldn't be for long.

Everything inside of him said 'don't do it, you'll both drown'. He realized there was no chance of Alan making shore almost fifty yards away unless he took action at that moment. Without another thought, he dropped down into the turbulent dark water twenty feet behind the rapidly moving boat. He took a bearing on Alan and started swimming toward him with all the strength he had. With powerful strokes, he was beside him in less than two minutes. His mother always said he was a child of the sea. For him, swimming came as easy as walking.

"Alan, you hear me Alan? Answer me!"

The only reply he could get from his friend was a groan. Even with the waves constantly washing over Alan's head he could see a strong flow of blood pouring from a nasty cut on his forehead. He'd be no help getting to land.

Under normal conditions, the river had little current but the massive amounts of runoff from the storm had increased it tenfold. He knew he couldn't swim against it, especially while hanging on to his friend. He had never tried it before but he'd seen pictures of how someone could swim and tow another person by grabbing them around their neck in the crook of the elbow and then attempting a side stroke. He slid his arm around Alan's neck and started stroking toward the last point of land he saw before the river opened up. Beyond that, the next chance of making shore was on the other side of the river, more than a mile away. He thought making it that far was impossible. He looked back toward the bridge. There were several other young boys trying to walk out on the bridge just as they had done.

"Help! Help us! Guys...can you hear me?"

One of the two boys was distracted by the unfamiliar noise even though it was mostly drowned out by the strong wind. He looked toward the river and couldn't believe what he saw. Jimmy continued to yell. The kid on the bridge raised up both arms and waved to let him know he saw them. He turned to the other boy who was with him.

"What do we do? They'll be out of sight in just a minute."

"I'll knock on the bridgetender's door. He'll know how to handle this."

As Jimmy guessed earlier, the bridge operator was fast asleep in a chair sitting in front of the large window that looked out over the span he was responsible for. Initially, he suspected the strong wind had blown something up against the bridgetender house. With only a door, the observation window and a small desk, it looked more like a tool shed than an office.

He listened again and realized someone was pounding on his door. He was barely awake as he opened the door and saw a young kid wearing a soaking wet sweatshirt and boots.

"What are you doing here? You shouldn't be out in this storm."

"Mister, there's two people in the water over there. They're screaming for help."

"Where? This better not be a prank."

He followed the boy out into the driving rain where his friend was staring intently across the water.

"Where are they?"

The kid pointed at two small dots on the water.

"I see them. How the heck? Alright, I'm calling emergency services. Keep an eye on them. Run down to the point where you can get ahead of them. I'll be right behind you as soon as I make this call."

Jimmy knew they'd been seen but realized he couldn't hang on to Alan much longer and still make it to the point of land he had to reach. The current was moving them offshore far faster than he could swim. The last point of land was now only fifty feet away but the course he was on would just miss it. He poured more strength into each stroke. His arms were burning. He knew only one thing for certain; whether or not he made shore, he was not letting go of Alan.

"Over here, son! Look over here."

Jimmy saw a man standing knee deep in the water off the point. He had no idea it was the bridgetender. Behind him on the shore were the two young boys who spotted them.

"I'm going to toss this rope to you. Try to grab hold. I'll pull you in."

On the first toss, the rope tangled into itself so badly it didn't go more than five feet from his hand. He pulled it back in and with his fingers shaking with nervous energy he straightened out the tangled mess and prepared to make another toss.

"You have to catch this one. It's your last chance."

The rope fell about ten feet short of Jimmy's outstretched hand. He was in desperation mode and began to kick and stroke with the one free arm harder than he'd ever swum before. He felt the rope touch his hand and grasped it as if it were the door to salvation. In fact, it was.

The bridgetender pulled them to shore with Alan still tightly held under his arm. Jimmy was too tired to even stand. He laid on the shore gasping for breath. Alan was moved onto a grassy area where he laid still until an EMS crew arrived. They loaded him into their ambulance and headed to the hospital. Not showing any sort of injury other than complete exhaustion, Jimmy was driven to his home by a city police officer.

Alan recovered quickly after five stitches to his forehead and a night's stay at the hospital. He recalled nothing of the incident after deciding to walk out on the bridge. Once he heard the details of what occurred, he was astounded. When he arrived back at his house, Jimmy was waiting for him.

"Jimmy, man, you saved my life. I mean it. If you hadn't been crazy enough to jump in after me, I was a goner. I mean it, man. There's nothing I can say but thank you. Oh, and did we get the boat? I mean we deserve it, right?"

"Forget the boat. Just promise me that this was the last time I'll have to jump in the water after you. I don't want to ever go through that again."

"You have my word on it."

The events of that day made a profound impact on Jim Harrison and set the course for a life of service and sacrifice.

2

Hurricane Irene – August 26, 2011
Twenty Miles Offshore Cape Hatteras 7:30 P.M.

TED CLARK AND Don Knight were in the cockpit of Don's forty-three-foot ketch, *Last Dance*. They were north-bound for their home port in Annapolis after a winter spent enjoying the Bahamas and Florida Keys. It had been such a great trip that neither of the retired firefighters wanted to return home, even when prudence dictated they should. Most cruisers made it a point to be back up north prior to the start of hurricane season, around the first week in June. It was turning out to be a disastrous oversight.

"You're certain we can outrun this storm? You know Cape Hatteras is the last place on Earth we should be in a blow, especially a hurricane."

"Don't worry, Ted. We're making great time around the Cape. We'll be at the mouth of the Chesapeake by lunch tomorrow and we can put in at Norfolk till this thing blows past. The wind from the storm is actually helping us sail northward. This old girl loves heavy weather."

The ketch was an old but lovingly maintained wooden Dickerson. She was well-found and a capable offshore vessel. Don had owned her for years and been through strong storms with her on many previous trips.

"She's really making tracks. I've seen eleven knots surfing down some of these swells. I'm glad we got away from the Gulfstream though. It would be getting pretty nasty out there about now."

"When she's set up with jib and jigger like this, she can take a lot of wind and stay on her feet. That's what I love about this ketch rig."

Jib and jigger is slang for a sail combination that could be used on a ketch rig when the mainsail wasn't raised. The only sails used were the jib on the bow and the smaller mizzen sail that hung from the smaller mast on the boat's stern. It allowed a boat to sail balanced and yet not be overpowered by too much sail area. The boat was handling the conditions with no problem. At least until the unforeseen occurred.

Ted yelled over the roar of wind and waves.

"What's that loud crack?"

"Oh, God. The upper shroud on the main mast just

parted. I've got to head her into the wind and lower sail or we'll be dismasted."

Don spun the boat's pedestal steering wheel hard over to starboard. *Last Dance* needed to be pointed straight into the wind to reduce all of the strain on the barely supported mast while the sails were being lowered.

"Take the wheel, Ted. I'll lower the mizzen first and then the headsail."

Don moved to the rear mast and started to untie the halyard which held the sail up the mast. Strong wind bursts shook the entire rig as he strained in the driving rain to untie the line and lower the sail. Halfway into the process he felt the entire vessel shudder. He looked forward and watched in horror as the vessel's main mast shook violently several times and then toppled over to the side of the ship's hull. Lying in the water it forced the boat over to its side at such an angle that water began to pour into the cockpit.

"I'm going below and get the cable cutters. I've got to cut away the rig so it's not trapping us on our side. Otherwise, we're just at the mercy of the waves with no steerage. Fire up the engine but don't put it in gear. Don't want to foul the prop with our lines."

Stress and fatigue were beginning to take their toll on both men. Both men were in their seventies and neither had a ton of extra strength to deal with the events that were occurring. Concern was showing on their faces as they tried to deal with life-threatening problems. When Don went back up to the cockpit holding the cutters, the boat took a severe blow from a combination of wind and seas. The domino effect began to expand.

"Don, the wheel is free spinning. There's no rudder response. We've lost steerage."

"That's more than we can deal with. I'll set off the EPIRB and call the Coast Guard."

The EPIRB was a satellite-based alarm that sent out a distress signal containing their exact latitude and longitude to anyone monitoring the proper channel. Don grabbed the VHF radio mic and broadcast a Mayday. That was the highest-level distress message a vessel could broadcast and was used to alert everyone listening that their boat and crew were in a life and death situation.

"Mayday, mayday, mayday. This is sailing vessel *Last Dance*, approximately twenty miles off Cape Hatteras. Northbound and disabled. We've been dismasted and lost steerage. Request emergency assistance immediately."

"*Last Dance, Last Dance.* This is the US Coast Guard, Elizabeth City. We copy you and have picked up your EPIRB signal as well. Does everyone onboard have on a life jacket?"

"Yes, there's two of us and we're in the cockpit. We've lost our rudder and our mast. We're broadside to the waves and they're getting huge. Don't think we can stay afloat much longer. I'm going to activate our life raft in case we have to abandon ship."

"We copy, *Last Dance.* Do you have flares aboard and a handheld VHF?"

"Yes, they're in my ditch bag. Oh, jeez! She's coming apart. Water is pouring in through the coach roof. We're...."

The radio went dead as the battery connection to the radio was lost.

"We've got to abandon ship, Ted. I'm going to inflate the raft and we have to get off. She's going down fast."

Don pulled the compressed air release valve to inflate the life raft which responded in seconds. He threw the small emergency craft over the side of the ketch.

"OK, Ted. Careful. Step into the raft quickly. If it keeps slamming up against *Last Dance*, it'll blow out."

Ted tried to time his move so he could jump into the open door of the inflatable life raft. Just as he attempted the maneuver another wave slapped the stern of *Last Dance* and he fell forward, tangling his leg in the stainless lifeline that ran around the deck of the ketch. The snap of his leg was audible. He screamed in pain as he fell forward into the raft.

"It's broke, I've broken my leg. Can't help you. God, it's killing me. Hurry."

Don made the same leap into the rubber raft but without incident.

"I'm aboard. I'm cutting us free. *Last Dance* is filling up fast."

Don took out his pocketknife and severed the line connecting the two vessels.

"We're free but it kills me to see the old girl go down like this. She was strong for fifty years. I should have checked the rig more often. My fault. There she goes. She's going under."

It took only seconds for the beautiful old ketch to slip beneath the surface of the waves. The two men were now adrift in a rubber life raft, twenty miles off one of the most dangerous coastlines in the world with a hurricane moving like a runaway stallion in their direction.

9 P.M. United States Coast Guard Station Elizabeth City, North Carolina

The motto of the United States Coast Guard Rescue Swimmers, SO OTHERS MAY LIVE, was never tested so thoroughly than the night Hurricane Irene hit the coast of North Carolina. With a strong hurricane bearing down, the station was in a state of high alert. The storm had winds in excess of a hundred miles per hour and was beginning to lash the coastal counties with a fury. Hurricane warnings had been issued by the National Hurricane Center. This was not a storm to take lightly. The eye was predicted to pass over Cape Lookout, directly in the center of the state's coastline and located just south of the notorious waters of Cape Hatteras. Conditions were already deteriorating even though a landfall would not occur until shortly after sunrise. Every Guardsman at the station understood clearly that they'd soon be operating in the center of the storm track. Hurricanes brought horrific flooding to the low-lying coastal counties of North Carolina and there would be numerous calls for help from those who didn't heed the warnings to evacuate. There were always a few who thought they could ride it out in their homes or beach cottages up on pilings. They quickly came to the realization that wooden frames and shingles were no match for the forces of an angry mother nature.

The ready room was full of men and women who prepared their entire career for events like this. They were filling up on caffeine from the huge stainless coffee pot on the ocean blue laminate counter. Most were in their late twenties and exceptionally fit. There was little relaxation at the station. The Coast Guard maintained its own vessels and aircraft so if they weren't being used, the staff would be hard at work making sure they were ready to go when the time came.

Jim Harrison, (Petty Officer 1st class) and his friend William Flynn (Petty Officer 2nd class) were dressed in their utility uniforms waiting to get orders to head out on any type of rescue. Jim was known as Jimmy to his friends and Jim Bob to Bill. The nickname continued to follow him no matter how much he protested. He was one of just two highly-skilled rescue swimmers stationed at Elizabeth City. He could be called on at any time to board one of two H-60 rescue helicopters and head out to sea in horrendous conditions where he'd be lowered into a violent ocean to pluck otherwise doomed sailors to safety. It was an occupation he lived for though it carried with it a high degree of difficulty and life-threatening risks.

Jimmy was a lean six-footer with a thick crop of sandy hair, a great smile and an easy-going disposition. His physique and high energy level made him seem much younger than his thirty-eight years. He was one of the most senior rescue swimmers in the Coast Guard. He realized that before long he would be too old to continue and would either have to be reassigned to a shoreside career or call twenty years enough and look for work back home. Bill and Jimmy were discussing the storm and what it might require of them.

Bill was only twenty-nine years old, at peak physical condition and the constant jokester at the station. His hair was red and his complexion ruddy with freckles.

"This is going to be a long night, Jim Bob. I'm already getting an adrenaline rush and we don't even have the first assignment yet."

"It's coming, trust me. And don't call me Jim Bob. I don't want to get that crap started here. It's Jimmy, Jim or James. Jim Bob is something you'd hear out of Andy Taylor of Mayberry."

"That's where you're from, isn't it?"

"New Bern is nothing like Mayberry. It's a sophisticated little town."

"I've been there, but it never struck me as sophisticated. Neither do you."

"That's because you wouldn't know sophisticated if it tapped you on your shoulder."

"And, you're always calling me Wild Bill. How is that any different?"

"Wild Bill has a kind of a flair to it. Jim Bob is like calling me Bubba or even worse, Junior. So, I'm just saying don't do it. That's my last word on the subject. Don't forget I am your superior officer so consider it a direct order!"

"Yes, Sir. Jim Bob. I got it"

Their sparring was interrupted by a call on the station's loudspeaker mounted in the corner of the ready room.

"HH60 Unit Two report to ready room."

Wild Bill and Jimmy both jumped to their feet. Bill patted Jimmy on the back.

"Well, Jim Bob. That sure didn't take long, now did it? Storm's still eight hours out and our phone is already ringing."

"This is what we came for, ain't it? Let's go earn our pay."

They half ran to the ready room where two other crew members were already sitting at a small table with the station's commanding officer waiting on the full crew.

"We had a Mayday about four minutes ago. A forty-three-foot ketch is taking on water twenty-two miles off Hatteras. That's getting close to the shoals so time is of the essence. Skipper said they lost the rudder and both masts when his rig gave way. Life raft is already deployed over the side and they'll be hitting it when the vessel starts to go under. NOAA says it's already Force 10 that far out. Everything's getting worse by the minute and it's probably going to be a Force 11 by the time you get to them. Their ship's radio died with their batteries. They'll be on a hand-held

VHF when you get over them. We've got their last position. When they see or hear you, they'll light off flares. Let's go get 'em. This one is about as bad as it gets so use every caution. Harrison, if it's too bad out there, don't kill yourself. It's your call whether you go in after them. I don't want to be writing any letters about you to your family. Dismissed."

Bill, Jimmy and the other two crew members grabbed their gear and jogged out into the pouring rain where their HH60 Jayhawk helicopter was waiting. The wind was blowing a steady forty knots. The rain felt like sand as it hit their faces. Without the engine running, the chopper's rotors were moving up down being pounded by the wind. The pilot, Chuck Hutaff, started getting checklist responses from co-pilot Buddy Jewell. Both were more experienced in bad weather flight than most senior pilots at major airlines. They didn't get to fly around storms. More often than not, they headed straight into the worst of them. With urgency and great precision, they went through all the pre-flight details. Nothing could be overlooked when you knew you were heading into a maelstrom twenty miles out over open ocean with no chance to be rescued if you went down. They were the court of last resort.

The entire crew was connected with helmets that contained the speakers and mics they required to communicate with each other. Chuck asked them if they were in place for takeoff.

"Checklist complete, engine temp is go. How 'bout you guys back there?"

Jimmy looked over the cable spools hanging by the chopper door.

"As good as it's going to be. Let's do this thing. Folks are waiting on us"

Chuck engaged the controls into liftoff position.

"Clear, we have rotation. This is going to be one hell of a ride. Hang on to something, fellas."

Bill had a strained grin on his face as he replied.

"You must be the worst pilot in the world. I don't think I've ever been up with you when the whole durn chopper wasn't bouncing like a ride at the county fair."

"Well, guess what? Get your ticket punched because you're about to ride the world's biggest Tilt-A-Whirl."

"We expect nothing less, Chuck. Try to scare us."

"Count on it."

Jimmy carefully examined the cables and pulleys he'd be trusting his life to in short order. No detail was too small to be overlooked. Bill shared his thoughts out loud to the crew.

"I'm a little nervous about this one. We normally go out after a storm and pick up the pieces and anybody left floating. This time the storm is almost on us and we're flying straight into it. What's wrong with us? Are we insane?"

Jimmy nonchalantly answered.

"Probably."

Even with helmets covering their ears and speakers inside located directly in front of them, it was still difficult to hear. There was tremendous external noise with rotors screaming and the raging wind pounding on the chopper's fuselage as they headed out into a turbulent dark sky. Their high intensity spotlights were illuminating otherwise black clouds that were charging onto the coast. They weren't running away from the hurricane; they were heading dead into the teeth of it.

Chuck was in constant communication with the control tower at the station. They gave him the exact latitude and longitude of the distressed sailboat's last communication. They would have to get there quickly or the wind and seas would carry the sailors' life raft so far away from their last position that it would be impossible to find them in conditions this severe. Winds were now approaching hurricane force and the occasional glimpse below through the clouds revealed waves the entire crew knew would exceed forty feet. The control tower called them with yet even more news they did not want to hear.

"HH60 Unit Two, doppler out of Newport shows rotation in your area. There are two distinct centers, both within a couple miles of your projected course. Can you see them on your onboard radar?"

"Base Flight Control, yes. They look pretty dramatic on the screen. I'm going to veer off about thirty degrees south until we're clear."

Chuck then relayed the Flight Control tower's weather alert to the crew.

"We're going to have to take a turn to starboard to avoid a couple of good-sized waterspouts just ahead. Can't afford to take any chances of getting too close to either of them.

Not a problem but it will cost us a few minutes we don't really have to spare."

The rain had gotten intense with visibility down to almost zero. The wind on the chopper's fuselage was hitting like a wrecking ball being swung into its sides. It was all Chuck could do to maintain course. They needed every minute possible to perform a rescue this far out. Their window was being reduced with every intensification of the storm. Though it went by quickly, the twenty-mile flight would have been terrifying to an inexperienced flyer. It was as if they were on a passenger plane in the worst turbulence imaginable. It was astounding that the chopper could remain flying enduring this severe battering. Chuck announced to the crew.

"We're over the last reported position. As expected, there's nothing. Winds out of the northeast so we'll head southwest and see how far they've drifted in this wind. It's been an hour since they took to the raft so I'm thinking they could be five miles or more. Keep an eye out for a flare."

The skilled pilot turned the chopper out of the wind to run before it as the life raft would have done. The stick jerked in his hand as he attempted to keep the chopper level and headed in the downwind direction. The whole plane was much like a boat in a violent storm, but the waves it was pounding through consisted of nothing but air. Nonetheless, they carried the same sort of power and violence as the ocean.

"Got to be around here somewhere. Anybody see

anything? We've only got thirty minutes left before we have to terminate."

Bill was the first to see the flare.

"Three o'clock to starboard. Definitely a flare. Maybe a quarter of a click. Barely cleared the waves. They're mammoth."

The pilot brought the chopper around and headed in the direction of the reported flare. Jimmy strained to get a visual on the life raft in the black sea through a driving rain. The high-intensity spots offered only brief glimpses of the water.

He finally located a tiny orange dot floating precariously on the surface of the ocean. The door of the raft's overhead canopy was partially open with an arm sticking out holding a white towel, waving for all it was worth. Jimmy was the one going down after the two sailors so he directed the pilot to where he felt was the best position to make good his descent.

"I got a bead on him. Head back upwind so I can swim down to them. Seas are huge, I gotta make it to them on the first pass. That's it, hold us right here if you can. I'll time my jump. Bill, I'll give you the word and you let down the hook to me."

"You got it, Jim Bob. Don't make me come down there after you."

"I think you've got a lot on your plate right now, Wild Bill. We can discuss this later."

"Count on it."

Argumentative banter was the common ploy the crew used to try and lighten an otherwise horrendous moment. Chuck timed the helicopter's elevation in relation to the huge seas below. Too high up and Jimmy's plunge would be disastrous. Too low and they'd all be in the water. He had to hit the crest of a wave as it passed under the chopper to shorten his fall.

"Almost, skipper. Keep the spot on the raft. Five, four, three, two…I'm in."

In a display of pure nerve and willpower, Jimmy plummeted into the water and started swimming with powerful strokes toward the raft. A massive wave lifted him thirty feet above the raft which was less than forty feet downwind from him. He continued kicking his oversized flippers until he came up to the side of the raft and grabbed a rubber handle built into the floating tubes.

"Anybody home in there?"

The zipper holding the canopy shut opened again and the harrowed face of a scared and exhausted sailor lit up as he saw that help had arrived.

"Thank God! Thank God! You're the answer to our prayers. We've been praying straight away for the past two hours. Can't believe you came out in this to get us."

"No time for praise right now. You got a life jacket on?"

"Yes, you want us to come out now?"

"In a second. How's your partner?"

"He needs to go first. I think his leg is broken."

"Nothing we can do about that now. Let's get him outside here with me."

The raft was jerking violently from side to side with each wave and Jimmy had to tighten his grip to stay with it. He relayed the injury to Chuck who had his hands full trying to keep the chopper in position overhead.

"Skipper, we've got a broken leg down here. I'll put him in the sling first. Bill, be careful getting him aboard. No way to lower a cage down here. I'll get him in the sling and he's going to have to just grin and bear it till we can start moving."

"Roger, speed this up as much as you can. The wind has picked up ten knots since we got here. It's getting real dicey up here, too."

Jimmy turned back to the open slit on the raft's canopy. The first sailor was helping to get his injured partner out of the doorway. He was in tremendous pain and not holding back on the gasps and screams as he got into the sling. Trying to not move the injured limb was an almost impossible task in the middle of the violent swirling seas and torrential rain. Jimmy tucked the last leg in the sling.

"What's your name?"

"Ted, Ted Clark."

"OK, Ted. Hang in there just a little longer and we'll have you aboard the chopper and on the way home."

"I'm trying. Swear to God. I'm trying. If you get me home safe, I'll never get on a boat again."

"Don't worry, if you don't get home, it means I don't either, so trust me. You're getting home. Ok, skipper, number one is in the sling. Get him up. Bill, he's really going to swing in this wind. Do what you can to not touch his right leg when you pull him in. He's really hurting right now."

"Gotcha, Jim Bob. On the way up. Five, four, three, two…at the door."

Bill reached out and grabbed the cable to stop the sling from turning and as smoothly as he could under the circumstances, pulled the sailor aboard the chopper. Again, as carefully and swiftly as possible, he removed the sling and pushed it out the chopper door. With each statement from Jimmy back to the chopper, he reinforced his words with predetermined hand signals. If voice communication was lost, they could still coordinate their actions.

"Sling is headed back to you."

Jimmy was still holding onto the rubber handle but finally had to let it go for just a second to grab the sling. A huge breaking wave poured down on him and the raft turning it upside down. He heard the remaining sailor screaming for him.

"I'm coming. I won't leave you. Get outside the raft if you can."

The raft was floating upside down and the slit was now under water. Jimmy let go of the sling and dove down under the raft. With only touch, he worked around the raft until he felt the opening and pulled himself half inside. He saw the man gyrating furiously with both hands and bubbles of oxygen pouring out of his mouth and nostrils. He lunged for him and grabbed the strap on his half-dislodged life jacket. With every ounce of strength, he jerked the man through the slit and into the ocean alongside him. He wasn't responding to his commands and Jimmy knew if he let him go for even a second, he'd never be able to grab him again. He took the lifeless body under the chin and started stroking toward the end of the sling now twenty feet away and swinging wildly. On the third pass of the metal hook, he grabbed out with his free hand and snagged it. He held the hard, undulating sling in one hand and a lifeless body in the other. With all the strength in his now spent body, he pulled both arms together. He quickly ran the cable on the sling around the chest of the sailor and gave Bill the command to hoist him up.

"No help from this one Bill. I don't think he's done for, just out of it. Get the sling back here quick. I don't have much left."

"I'm on it. You hang on, Jim Bob. This is gonna be quick."

With well-timed and precise maneuvering, Bill got the unconscious victim into the chopper alongside his friend who, in spite of his damaged leg, pulled him close and held him by the arm. Bill removed the sling and hurriedly swung it back outside the chopper door and lowered it to Jimmy. He shined the spotlight so Jimmy could see it on the way down. When it got close, Jimmy dove toward it, took hold and clipped it on to his harness. Totally spent, he let Bill hoist him back up and into the chopper. He reached out and pulled his totally drained buddy into the fuselage.

"Ok, skipper. We're good back here. Let's get the Hell out of Dodge!"

"Good job, you guys. We'll be home in twenty minutes. Hold on to our passengers. It's gonna be like riding a bucking bronco on the way in."

As the chopper approached the tarmac at the station, they saw an ambulance on the edge of the asphalt waiting to transport the two rescued sailors to a nearby hospital for treatment. Station Commander Phil Hewett greeted them.

"Tremendous job, guys. Let's hope that's the worst one in this hurricane. You need to go get a few hours' sleep. Irene is getting closer all the time. Unit One is already out picking up the first group of idiots who thought they could ride it out. The eye is going to come ashore around Cape Lookout about seven a.m.. I'm sure we'll have our hands full. You're going to be needed. So, get a little shut-eye. We'll handle it without you as long as we can but that's more than likely going to be only a few hours. Again, a great mission, guys."

Over the next twenty-four hours the crew of the HH60 would stay in the air almost continuously stopping only long enough to refuel and stuff a sandwich down their throats. When the storm departed, they had flown fourteen missions and pulled over thirty individuals from the flood swollen towns Irene had passed over.

❧

September 15, 2011 – USCG Elizabeth City

Becky Pollard, first female Republican Governor of North Carolina and a New Bern resident, was in the station's large hangar standing next to Base Commander Hewett and a few other dignitaries. She was there to thank the station and staff for their help during and after Hurricane Irene. Jim Harrison was to be the recipient of the United States Coast Guard's Gold Lifesaving medal. The medal was presented by the Coast Guard Commandant and was reserved for only the most daring and heroic actions of just a few among a group of men and women who routinely risked their lives to save others. The citation detailing his actions was read aloud and then the medal was pinned to his chest.

Governor Pollard took the podium.

"What a tremendous group you are. I can't tell you how grateful our State is for your incredible service during a dangerous storm. We're not only in awe of what you consider 'all in a day's work' but we're so thankful this station is on our coast. We are truly blessed to have you in our state. I'm particularly proud of Petty Officer 1st Class James Harrison. I've known Petty Officer Harrison for a long time. We even go to the same church in New Bern where he is known as Jimmy. So Petty Officer Harrison, well done. You make us proud."

The ceremony was brief. Within the hour, the station was back to business as usual. Jimmy, Bill and crew were going over their HH60 making sure every detail had been examined to assure it would be in perfect condition when the next mission required their attention. A young guardsman came to the hangar door and yelled out.

"Harrison, phone call in the break room."

"Thanks, I'll be right there."

Jimmy wiped the grease from his hands with a red shop towel and headed out to take the call. He had a good idea who it was and thought it might be bad news about his mother. Fortunately, it was not the call he thought it might be.

"Hey, Jimmy. It's Mom. How are you son? The night nurse told me that you were a hero and saved a bunch of people out in the ocean."

"Not a bunch of people, only a couple of guys from a sailboat. Just doing what they pay me for. I'm a lot more concerned about you than anything going on around here. How're you doing?"

"I'd like to say I was OK, son. But I'd just be lying. Can't seem to catch a deep breath anymore. I don't think I can keep going much longer, son. I really want to see you. Could you come visit with me soon? I think it needs to be real soon. I hate to be a burden, but I need to see you before…before, well…you know."

"Today is Thursday, Mom. I'll leave right after work and see you tomorrow evening. You stay strong, Mom. I love you and I'll see you shortly."

"Thanks, son. You made my day. Love you too."

After the call, Jimmy sat in the folding metal chair in

the break room and thought about what was happening. He knew his mother, Margaret, was nearing the end. She'd been sick and in Lakeview Nursing Home for the past two years. It always broke his heart that he couldn't be there with her more, but it just wasn't possible to leave work that often. With only two rescue swimmers at the station, he was indispensable to the operations there. He would see her tomorrow though, no matter what else happened.

3

New Bern, North Carolina – Late Afternoon

JIMMY LOOKED OUT over the Neuse River as he drove across the bridge spanning the large body of water. Truth be known, it was the Neuse and countless days he'd spent on her as a young man, sailing, swimming, fishing and just hanging out with friends that steered him to the Coast Guard. The incident with his friend, Alan, made the path even clearer. His love of the sea was born there and had only grown stronger as he got older. It was in his blood. He always said he couldn't breathe when he got over ten miles from the coast. Even though he didn't get much time to use it anymore, he kept his old thirty-foot Tartan sloop, *Sugarcane*, at Edgewater Marina on the Trent River. The Trent ran into the Neuse at Union Point, a prominent landmark and park in downtown New Bern. The Trent was more protected and he felt comfortable that his boat was being looked out for even when he wasn't able to do it himself.

As he arrived at the top of the high-rise bridge, he looked over at his hometown. The steeples and spirals shot up over the skyline and the old town hall clock was beautiful as the light from its illuminated face bounced off the roofs and windows of the surrounding buildings. From the water it was particularly beautiful, reminding him of a smaller version of Charleston or Annapolis. The waters of the Neuse and Trent would be full of sails on any nice day and, even though the town was forty miles from the ocean, it offered down river passage to anywhere in the world that wind and waves could take you. There were hundreds of homes in the historical district dating back to early colonial days when New Bern was the capital of North Carolina. Over the last twenty years, the town's fathers had come to realize the value and marketability of a city that dated back over three hundred years. The town now emphasized its history and was attracting large numbers of tourists from all over the world to see what Jimmy already knew. It was one of the most beautiful and unique historical towns in the entire country.

The historical business district, with its dozens of restaurants, shops, and watering holes was brimming with tourists that evening. The narrow streets offered only a few remaining parking spaces and Jimmy knew he would be back later that night after spending time with his mother.

He headed out onto Neuse Boulevard about four miles until he arrived at the shaded grounds of Lakeview Nursing

Home. He thought it was a well-run facility and the employees took excellent care of his mother. She thought of them more as friends than staff. They all called her Miss Margaret and most took the time to chat with her beyond what their duties required. Jimmy had to own up to a lot of guilt that she had spent so much time alone there the past several years as he was her only remaining family. His dad passed away almost ten years earlier and there just wasn't anyone else who was close enough to call family who could check in on her. She never fussed about how things were and always lit up like a Christmas tree every time he walked into her tiny room. This night was no exception.

"Jimmy! You made it, son. I'm so happy you're here. Come over here and give your mama a hug."

He walked over to her bedside, sat down on the edge beside her and bent over to give the fragile woman a warm embrace. He knew there would not be a lot more hugs between them, so he stayed wrapped in her arms until she had to release him for lack of strength to hold on any longer. He could see how weak she was and how shallow her breathing had become. Even her voice was less than half the joyous and happy instrument it had been for so many years. She was only in her early seventies but diabetes and kidney failure set her on a downward slide that she was never able to stop. Jimmy was her only child. For years, she didn't think she'd be able to have children even though it was her fondest desire. When she finally became pregnant, she was in her thirties. Her entire world became a much brighter place.

He'd been the light of her life. Even though she was nearing her final days, he made hers a life she thought well worth living. Jimmy continued to sit beside her on the bed and tenderly held her small weatherworn hand.

"How are you doing, Mom?"

"I think I'll be seeing my sister Doris soon. That'll be good. I miss a lot of my family and especially your Dad."

"I'm sure you will. I have to tell you that you and Dad were the best parents anyone could ever ask for. You were not only supportive and loving, you were always a good example of how I should try to live. I'm afraid I've not been nearly as good a person as you both were."

"Don't even try to tell me that. You risk your life every day for people who would most certainly die if you weren't willing to jump in the ocean after them. These are people you don't even know. I couldn't make myself do that. I don't know many who could."

"I'm not saving somebody every day, Mom. Just now and again."

"But, you're ready to do it and that's the same thing."

"Now, let's talk about more pleasant things."

"Such as?"

"You pick the subject, Mom. I'm interested in what you're thinking about."

"For one thing, I'd like to know what's going on between you and Kay? You haven't been talking about her hardly at all. You know she's the one you're supposed to be with. When are you going to ask her to marry you? You don't want to wait until you're in an old folks' home like me. You're missing out on some of the best years of your lives. You should be having kids of your own and building a life together."

"That all sounds wonderful, Mom, but life just isn't that simple. Kay has been away in law school and you know what a gypsy I've been with the Coast Guard. It hasn't been possible to spend much time together. It's not like it was when you and Dad were dating. I think Dad only held two jobs in his entire life and you taught at the same school for thirty years. It was a simpler time."

"It only sounds simpler because you weren't around then. It was all a blur of bills, feeding you and your father, Korea, Vietnam, the assassination of President Kennedy and his brother, Bobby. There were race riots everywhere and just all kinds of things. Life is full of struggles no matter the time. Finding someone to love you and build a life with you is the best part of it all."

"I know there's a lot to what you're saying, Mom. Let me give it some thought."

Margaret started a coughing spell that continued for almost a full minute. A nurse in the hallway heard her and came into the room to see if she could help.

"Here, Margaret. Let's get you some water. It's time for your pills anyway. You must be her son, Jim."

He stepped back to give the nurse room to help his mother.

"I am."

"She talks about you all the time. She thinks you're pretty special. She tells me you're in the Coast Guard."

"That's right."

"What do you do? Are you a boat captain or something like that?"

"I'm a rescue swimmer."

"Oh, my word! You're one of those people who jumps out of helicopters during storms and saves people?"

"Occasionally. It's something we're trained to do. Thankfully, that doesn't happen a lot."

"Just the same. I can see why your mother's so proud." Margaret stopped coughing long enough to say.

"He is a hero. My boy's never been afraid of anything." He was embarrassed by his mother's proclamation.

"It's really just my job." The nurse understood Margaret's praise.

"Just the same. I know where your mother's coming from. She should be proud of the young man she brought into this world."

"I am."

Margaret started to cough some more. The nurse took her temperature. She checked her pulse while he watched.

"I think your mother's ready for a nap. She knew you were coming, so I don't think she slept much last night and certainly not a wink this morning. Let me clear this tray off her bed stand and I'll walk out with you."

Jimmy and the floor nurse left Margaret's room and stopped a short way down the hall.

"Mr. Harrison, I don't know how up to date you are on your mother's condition, but I have to tell you that she can't last much longer."

"I can see she's really gotten weaker. What's her main problem?"

"Dialysis is no longer taking enough fluid from her. It already puts so much of a strain on her body to go through it every other day, the doctor says it's close to the time to stop the process. That would mean she's probably down to the last several weeks at the most. I'm sorry."

"I'm stationed in Elizabeth City. I can be here in about three hours. Promise you'll call me if she starts to go downhill any sooner. I'll be back next weekend for certain and when the end is near, I'll take off no matter what time it is and head back here to be with her."

"You can count on that. Don't worry. I'll be checking on her several times every day myself so I'll see if she starts to get much worse. I'll call you right away."

"Thank you so much. I appreciate you looking out for my mother."

"I'm glad to do it."

⤴

Later that evening – Morgan's Tavern and Grill

Morgan's Tavern had been a favorite in New Bern for years. Patrons were a combination of locals and tourists who came in large numbers to explore the restored historical district of North Carolina's second oldest city and its first State Capital. Morgan's was a popular restaurant. Tucked into the back corner was a small bar with a quaint atmosphere where people became a collection of friendly and interesting conversationalists. Jimmy grabbed a stool. The bartender, Russ, knew almost everyone in town. He was about Jimmy's age and considered working at the popular restaurant a full-time career. He enjoyed talking with the regulars and tourists alike.

"Hey Jimmy. How are things in Elizabeth City?"

"It's a nice place, Russ. It's just not home. Hard to beat New Bern."

"I'm with you there. I don't know whether it's just because I grew up here and have lots of friends or maybe I'm just too lazy to head out into the great unknown."

"I've seen a lot of the rest of the country. There's not many places that offer what we already have here. Don't feel like you're missing anything. You're not. How are the Bears doing?"

"On their way to another State Championship. Haven't lost a game all season. I think they're as strong as they were back when you were on the team. I'll never forget that game against Havelock when you caught that pass out to the sidelines and carried it down the field for a TD. If I remember right, it was the go ahead score, wasn't it?"

"Yeah, but don't forget they came back with a minute to go and scored. We wound up losing with only fifteen seconds left. Tough loss. But I still remember the great guys on the team. Those were really good times."

"You heard about Benny?"

"No. What about him?"

"Died. Got in a wreck about two weeks ago. Cops said it was instant. I really thought the world of Benny. Left Ginger and two little kids. Makes you think though. Life can turn on a dime."

"Tell me about it. I always liked him. That's tragic."

Several hours passed while Jimmy and Russ chatted about days gone by and where mutual friends wound up. Jimmy wasn't much of a drinker though he enjoyed a couple of cold beers from time to time. He preferred the darker craft beers. He'd just sip on them and try to imagine where all the tourists in town were from by listening to snippets of their conversations. The New York accents were always the easiest to figure out.

He was looking back toward the main dining room when he was startled to see Kay sitting in a small room with some polished looking guy wearing a sport coat and turtle-neck sweater. Since the first time he saw her, she'd been the love of his life. Instinctively, he didn't like the guy she was with. The guy was looking at the woman Jimmy had fanta-sized about since grade school with a hunger in his eyes that made him instantly detestable. Not wanting to be caught staring, he turned back toward Russ.

"One last beer and I'm outta here, Russ."

"The same?"

"Yep. Don't want to switch this late in the evening. Let me ask you a question."

"Ask away."

"Over there in the small dining area, who's that sitting with Kay Burwell?"

"I didn't see her. She was your old main squeeze, wasn't she?"

"Sort of."

"I don't know his name but I've seen him in here quite a bit at lunch. He's a lawyer. He always comes in with a bunch of them and they have a two-cocktail lunch. Wears a Rolex and likes to flash the cash paying for the other guys a lot. Don't like him myself."

"Why's that?"

"For starters, he's hot for Kay. She's too good for somebody like him. He's too polished and you almost see a flash of light from his teeth when he smiles. You know the kind."

"That's a shame. She deserves better."

The conversation continued. Every so often Jimmy would turn and take a quick glance toward Kay. Then, he looked over and noticed they were getting up. He took one last look and turned back to the bar.

"I guess I'll settle up now, Russ."

"You going home tonight? That's a long ride to Elizabeth City."

"No. Figure I'll go to church in the morning, see a couple more friends and leave after lunch. I want to drop by Lakeview and see Mom one last time before I head out."

"How is she?"

"Down to probably several weeks or so. She's fought this kidney thing for quite a few years but she's about to give out. I'll come back next weekend to see her again unless they call me sooner and say I need to get back here."

Jimmy was startled by a hand on his shoulder. He turned around to see Kay and the guy she had been sitting with standing behind him. Kay smiled as she spoke.

"I thought I saw you over here. How are you, Jimmy?"

"Good, good. You look well, good too. Great, actually."

The guy with her stuck out his hand.

"Morrison Brooks. Great to meet you, Dennis."

"Jimmy, Jimmy Harrison."

Not really wanting to, but forcing himself to be polite, Jimmy shook his hand.

"Oh, great to meet you Jimmy. How do you know Kay?"

"We were friends back in high school. Haven't seen her in a long time."

Kay smiled.

"Jimmy was my first boyfriend. I thought he was overseas with the Coast Guard."

"I'm stationed right here in Elizabeth City."

The attorney was not impressed.

"A Coastie, eh? Good to know there's some strapping young guys like you out there to come get us when we run out of gas in our sportfisherman. Good for you."

Jimmy didn't reply. Kay could see that Morrison had just given Jimmy a putdown to display his own superiority.

"Great meeting you, Jimmy. I've got to get this beautiful young lady home. Big day at the office tomorrow. What do you say, Kay? The Mercedes waits outside."

Jimmy knew a lot of guys like this one. He couldn't just say they needed to get in the car. He had to let everyone within earshot know he had a Mercedes. He put his arm around Kay's shoulder as they walked away. As they stood at the register for Brooks to pay their bill, Jimmy took one last look toward Kay just in time to see her make the 'phone me' gesture and silently mouth the words "call me" to him. He smiled at her and nodded.

Jimmy drove home through the now empty streets. New Bern, with the exception of the restaurants and bars, shut down every evening by six p.m. The small clapboard home he was raised in had been purchased in the seventies by his parents and they never thought about leaving it for something larger or more modern. To them, as it was with Jimmy, it was home and always would be. He realized that when his mother passed away, he would probably have to sell it to pay off her medical bills.

The bar in the kitchen had bills from clinics and the hospital sitting in a shoebox, full to overflowing. She'd lived off a small pension and a meager Social Security check for the past twelve years. There was no money for anything other than the basics. Jimmy was grateful that Paul Canady, Rector at Christ Episcopal Church, and few other old friends had gotten the powers that be at the hospital and then at Lakeview to get Margaret signed up for every kind of assistance she could qualify for. Even though she received the treatments she needed to stay alive, a great many things didn't get paid. Jimmy just hoped the sale of the family home would be enough to satisfy the bulk of the debt. He figured he would know fairly soon how things stood. Working in the Coast Guard meant he was in no position to help her financially. He laid down on the bed, the same one he'd slept in for all the years he lived at home.

Jimmy started thinking about Kay and the great times they'd shared. He could remember every detail of the first time he saw Kay. They were both around twelve years old and were spending a warm summer afternoon outside with a group of kids from the neighborhood. The boys were tossing around a football. The girls were playing under a dogwood tree that was in full bloom, covered with a white crown of flowers it shed it each time a light breeze passed through its branches. Kay was wearing a yellow summer dress with puffed out lace fringed shoulders that highlighted the thick, dark hair that hung down the middle of her back. She held onto the tree trunk and skipped around it like a Maypole, her hair extending out away from her head as she made tight turns around the tree. He instantly thought she was the most beautiful thing he had ever seen. If it was possible to happen this young, it was love at first sight. He stared at her until she finished dancing around the tree and sheepishly walked over to her. She had no idea how much courage it took for him to go over to her and ask her name. Her face was even more beautiful up close than he thought it would be while watching her twirl.

"Hi, I'm Jimmy Harrison. I live just down the street. Last house on the left. Do you live around here?"

"My family just moved here. We're in that house over there with the green shingles and the big front porch. My room is right up top on the right. That's my window with white curtains. I'm Kay. Kay Burwell and we moved here from Texas."

"Wow, Texas! Is your Dad a cowboy?"

"Not hardly. He's a lawyer. I'm gonna be one too."

"You already know what you want to do for a job?"

"Yep, my dad says I'll be a great one. So, that's what I'm going to be."

Jimmy was smitten. He wanted to stay and talk with her all afternoon, but the beautiful young girl's mother called her to come home before he even got started. He would be on the lookout for her from that day on. And, here it was many years later and she was still the only woman on his mind. He couldn't deny he was excited by her asking him to call. That would be the first thing on his mind when he woke up the next morning.

∽

Sunday Morning – Christ Church

Jimmy had just attended services at the church he grew up in. Christ Church had been a centerpiece of life in New Bern for over three centuries. On his Southern Tour in 1791, President George Washington attended services there. Over the years, countless dignitaries and persons of note had visited the historic old chapel which had been rebuilt over the years. It sat in the midst of a grove of trees draped in Spanish moss. The lawn outside was filled with ancient gravestones that included names of the city's most distinguished citizens dating back to the town's founding. Its steeple rang out with chimes throughout the day letting everyone for many blocks know the hour. It added a charm to the town no longer found in most cities. He was about the same age as Jimmy and the two had been friends since Paul moved to the area following the directions of his employer, the Episcopalian diocese. The always friendly priest stood at the door to the chapel after services shaking hands and chatting with each person who attended the service that morning.

Jimmy looked over the group of mostly familiar faces. The line slowed as a young woman in a wheelchair was pushed toward the huge wooden door. It was apparent that she suffered from a debilitating physical condition. She was unable to sit upright in the chair and leaned toward one side. She raised her trembling arm up as best she could to shake hands with Paul. Smiling as he saw her, he bent over, taking her hand in his and gently placing his other hand to the side of her face.

"Good morning, young lady. I'm so glad you could come to service this morning. And don't you look beautiful in your Carolina Blue dress. It's always wonderful to see you."

Paul placed her hand back down on the side of the wheelchair and her escort carefully pushed her down the small ramp leading from the church. Jimmy moved toward the door. The priest again lit up with a huge smile as Jimmy walked over to him, hand outstretched.

"Jimmy, it's good to see you here. How is your Mother doing? I was out there last week and she didn't appear to be doing well at all."

"The end is near, Paul. I know she would want you to go by and see her. It probably needs to be real soon."

"I'm sorry. That bad, heh?"

"Yeah. She hasn't got much time left."

Noticing a line building up behind Jimmy, the priest had to let him go on though he would have liked to talk with him longer.

"I'll definitely go by and see her tomorrow. I promise."

"Thanks. That would be great."

Jimmy walked to his car and retrieved his cell phone from the glove box where he placed it during church. He had to admit he was excited just thinking about speaking with Kay. She answered the call on the second ring.

"Hello, this is Kay."

"Hey there. It's me, Jimmy."

"I'd know your voice anywhere. It's so great to hear from you. I felt like I'd never see you again. I thought the Coast Guard sent you somewhere like Alaska or Australia or God knows where."

"I'm stationed just a few hours from here, in Elizabeth City. I came home to check on my Mom. She's over at Lakeview Nursing Home."

"How is she?"

"Not well. I don't think she'll last another month."

"I'm so sorry. If there's anything I can do, I hope you'll call. Actually, I'm glad you called me now. We should get together and catch up. How about we go somewhere and grab a sandwich this afternoon? Do you have the time?"

"I'm going to go see Mom for about an hour and then I could meet you over at the Country Biscuit. Would that work for you? Around two?"

"It's such a beautiful day. Why not meet over at Union Point Park and then walk over to the diner? It's only a few blocks and I love being outside.

"I'll see you there."

Jimmy hurried down the hall at Lakeview. He was excited to tell his mother that he and Kay were going to meet later in the day.

As he entered the room, two nurses and an orderly were just putting a hospital gown back on Margaret after bathing her. He waited outside the room until he got the all clear signal from Jessica, the head of staffing at the nursing home.

His mother was propped up in bed when he walked in. She smiled as he entered but even her happy countenance couldn't conceal the fragility that enveloped her. She was certainly drawing near to her final days. He walked over to her, bent forward and gave her a kiss on the forehead.

"Hi, Mom. How're you feeling today?"

"A little weaker every day and I know it. If I said great, you'd know I wasn't, so let's just say I'm a lot better now that you're here. Did you call Kay like I asked you to?"

"I did and you were right, as usual. She seemed happy that I called and we're going to have lunch together after I leave here today."

"My prayers have been answered. My boy isn't going to be a lonely old bachelor after all."

"What? Do you think if Kay doesn't want to have anything to do with me, that nobody else would either?"

"Somebody might have taken a liking to you, son, but Kay's the one I know will take care of you after I'm gone. You know, I won't be around that much longer. Besides, son…you're in your thirties. Almost your forties. She's not going to wait for you forever. I want to know you two have tied the knot before I'm gone from here."

"Don't say that, Mom. You're gonna outlive me more than likely."

"We both know what the truth is, son. I might have a month or two but that's about it. I'm not sad. I'm ready to go. No regrets now that I know you and Kay are going to get together again. I always knew it was going to happen.

And, when I'm gone, you and Kay can have the house and then there'll be some grandkids running around in my yard. How great would that be?"

Jimmy couldn't bear to tell her he'd already spoken to a real estate agent about selling the house. It was the only way to pay the mounting medical bills for her care. He would just deal with all that after she was gone. That was the last thing she needed to be worrying about now.

"That would be great, Mom."

"Not would be great, it's gonna be great. Now you go meet that girl and make it happen. Here, give me a little kiss and then get your butt in gear and propose to her."

"I don't think that's going to happen today, Mom. But who knows? You could be right."

"I am right. Now get on out of here. Call me and let me know how things went, won't you?"

"I'll call you tomorrow. Love you, Mom."

As he left Lakeview, he realized there wouldn't be many more visits to see his mother. He just hoped she could make it a few more weeks. Maybe he could bring Kay over to see her. He knew how much his mother loved her.

The afternoon sun was bright and Union Point Park was packed with families young and old. Kids were running everywhere. Parents and small children were feeding crackers to the collection of birds at the water's edge. He heard someone call his name.

"Jim Harrison, is that you?"

He turned to see Dave Santiago and his wife Mary with

a young girl sitting on a park bench enjoying the warmth of the day.

"How are you, Dave? And the ever beautiful, Mary? Man it's been a long time since I've seen you."

Mary Santiago smiled and pointed to a young boy throwing a football with a friend.

"We're here watching our son, Jason, play ball with his friend, Luke. Do you remember him? I bet you haven't seen him since he was tiny."

"You're right. I don't think I've seen him since he was back in kindergarten. Who is this beautiful young lady you have with you?"

"This is our daughter, Lisa. She's the dancer in the family. Jason's our football player. He plans on playing at the high school soon, just like you did. He's a good athlete."

"Wow, he's really getting big, isn't he?"

"He's twelve now. Loves all sports. Mainly, football. Hey, Jason, throw the ball over here to Jim Harrison. You remember him, don't you?"

The young man ran over to Jimmy.

"My dad said Jimmy Harrison was the best football player to ever play for the Bears. Was that you?"

"I'm Jim Harrison all right but I don't know about being the best football player ever at New Bern High."

"Don't let him kid you, Jason. He was the best. Jimmy, throw him a pass or two, won't you?"

"Sure. Jason, you run out toward the gazebo over there and I'll hit you with one."

The two young boys were thrilled to have such a distinguished football player willing to throw the ball to them. He threw four or five passes to each of them before he heard a familiar voice calling his name.

"Jimmy, always playing ball, huh? Never too old to give it up."

"Kay, just trying to keep my arm from getting stiff. Haven't thrown a football in years."

He threw the ball while he was talking, a perfect bullet to Jason.

"But, as you can see, I still got it."

"You do."

Jimmy turned to the Santiagos.

"Do you recognize Kay Burwell? She was in high school with us. She's been off at Law School the last several years and we're just going to have a bite together."

Mary smiled.

"Of course, we remember her. We never saw you without her. It's wonderful that you two got married."

Jimmy quickly interjected.

"Oh, we're not married. Still just good friends. Great friends actually."

Looking at them together, Mary saw the electricity apparent all around them.

"That's so sweet that you've stayed in touch all these years. History between friends is one of the most important things we have in life. You shouldn't ever lose touch with someone who's been a big part of that. Now, you take Kay to get some lunch, Jimmy. It was wonderful seeing you both."

"You too, Mary, Dave."

Jimmy looked back at the two young boys as he and Kay walked away.

"See you later guys. It was fun throwing the football with you."

"Bye, Mr. Harrison."

As they walked away, Kay opened up a subject area they had never discussed before.

"You like kids?"

"Love them. Actually, I was one. But, that was many moons ago."

"If you were ever to get married, would you want to have some?"

"I think I would. If my wife wanted them. I mean, that's kind of the next step after you get married, isn't it?"

"Some people think so. I guess most people do. I'm not so sure I would be a great Mom."

"Why do you think that?"

"First, I'm getting a little too old to even think about it. Besides, I'm just getting into the best years of my career. It seems like I went to school forever to become a lawyer and now that I'm there, it would be hard to have kids and become the next Clarence Darrow. I don't know. I guess I'd have to think long and hard about it."

"Well, I think you'd be a wonderful mother. I hope you get to make that choice someday."

"It would need to be soon. I don't want to be on Social Security and going to PTA meetings."

"Who knows what's going to happen? You might even be married by this time next year...and maybe even pregnant!"

"Sounds like you've been thinking too much."

"I'm just saying, stranger things have happened."

The old diner was almost empty since the lunch crowd had pretty much departed. The former fast-food franchise which failed and sat abandoned for years had a rebirth as a blue-collar hangout. The locals loved the home cooking menu and casual atmosphere. There was nothing fancy inside. The tables were steel with Formica tops and chairs were the same metal with blue vinyl seats. Most of the seats had at least one tear with the padding sticking out. It was clean and the kitchen was staffed by some old-timers who knew how to cook cabbage, meat loaf, mashed potatoes and any kind of breakfast all day long. Jim and Kay had spent many an hour there over the years.

They grabbed a small table near the window and ordered their usual, a BLT on toast with coffee. It had been well over a year since they'd spent any time together and Jim felt a little nervous seeing her after all that time. He had pretty much decided that their long-time separation and her new, uptown career as a lawyer had pulled them in widely different directions. He broached the subject.

"I was surprised you wanted me to call you."

"Why is that?"

"I mean, I just saw you out on a date with someone and I figured you'd have a steady guy by now."

"I do."

"That gold watch lawyer I met the other night?"

"I know you're joking. He's just a nice guy I have to work with. He's not nearly as smug as he came across with you. You probably got him feeling a little insecure."

"I guess I was just a little surprised to see you with a guy like him."

"How's that? I mean what kind of guy do you think he is?"

"He looks to me like he probably has a monogram on his pressed boxer shorts. I'm sure he practices everything he says to you in front of a mirror before he takes you out. I could be wrong. You know I'm not going to like anybody who takes you out other than me. So, if you're not interested in him for anything more than a free lunch, who's the lucky guy?"

"For almost twenty years, you've been the only guy in my life. I thought you understood that. Even though my law career has taken almost all of my time for so many years now, I always believed we were destined to be together. I think I was thirteen years old when I first told you this, wasn't I?"

"We were just kids back then. I never took that as a vow."

"I did."

"You don't know how it makes me feel to hear you say that. I never stopped thinking about you, pretty much all day every day. I hoped one day we'd be together but after so much time, I figured you'd moved on."

"Not going to happen. But, on a more serious note."

"What's more serious than this?"

"I just have to ask you this. I think about it from time to time."

"Ask away."

"Do you think you'll always work in such a dangerous job? I would have no interest in being a widow."

"Yes, probably. It can be dangerous, but I don't think about it that much. If you really think about it, there is danger in everything we all do. The riskiest thing any of us do is drive in our cars. You don't have to be doing anything wrong and suddenly another car runs a stop sign and you're pushing up daisies."

"When that recent hurricane came through here, did you have to go out and rescue anyone?"

"There were a lot of people who stayed in their homes that we had to pick up from their rooftops. That happens literally every hurricane. Everybody thinks they won't be the ones that have to call us. Never ceases to amaze me."

"But how about out in the ocean? Were there any rescues out there during the hurricane?"

"We just had one. They were about twenty miles off Hatteras when their boat sank. We just took the chopper out and picked them up. Nothing really to get all that excited about. All in a day's work."

"I'm sorry, but you're underselling what you do. You

couldn't pay me to go out there in that kind of weather. You must have a lot of the riverboat gambler in you. Tell me this. When you go out in a really bad storm, way out in the ocean and you know you're going to have to jump in the water to save someone, do you ever think about what the odds are you're not going to make it back yourself? Do you even think about things like that?"

"To be totally honest, I don't think I could be any better trained and prepared. I really feel like I'm going to be successful every time I jump in."

"What if conditions were so bad that you had doubts? What if you thought there was a fifty/fifty chance you wouldn't make it back to the chopper? Would you still jump in and try to save somebody?"

"Man, you lawyers ask some tough questions. I haven't really thought about it. Seems like a negative approach and it could give you second thoughts. Tell you what, if I ever have to go through something like that, I'll let you know what I did. I hope I'd still try and save them, but that's a split-second decision and I haven't had to make it yet. Not looking forward to a situation like that."

"One more important question."

"You always did have lots of questions."

"Do you still have your old sailboat, *Sugarcane?*"

"Sure do. I want to be buried in it. I'll never sell it."

"When can we take her out?"

"If you're serious, I'll try to get a day off later this week and we can sail down to Oriental and back."

"I'm in."

"That's exciting. I'll call you tomorrow when I get back to the station and beg the CO to let me have a day off."

"What's the CO?"

"My Commanding Officer."

"Got it. I'll be hanging onto my phone all day. You better call."

"You won't be waiting long. And one last thought."

"That would be what?"

"I noticed a few minutes ago that you said you don't want to be a widow."

"That's right, I don't."

"You can't be a widow if you aren't a wife. You do understand that?"

"I do."

"That's good to know."

The two hours they spent together passed like a couple of minutes. It was as if they had never been apart for these last several years. After they walked out of the diner, Jimmy nervously tried to give Kay an awkward hug. Not nearly satisfied with just a polite hug, she pulled Jimmy closer to her and gave him a kiss on the lips. There was no mistaking that she still felt an intense fire inside for him. His mind raced and he paused against her lips long enough to let her know that she was not alone with those feelings. He held her hand as they walked back to her car at Union Point. As she opened the door, she turned back to him.

"This will go down as one of the greatest days. I think it was a turning point."

Jimmy looked into her dark eyes.

"I know it will for me. I don't remember any others quite this like this. I'll call you tomorrow as soon as my CO says I can get a day off."

Kay sat in the driver's seat, looked up and smiled.

"Don't let me down. I'll be waiting for the phone call."

"I'll never let you down, about anything."

He bent over and gave her a kiss and then closed the door. He watched as she drove away over the Alfred Cunningham drawbridge, continuing to keep an eye on her car for several minutes until it was completely out of sight.

4

The Sail

CHARLES BREWER AND his fiancé, Chrissie Spaight, launched their small dinghy from the shore of Flanners Beach/Neuse River Campground, a few miles east of New Bern. Known mostly to the locals, the small national forest site was where the public could access the dark waters of the Neuse. Like many beaches, it attracted a good number of people who knew nothing about dealing with the dangers found in larger bodies of water. The Neuse was no exception.

The young man from Havelock was not a boater and had only recently purchased a molded plastic dinghy from a friend for a hundred dollars. With no motor, it was propelled by two aluminum oars. He had only the vaguest idea of how to row it. His fiancé was more than nervous when he asked her to sit up front in the tiny craft.

"Are you sure this thing will hold both of us? It seems small and tippy to me."

"Can't you see it has two seats? Of course, it'll hold us."

"How far out are we going?"

"Just to that little float out there. It's hooked to a crab pot. We can pull up the rope under it and get some crabs to eat. A free dinner."

"But it belongs to somebody, doesn't it?"

"I don't think they'll miss a couple of crabs. We'll just take them out of the trap then throw the float back in the water. They'll never know we were here."

"I don't like this. I'm getting wet. There's a lot of waves out here."

"They're just a foot tall. We'll be fine. Quit being such a worry wart."

With his fiancé seated forward, Charles waded behind the boat pushing it out to where the water was deep enough to row without the oars hitting the sandy bottom. Grasping the stern with both hands, he pulled himself aboard. The dinghy drank a couple gallons of water as he climbed inside.

"Take that small pail and bail out the water, Chrissie. I'll keep rowing."

In their excitement they paid no attention to the dark clouds moving up behind them. The wind began piping up and within a few minutes the small chop on the water's surface became two-foot waves."

"Please, let's turn back. I'm getting soaked and the waves are pouring in. We're going to sink this thing. Please,

Charles. I'm scared! I can't swim. We don't even have life preservers with us."

"We're almost to the float. Just a few more strokes and I'll have it."

As he reached out for the float, the oar on the opposite side of the dinghy slipped overboard. Chrissie tried to reach for it with no luck.

"Charles, the oar is in the water."

He turned to look toward the drifting oar and lurched out to grab it. It was just out of his reach and as he leaned toward it, the small water-logged dinghy put its rail under water, immediately filling up the boat. In only seconds, it rolled over on its side and flipped upside down. Chrissie thrashed her arms wildly trying to keep her head above water.

"Don't panic, Chrissie. I'll get you. Hold onto the bottom of the boat. I'm coming."

As he swam toward her, the rope holding the crab pot float to the chicken wire cage on the river bottom caught his foot. The more he fought it, the tighter it wrapped around his foot. Chrissie watched helplessly as he went under several times trying to get his leg free. Thrashing helplessly with panic in his eyes, he resurfaced five or six times gasping for air. Then no more. Chrissie screamed for all she was worth until she was almost spent, but soon realized the horrible truth. He was gone and she was alone clinging to a small overturned dinghy being blown toward the far side of the river, more than two miles away.

The river was covered with whitecaps and she held on to the narrow keel that ran the length of the overturned boat. She was just beginning to notice the bone-chilling temperature of the water. She knew she had little time and almost no chance of anyone finding her before she would lose her grip.

Jimmy and Kay walked down the dock of Edgewater Marina where his thirty-foot Tartan sloop had been berthed for over a decade. Though his job kept him on or beside the water constantly, it never gave him the satisfaction he got sailing his own boat in waters he knew like the palm of his hand. As they came alongside *Sugarcane*, he jumped into the cockpit and reached back to grab a bag of drinks and snacks that Kay brought along for the afternoon. He set it down on the cockpit floor and then reached back to place both hands on Kay's waist.

"Permission to come aboard, Captain."

"Permission granted, Admiral. You don't even have to ask."

He effortlessly lifted her and helped her step onto the boat's seat and beside him in the cockpit.

"How does the weather look? I watched the local news this morning on WCTI and Les Still said there was a good chance of afternoon squalls. Anything for us to worry about?"

"*Sugarcane* loves a little wave action on the water. We'll just keep our eyes open. If a storm starts heading our way, I'll reef the sails and we'll just keep on trucking. I'd like to get all the way to Oriental for lunch and then back here before dark. We'll need some strong winds to make that happen. You couldn't be in better hands on this river."

"I know that's a fact. I'm just always cautious."

"A good sailor is always cautious. Safety first. Otherwise, you screw up out there and they call some nut like me to fly out in a helicopter and jump in the water to save you. And, the water is pretty darn cold right now. Not fun without a dry suit on. Most folks wouldn't live thirty minutes in fifty-degree water. Ok, if you'll help me store this stuff below in the galley, I'll get the dock lines and we're outta here. Gotta tell you. I'm excited."

"How's that?"

"My favorite girl on my favorite boat on my favorite river, all at the same time. In my world, it doesn't get any better than this."

He started the old gas powered Atomic Four engine and began to back the forty-year-old boat away from its slip and out into the Trent River. After a short trip under motor alone, he cleared the Trent River fixed bridge and approached the Alfred Cunningham Bridge. He called the bridgetender on the VHF radio.

"Cunningham Bridge, Cunningham Bridge. This is the sailing vessel *Sugarcane* approaching you from the Trent River requesting an opening at your convenience."

"Roger, *Sugarcane*. Give me a couple of minutes to let some of this traffic clear and I'll open up for you."

"Thank you. *Sugarcane* standing by on channel thirteen."

"Why channel 13, Jimmy?"

"In North Carolina, all the bridges monitor this channel. It's the proper etiquette for requesting an opening."

"Got it. There's lot of rules aren't there?"

"There are quite a few, but no amount of rules can replace common sense. You wouldn't believe some of the things we've seen people do out on the water. It's got to be one of the best places on the planet for cleaning up the gene pool."

As they watched, a siren went off on the bridge alerting traffic of the upcoming stop. crossbars were lowered across the bridge bringing traffic to a halt. The center span of the bridge began to turn until it was at a ninety-degree angle to the rest of the structure. That opened up two different boat lanes with the turning section of the bridge between them. In only a minute, they were completely open and Jimmy started motoring *Sugarcane* forward through the narrow passage. When they were through, he called the bridge-tender once more.

"Thanks, bridgetender. *Sugarcane* is clear."

"No problem, Jimmy. That is you, isn't it?"

"It is, who am I talking with?"

"Rich Cipolla, we went to school together."

"Right, I remember you. We'll have to get together soon."

"I'd like that. You have a safe sail. Some storms possible this afternoon."

"We heard that. We'll be careful. Thanks again. *Sugarcane* back to channel 16.

The siren rang out again signaling the bridge was heading back to its original position. The backed-up traffic started moving in and out of New Bern again.

Jimmy steered his small sloop to the first channel marker on the Neuse. Union Point was the spot where the Trent River emptied into the Neuse. Jimmy turned the bow to starboard and headed under the high-rise Neuse River Bridge. This bridge was high enough in its center span that sailboats with masts less than sixty-five feet high could pass under without a problem. Masts taller than that were out of luck with no entrance to New Bern possible by water. The wind was brisk with a slight chill as it was late November. The north wind always brought the temperature down, but offered a downwind run toward Oriental, just over twenty miles to the southeast.

Once they were clear of the second bridge, Jimmy turned *Sugarcane* into the wind and raised the large foresail. It was a hank-on sail. Jimmy never had the money to buy a roller furler for the headsail. He had to go forward onto the top deck to reach the mast and pull the sail up by its halyard. He felt that was a small price to pay for the pleasure of having such a great performing boat to sail. *Sugarcane* was an older boat, designed by Sparkman and Stephens, the greatest yacht designers of all time, to his mind. There were over six hundred of this model boat made in the seventies, but only sixteen of them were the high-performance model with more sail area, taller mast, deeper keel, and a little more ballast. She was a good performer in all conditions.

With a fixed keel, it was a stiff boat and could handle a lot of wind and waves. He always felt secure in her. With the sail raised, he turned the bow back around for its long downwind run to Oriental. She accelerated immediately to six and half knots. Jimmy reached down to the controls and shut off the engine.

"Enough of that noise. My favorite sound now, just the water lapping against the hull as the old girl makes tracks. I love this."

"I know you do. This is what you were meant to do. Since there aren't any more clipper ships sailing the world, I guess the next best thing for you was joining the Coast Guard."

"No question. I have a home there and a job I love. Not many people can say that. What about you? Is working as a lawyer all you thought it would be?"

"It has its headaches like anything else, but overall, I'm pretty happy. I can tell you one thing about it."

"That is?"

"It's a lot more paper work than I ever dreamed. When I first thought about becoming a lawyer, I envisioned standing in front of a packed courtroom and arguing a case for my defendant. That turns out to be a small part of the job. There's hours and hours at a desk researching laws and old cases trying to figure out what to do. My firm does a lot of corporate work. Contracts and business disputes. You talk about boring. Of course, they do charge a goodly sum for their services so I can make a decent living. And, I do get to live in my favorite place in the all the world."

"Agreed, there's no better place. No place more beautiful and might I add, more romantic, than New Bern."

Kay slid along the cockpit seat closer to Jimmy. She laid her head against his shoulder.

"I've missed you like you wouldn't believe. Sometimes it got so bad I thought I should drop out of school and come home. I'd just corral you and force you to propose to me. We'd get married and live happily ever after, just like the old Walt Disney stories. Apparently, those are not based on truth."

"Don't be so sure. You're back home now. I'm here with you. And if you're exceptionally kind to me, who knows what might happen. I mean, we're already in the same boat, right? And, we are moving nicely down the river."

Sugarcane was leaving a wake behind her and occasionally reaching seven knots of hull speed. Her rising and falling bow and gentle heel made the ride almost hypnotic. They both noticed dark clouds moving in behind them.

"Looks like one of those squalls Les Still predicted is headed our way. The old rule sailors should always follow is when it first crosses your mind of the need to shorten or reef the sails, just do it. Don't second guess yourself. It will get you in trouble. That being said, I'm going to switch the genoa for my working jib which is about half the size. It's down below in the vee berth. If you will, how about taking the tiller and keep us heading on this course? When I tell you to, push the tiller hard over to the side of the cockpit and keep the bow pointed directly into the wind toward

New Bern till I get the jib raised. Then you can turn us back around when I tell you to. Got it?"

"I think I do."

"If you mess it up, no problem. Nothing serious will happen with the wind at this strength. So, let's do this."

Jimmy went below and grabbed an old sail bag from the hanging locker. He carried it up to the foredeck. He gave the signal to Kay to turn the boat into the wind. He quickly untied the jib halyard and lowered the genoa onto the deck. The wind was already strong enough to cause the sail to slap loudly as it came down. He released each hank of the sail from the stainless-steel stay that held the mast upright. He emptied the smaller jib from the bag and stuffed the larger sail back in its place. He ran the working jib up the stay and tied it off to a cleat on the mast. He made a circular motion with his hand to let Kay know it was time to turn the boat back around. The jib filled with wind and *Sugarcane* continued its romp down river. The whole process took only a couple of minutes. It was a task that appeared to be simple when the person doing it had years of experience. To a novice, it could quickly become challenging.

"Done like an expert, Kay. With this smaller sail, we can handle an awful lot of wind. We'll be fine. Nothing turns me on like seeing a beautiful young woman steering a sailboat. I guess that's what I love so much about you."

"Just that I can steer a boat? That's all I have to do?"

"Well, you can also help me wash her from time to time and maybe even sand and paint the bottom."

"Dream on, sailor man. Dream on."

Their sail change timing was excellent. Within fifteen minutes, the dark clouds were closing in and the wind increased to a steady twenty knots, occasionally gusting to thirty. *Sugarcane* was completely under control and Jimmy was enjoying how well his little ship responded to the heavier conditions. For about ten minutes they enjoyed the ride silently, looking out across the river at building white caps and lines of wind making dark patches on the surface of the water. The rise and fall of the boat's hull and its powerful slice through the waves had a predictable rhythm. To Jimmy, it had the feel of a choreographed dance between the boat and the sea.

"What's that over there, Jimmy? Looks like debris in the water. You don't want to hit it."

"Where?"

Kay pointed to the starboard side of the boat, about thirty degrees off the bow.

"Right there, see where I'm pointing? Oh my God. It's an upside-down boat with somebody laying on it."

"You're kidding. Take the tiller."

Jimmy grabbed a pair of binoculars from their perch just inside the cabin door. He focused on the spot where there was definitely something floating.

"You're right. It's a girl hanging onto the bottom of a dinghy. We need to get to her right now. The water is super cold. No way she can last more than a few minutes."

Jimmy turned the engine back on, pushed the shift lever forward into gear and directed Kay.

"Turn back into the wind. I've got to lower the jib so we can get to her. Use more power this time. The wind is going to fight you."

Kay cranked up the throttle and Jimmy went forward to the mast, quickly untied the halyard holding up the jib and let it fall to the deck. He hastily lashed it to a lifeline so it would stay on board and then raced back to the cockpit and relieved Kay at the tiller.

"Kay, you're going to have to help me here. You okay?"

"Whatever you tell me to do, I'm going to do it. I'm fine."

"We need to get close to her without running her over. We need to stay a few feet away from her. I don't think we should be either upwind or downwind from her. I don't want her banging into us or vice versa. I'm going to just come up off to her side. I'll throw us into neutral and don't put it back in gear unless I tell you to. Don't want her to be run over or hit the prop. Got it?"

"I do."

Jimmy stripped off his clothes down to his briefs.

"You're going in with nothing on?"

"It's cold, I want some dry clothes to put on when I get back on board."

Jimmy pulled *Sugarcane* within ten feet of the girl on the overturned craft.

"Listen to me. If you get blown away from me, you'll need to bump her in and out of gear to get closer. If the wind starts hitting you hard you might get blown away faster than I can swim. We're good for right now. I'm going to swim over to her and bring her back to the boat. I'll lower the stern swim ladder and come around back there to get her aboard. Be ready to help me pull her onto *Sugarcane*. It'll be a lot harder than you think."

With that, Jimmy jumped straight into the frigid water and swam over to the woman. His powerful strokes helped him close the distance between *Sugarcane* and the dinghy in mere seconds. He could see the woman was motionless with almost no strength left.

"Can you hear me? I'm right here beside you."

The woman tried to raise her head up and look toward him but could only manage an almost imperceptible nod. She mumbled, barely audible.

"I can't swim. I can't let go. I'm going to drown. I'm going to drown. I know it."

"You're not going to drown. I'm not letting you go anywhere except over to my boat. I'm going to hold you by the waist while you let yourself down into the water. I'll turn you on your back and grab you above your shoulders and swim over to the other boat. Do you understand what I'm saying?"

"I'm scared. I can't swim. I don't want to let go."

"You have to. You can't last much longer. Let the boat go. I'm right here. Let it go."

Chrissie was not responding. Either she was overcome with fear or too weak to make any conscious movements. Jimmy increased his grip around her waist.

"Let go. I'm going to pull you free. Don't fight me. Here we go."

Jimmy was surprised at how little effort it took to break her grip from the dinghy's keel. She dropped quietly into the water beside him. It was obvious if he wasn't there to catch her, she would have just sunk quietly out of sight. Jimmy positioned himself to where he could sidestroke with one arm and hold her tightly around her neck, her head facing the sky. The wind was now raging and the waves were approaching a three-foot chop. Only the strongest of swimmers would have any chance of succeeding at carrying her toward *Sugarcane* in these conditions. Jimmy yelled out to Kay.

"Bump her forward for just a second and then turn 180 degrees to give me the stern. Quickly, it's hard to hold my position."

Kay put the boat into forward to get up just enough speed to turn it around. Once she had *Sugarcane's* stern toward him, she put it back into neutral. He was already starting to weaken from the extremely cold water and he strained to make the stern ladder. He grabbed it with his left hand while maintaining a tight grip around the now unconscious Chrissie. He looked up at Kay.

"I don't have much left. You're going to have to help me get her aboard. I can't let her go until I know you have her."

Kay bent over the stern and grabbed Chrissie's arm.

"I've got a firm hold on her. Let's do this together."

Jimmy and Kay were both struggling, but were finally

able to pull and push the limp woman onto the stern of *Sugarcane*. Kay backed into the cockpit and pulled Chrissie down to the floor alongside her. At first glance she appeared lifeless. Jimmy was trying to climb up the stern ladder himself and finding it difficult to control his failing muscles. Kay extended a hand to help him up.

"Thanks. That was as hard a rescue as I've ever had to do. Get me a towel and my clothes. Let's get some blankets from the bunk below and wrap this girl up. She's got hypothermia."

Kay grabbed another towel, two blankets and started to dry off the frozen girl and get her body wrapped snugly to get her temperature up. Jimmy pulled on his clothes and went below to the cabin's VHF radio.

"Mayday, mayday, US Coast Guard Morehead City. Mayday."

Quickly, the monitoring station came back to him.

"This is the US Coast Guard Morehead City. What's the nature of your emergency?"

"I'm a Coast Guard swimmer. I'm aboard my own thirty-foot sloop in the Neuse River located mid-river between Flanners Beach and Kennels Beach. I just pulled a woman from the river. She's unconscious and in bad shape. Her breathing is shallow and she's hypothermic. How soon can you have a chopper here? It's critical."

"Can you give us your position?"

Jimmy looked at the GPS and relayed the coordinates to the Coast Guard.

"We're at 34° 59' 15.126" North by 76° 53' 47.3316" West."

"I copy. Unit CC 1 is already in the air on the way back from a distress call over at Goose Creek near Hobucken. We'll divert them and you're looking at maybe five minutes, max."

"That's great Morehead. We'll sit right where we are and monitor 22. Tell the chopper we're listening for them on the VHF."

"Will do. Please continue to stand by on 22 alpha and keep us updated if anything changes."

As promised, within minutes the chopper could be heard on the horizon even as the wind was howling.

"There they are, Kay. How's she doing?"

"She's still with us. I think she's got a little more color in her face. She breathing about the same, but she's still out cold."

Several times, Chrissie opened her eyes and tried to mouth words. Kay leaned over close beside her face and listened carefully to make out what she was trying to say.

"It sounds like she's saying Charles or Charlie. You think she had someone named Charles with her?"

"If that's all you can get out of her, there's no way to know. I didn't see anybody else near the dinghy. If there was, I don't think there's any way possible I could have swum another person to *Sugarcane*. I'll just let the chopper guys know and they can look over the spot and see if they can see anybody. If there is someone else, I guarantee you they didn't make it. It's been too long in water this cold."

"Ok. We're going to have to get her into the basket. They'll lower it to us alongside the boat. It'll be tricky. They can't risk getting the cable caught in our rigging and I sure don't want to have to get back in the water. There's no way this woman could stand it. We'll just have to do what we can to make it work."

"Vessel hailing Coast Guard on channel 22. Do you copy?"

"Yes, Coast Guard. This is AST Jim Harrison from Station Elizabeth City. We see you headed toward us. Do you have a visual?"

"Yes, Sir. What's the situation there?"

"We have a hypothermic female, about twenty-five years of age. She was in the water for at least twenty minutes to a half hour. She's unconscious and needs thermal gear ASAP plus evacuation to a trauma center. You're going to need to lower a basket to us. I can secure her if you think you can get it close enough to us without catching our rigging."

"We'll do our best sir. Please stay on channel 22 alpha."

"Will do."

This chopper crew was stationed in Morehead and capable of the same type of rescues that Jimmy handled out of Elizabeth City. They spoke the same language.

"OK, skipper, we're going to come in around forty feet since there's no wave height to speak of. We'll go upwind from you and hopefully the force of the wind will bring the basket to you without us having to get too close."

"Kay, see the door open on the side of the chopper? The guy sitting there will work the cable and lower the basket to us. It'll be swinging around and can hurt you if it hits you so stay on guard while I try to grab it."

The basket was pushed out of the chopper's fuselage and the flight crew began to lower it slowly toward *Sugarcane*. The wind speed was hovering around twenty-five knots steady with an occasional gust and the basket would then start to spin. A skillful yank on the cable by the guardsman at the chopper's side door would cause it to stop or slow down dramatically. Jimmy stood on the side deck of *Sugarcane* on the windward side of the boat. As the basket got within ten feet, he started to reach out so he could catch it on his first lunge. The maneuver would have to be timed precisely or he'd grab a handful of nothing and quickly be back in the river. Kay was startled by how loud the overhead chopper was and how much downdraft it generated.

"Kay, get on the radio and tell them the basket is ten feet up. Give me just a little bit more, maybe half that."

Kay relayed Jimmy's request and slowly the swaying basket was lowered just enough for Jimmy to grab hold of its side rail.

"Got it Kay. Tell them to give me slack and I'll take the basket."

The cable went slack as requested and Jimmy pulled the basket over to the side deck of the boat.

"We're going to have to lift her one more time. You take her side toward the boat and I'll lift the other side. OK, on three. One, two, three. Using all their strength they laid Chrissie into the basket. Jimmy secured the straps mounted inside the basket to her and then gave the chopper crewmember in the open door the thumbs up. Before the chopper lifted higher, it pulled sideways away from *Sugarcane*. Once the basket was clear the cable started retracting and pulled it up to and then inside the chopper. All in, it took only ten minutes. Jimmy hailed them on the radio."

"Guys, there's a chance she had someone with her. Do you see the overturned dinghy? Maybe a quarter mile from me by now?"

"Yes. Got a bead on it with binocs. Doesn't appear to have anyone near it. We'll do a circle over it as we leave and check it out. Thanks for your help. I'm sure this young lady will be more than grateful as well."

"Great job, fellas. I'll tell your CO how professional you were. And don't forget you'll owe me a beer."

"All in a day's work, sir. See you at Elizabeth City."

"Affirmative."

The chopper took a beeline course straight for the trauma center at East Carolina University in Greenville, only a few minutes flight from New Bern. Kay turned to Jimmy.

"That was the most incredible thing I've ever witnessed. It went so smoothly. Like a well-oiled machine. But you're blue and actually shaking. You need some more clothes on and we need to get to a marina where they have electricity and heat."

"It's only an hour or so more to Oriental. I'll get some warm clothes on. Then, let's put the jib back out, kill the motor and enjoy what's left of the day. I came here to spend time with you, not do more of what I do every day for a living."

"You were spectacular out there. So courageous in spite of the danger to yourself."

"Go on."

"And I hope you don't mind me saying this, but when you stripped down to your underpants, Wow, you looked like you did in high school. I don't think you have one pound of fat on your entire body. You're in fantastic condition. Everybody else is starting to get squishy around the middle as they get older. How do you do it?"

"It's part of my job. A rescue swimmer has to go through some of the toughest training on the planet and you can't afford to ever let yourself get lazy. You saw what it was like today. Add about forty more knots of wind and waves thirty feet high. There's no room for even the tiniest bit of weakness. You're not only trying to save people's lives; you're basically saving your own every time you go in after them. And, besides that, I have plans I don't want to miss out on."

"And what are those plans?"

"How about we discuss them tonight over an adult beverage at the marina?"

"I'd love that."

Oriental Marina was tucked into the heart of Oriental, North Carolina, and known up and down the east coast as the sailing capital of North Carolina. With only eight hundred permanent residents and over three thousand sailboats calling it home, Jimmy loved the feel of the place. There were several nice marinas but he'd been sailing there for many years and he felt most at home at the original Oriental Marina. There were only a few slips but the marina had a wonderful restaurant called the Toucan. In the summer, their swimming pool offered a great break from the burning hot sun. In the evenings, all year-round, the outside Tiki Bar kept a crowd of regulars mixed with cruising boaters from almost everywhere. The owner, Tom McIlhenny, met Jimmy at the dock to take the lines that would secure *Sugarcane*. He was a jovial, large man who wore shorts year-round. He'd known Jimmy for years.

"Well look here. Haven't seen you in a couple of years. To what do we owe the privilege of a visit?"

"Hey, Tom. I just needed an Oriental fix. A hot meal and a shower would also go a long way."

"What was all the excitement about on the river? I heard the Coast Guard talking to a boat but couldn't make out who it was or what they were saying. I assume somebody was in trouble."

"You'd be right. We picked up a woman in the river on an overturned dink. Had to get in the water to get her aboard. Let me tell you, that river water is cold this time of year."

"That was you talking with them? She survived?"

"Just barely. She didn't have another five minutes left

in her. Might have had somebody with her who wasn't so lucky. We don't know for sure because she kept passing out and was unable to tell us anything."

"I'm sure it was cold out there. They took her in the chopper?"

"Had to. She was almost comatose. I called the Coast Guard station at Morehead and they sent out a Jayhawk to pick her up. Hope she made it. Like I said, she might have had someone with her cause she came to a couple of times and all she said was 'Charlie'. Must be a boyfriend or something. He was nowhere to be found, so I'd say his chances are nil of turning up alive. Middle of the river in gale force winds in a ten-foot dink. I'll never understand where these people come from."

"I know. And, there's no shortage of them. Well, there's plenty of hot water so come on in and get a shower."

Tom saw Kay emerge from the cockpit.

"Well, well. Who have you brought with you?"

"You don't remember Kay?"

"This is the young gal you harassed all the way through high school?"

"I wouldn't consider it harassment but yes, this is the same beautiful woman you've seen me with for a long time."

"Welcome, Kay. Good to see you. So, you haven't been able to do any better than Jim Bob here, have you?"

Kay smiled up at Tom while taking his hand up to the dock.

"I tried to get away by going to law school for three

years but he just kept turning up. I guess we're doomed to be together forever."

"An attorney, heh? Beautiful and smart. Jim Bob, you've hit the motherload with this one. If he treats you bad, Kay, come see me."

"You can count on it, Tom."

Jimmy looked over at Tom.

"Tom, please, no more Jim Bob. I'm trying to get past that."

"No problem. I've got some other boats coming in, so guys just help yourselves. Crab cakes in the Toucan on special tonight."

"One of my favorites, Tom. I think you've sold me."

Jim and Kay headed to the marina showers, which they both looked forward to. After an extended shower with steaming hot water, they walked back to *Sugarcane*, dropped off their dirty clothes and headed to the restaurant for a seafood dinner. They filled up on crab cakes, hush puppies and topped off their meal with Key Lime pie.

It was already after dark as they headed back to the boat, just a few yards from the Toucan. They went below into *Sugarcane*'s salon. Jimmy lit two small oil lamps and cut on the portable electric heater that easily warmed up the teak lined main cabin. He loved the way the small boat felt down below with all the varnished wood and polished brass. Staying aboard was his idea of the perfect night. Whether docked in the marina or at anchor inside a small quiet cove, he always slept like a baby when staying aboard. This evening was special. His favorite person in the world was tucked in beside him in the place he loved the most. She sat down on the port settee, opened a bottle of Cabernet Sauvignon and poured two plastic goblets almost full. He learned years ago that wine goblets made of crystal or glass might work on a large yacht but not on a small sloop so easily moved around by the sea. Broken glass on the cabin sole was no pleasure to clean up and any tiny remaining shards would most certainly find a bare foot.

He sat across from Kay on the starboard settee. With a varnished mahogany table between them, they were separated only by a couple of feet. The soft flickering light from the oil lamps played off the varnish and added a gently moving shadow down one side of the most beautiful face he'd ever seen. Kay was small-framed with shoulder length auburn hair and a smile that lit up every room she entered.

"Here's to Oriental, *Sugarcane* and us."

"To us."

"It would be hard to overstate how much I missed you. I didn't realize how much until I saw you again in Morgan's. My spark was faded, but I took one look at you and the fire ignited. I'm probably blowing my chances by telling you right off that I want to be with you all the time. You make me feel better about everything. Is this what you'd call playing all my cards in one hand?"

"Those are the words I've been waiting to hear. Right now, this moment is the one I'll remember the rest of my life. Ever since I saw your face with that mop of uncombed hair, it has stayed with me. When I think of who I want to spend the rest of my life with, your face is the only one I see. If we don't grab this moment, I'm afraid we'll regret it the rest of our lives. Love like this doesn't come along but once in a lifetime and I'm not letting you out of these arms, ever again."

He moved over beside her kissing her with all the pent-up emotion that he'd been holding onto for years. They talked and reminisced, sharing their dreams till the music from the tiki bar no longer filled the marina. Around two in the morning, they crawled into the inviting and comfortable vee berth in the forward section of the boat. They fell asleep holding on to each other feeling they had solved life's greatest challenge. That night, they were both convinced nothing would ever separate them again.

The sun came up bright and even though it was late November, they decided to walk over to The Bean, a small coffee shop just across the street from the marina. The place was bristling with locals and sailors, most talking boats and cruising, not the politics and news the rest of the world dealt with in the mornings over coffee. That endeared the place to both of them. They were still floating in their own small world and didn't want to be anywhere else. Unfortunately, they were both still prisoners of the real world with bills to pay and jobs that were pulling on their leashes. They would find a way to cut the land lines one day and head out on their own adventure. Before long, they were full of coffee and Danish. The wall clock was showing ten AM.

"I don't want to even think about it, but I guess we better start heading back to New Bern. It's a three-hour trip and then I've got to secure the boat and drive back to Elizabeth City."

"I hate that. I miss you already. When can you come back?"

"Unless I have duty, I'll be back next weekend and every weekend from now on if they don't have me on call. Weekends are always busy for us. That's when all the folks from upstate come to the beach and pretend they're John Paul Jones for two days. You wouldn't believe how many of them we have to go and rescue every weekend."

"I can imagine. I do have an idea though I want to run by you."

"I'm listening."

"Every December, there's a formal dinner and dance in New Bern at the Convention Center. It's called the Heart Ball. Wouldn't it be great if we went together? You could go in your dress uniform so I can show you off to all the stuffed-shirt attorneys I work with."

"Did you say formal?"

"That's right."

"I don't think I've ever been to a formal. I've only worn my dress whites a couple of times, for award ceremonies and things like that. You don't think I'd embarrass you with all those Morrison Brooks types?"

"You'd make me prouder than when I graduated from law school. Tell me you'll do it, just for me."

"There's nothing I wouldn't do for you. You just have to mention it and my answer will always be the same. Whatever makes you happy is what I want to do."

The sail back to New Bern was calm with light breezes and temperature in the sixties. They played a stack of their favorite songs on *Sugarcane*'s stereo. Jimmy pulled Kay as close as he could and still work the tiller to steer the boat. He thought that in all the years he'd enjoyed sailing on the Neuse, this was best day he'd ever spent on it or anywhere for that matter.

It went by all too fast. In what seemed like minutes, they were back in New Bern tying up the boat. Kay gathered up her bag and stepped onto the old wooden pier. Jimmy followed her.

"Here, let me take that for you and be your official escort to your car."

"That would be lovely. I enjoyed every minute aboard your boat today. I see why you love it so much. What a peaceful, wonderful feeling to let the wind move you. It is so relaxing. I feel as refreshed as if I had been gone for a week."

"When I am at the tiller, those are the best times of my life. I'm going to keep this boat even if I lose everything else I have. She's my most prized possession."

"I understand. Now how about giving me a kiss to hold me till I see you again?"

He set her bag down, took her firmly in a strong embrace and gave her exactly what she asked for.

"How was that?"

"Remember what you did there. I'll be needing that again soon. And when will you be back?"

"If the CO approves, I'll be back on Friday evening. I want to spend some time with Mom. I don't think she has a lot of that left."

"Keep me posted on how she's doing and when you're coming. Maybe we could go to Morgan's for dinner on Friday when you get back. Where will you be staying?"

"I want to stay on the boat. We'll see how Mom is doing."

"Jimmy."

"Yes, Ma'am."

"You do know I love you, don't you?"

"I was hoping that was the case. I'd hate to think I just spent the most wonderful day and night of my life with a woman who was just toying with me."

"You would make a fine boy toy, but no. You are the one I want to spend the rest of my days with. If you ever get up the nerve to propose to me, I'd probably say yes."

"I'd do it this minute, but it needs to be in a more special place than this old dock. Consider it a gentleman's promise that an incredible proposal will be forthcoming from the man who loves you."

Jimmy kissed her one final time and helped her into the car. He watched as she drove out of the marina. He headed back down the dock to *Sugarcane*. It was getting late in the afternoon and he had a long ride ahead.

5

Coast Guard Station Elizabeth
City – Monday morning

JIMMY AND BILL Flynn were drinking coffee and relating their activities of the past weekend.

"I guess my tale of catching the largest bluefin tuna I've ever seen out of Oregon Inlet sort of pales in comparison to spending the weekend with a gorgeous woman and all but setting a wedding date. Am I right?"

"Catching a bluefin is pretty special, but from my own point of view, hearing Kay say she wants to get married is about as big a weekend as I could hope for. I think we both had a pretty great weekend."

"And you picked up some half-frozen woman in the middle of the river. What's the story there?"

"From what I found out about the survivor, she and her fiancé went out in a ten-foot dinghy for a ride with twenty-knot winds on the Neuse. The boat flipped and she hung on to it. They haven't found him yet. It'll probably be three days to a week until he comes to the surface. You know how long it takes to make a body float in cold water. I hate to see it when folks come down here and think being on the river is a game. They've got no concept of how bad things can get with very little warning. I got a call from a buddy at Morehead. He left a voicemail saying Chrissie, the woman I rescued, was stable at Greenville and will probably be okay. She'll be burying her fiancé before they even get married. That is, if they ever find the body. Life turns on a dime."

"You're telling me. How many times have they called us to bail people out of their own stupid mistakes?"

"More than I want to remember."

The intercom in the lounge interrupted their conversation.

"HH60 Unit two report to ready room. Unit two alert. All unit two personnel report to ready room."

"Well, so much for a quiet cup of coffee and discussing our wonderful weekend."

"No rest for the weary, Bill. One last swallow of caffeine and I'm on my way."

The rest of Unit 2's crew were hurrying in as Jimmy and Bill entered the ready room. Commander Hewett stood at the front as the group sat down in grey aluminum folding chairs.

"Good morning. Sorry to cut your coffee break short. A

group of surfers were taking advantage of the big waves left over from this past weekend's strong weather. One of them was apparently not as experienced as the rest and got too close to the mouth of the inlet. Some of the older boys tried to get to him but he was swept out to sea way too fast for them. It's rough out there, especially in the inlet. The report came in exactly six minutes ago. Let's go find him. He's wearing a wetsuit so we've probably got more than hour before the cold starts becoming a serious problem. You need to be in rotation in five minutes. Questions?"

The crew was silent, already going over the mental checklist they kept stored in the front of their minds. They grabbed flight gear from their lockers and jogged out to the chopper, already warming its engines. Each man took his position on the chopper. After clearance from the station tower, they lifted off heading southeast toward the inlet at Beaufort. This would be a forty-minute run for them, but they were the closest available crew. Jimmy was the only swimmer on call that morning.

The sun was out and the winds were nothing out of the ordinary. The biggest task would be locating the young surfer. Someone in the water with no flares and wearing a black wetsuit would be a difficult target to spot.

The inlet came into view ahead of the chopper. From the air it was easy to see the dark water of the deep channel bordered on each side by steep breaking seas caused by ocean swells crashing onto the shoals. Three crew members held binoculars close to their eyes and scanned everywhere looking for the needle in the haystack. Jimmy noticed the angle of the large channel buoys.

"Check out how much the buoys are laying over and the wake around them. No wonder the kid couldn't paddle his board back in. Must be five knots or better of current heading out. Chuck, think we should just follow the channel out?"

"I'm already on it. Kid could be miles out by now. Buddy and I'll look ahead and you guys each take a side of the channel. We're down to about twenty minutes so let's make this happen."

The sky was clear and even though the swells beyond the channel were four to five feet high, they weren't breaking and there were no whitecaps. The crew strained trying to not overlook any small stretch of water. A young man's life counted on it.

Chuck kept the crew apprised of the air time left. Running out of fuel was not an option. There had to be enough in reserve to make the return trip to the base. If needed, they could divert to Morehead City which was closer to the inlet.

"Fifteen minutes, guys."

Bill picked up something about three hundred yards off the port side.

"I think I see him. Straight toward the Cape Lookout lighthouse. Three hundred yards. Yep. That's our guy."

"Headed that way."

"It's him. He's still on his board. This shouldn't be too bad. Jim Bob, you ready?"

"Born ready. Get the cable boom out while I hook up."

Both men went about the tasks they'd done countless times before. Chuck lowered the chopper to forty feet off the water and started to circle the surfer. Jimmy sat in the open doorway of the aircraft, his feet hanging out with flippers on, ready to be lowered.

"Looks like a pickup right out of the training manual, Jim Bob."

"Start lowering."

After fifteen feet of cable was out with Jimmy suspended over the surfer who was staring straight up at him, Bill called out over the headphone.

"Jim Bob, you have company old buddy."

"Don't tell me."

"Sorry. About twenty feet out and circling the kid. As much as I don't want to say it, it's a good twelve-footer. It looks like a white to me. What do you want to do?"

"Just get me directly over the kid. I might not have to get in the water. I'll just get him on my lap. He's young and strong, he'll be able to just hang on to me."

Every one of the crew could clearly see the large shark circling ever closer to the surfboard and its lone occupant. The closer Jimmy got, the closer the shark got. They both had the same target in their scope. At ten feet above him, Jimmy yelled out to the surfer.

"Stay on the board. I'm coming down right in front of you. Jump into my lap and put your arms around my chest. I can't get into the water to get a harness on you."

"The water's not that cold."

"I'm not worried about the cold. You have a large shark circling you. Don't get off the board. I'm almost to you."

Now the kid was scared. It was necessary to explain why he should stay on the board. Any splashing or excited movement in the water might cause the shark to make his move. Chuck carefully held the chopper directly over the kid, which was challenging. Bill lowered the cable the last ten feet.

"Bill, you're going to have get me right on top of the board. I'll straddle it just long enough for the kid to get on my lap."

"You got it. Don't see the shark at all. He could be right under you. Make your move quick."

"Down, now."

As the cable let him down, Jimmy put one leg on either side of the board, facing the surfer and the rear of the surfboard. For about fifteen seconds, he rode the board like a horse with one leg on each side. Only a few feet away Jimmy saw the surface of the water break with the tip of a large fin. His heart racing, he watched as the entire body of the shark passed under them. Estimates of the shark's size were dramatically incorrect. Its back was as wide as a Clydesdale and it had to be fifteen feet in length. It was definitely a full-grown specimen. Suddenly his legs were feeling vulnerable. He grabbed the harness on the end of the swinging cable with a newfound urgency. He knew sharks normally made one pass or a bump before a final attack, which he guessed was only seconds away. He helped to get the kid seated and gave Bill the thumbs up. He quickly started pulling Jimmy and his passenger straight up and away from the board. In three minutes, they were both safely aboard the chopper. Bill came over to them.

"Son, what's your name?"

"Mark Bratton. Man, I'm so glad you guys got to me. Was there really a shark close by or were you just trying to hurry me up?"

"Oh, he was there alright. A big great white, just like you see on Shark Week. He was looking at you like lunch. And Jim Bob, you might want to check out your flipper. Seems one is a lot longer than the other one."

They looked at Jimmy's right flipper. It was bitten completely off about four inches below the bottom of his toes.

"That's way too close. I don't hate sharks, but all this stuff about them being here first and they really don't like to eat people doesn't seem comforting when one's trying to take your leg off."

"My buddies never told me there were sharks out here. A great white? Jeez, I don't think I'm going to be surfing around here anymore."

"Mark, if the water you're swimming in is attached to the ocean, there will be sharks in it. They normally won't bother you but it's not a good idea to poke a stick at a tiger if you know what I mean."

"I understand. Thanks again, guys. You literally saved my life. I owe you all."

"No problem, son. We signed on to this because we're adrenalin junkies. You just helped us get our fix today."

The chopper sat down at the Morehead City Coast Guard Station, located only a few miles from where the rescue occurred. If they had a helicopter on station there, it would have been a far simpler and quicker rescue.

The young man's parents were waiting on the tarmac and came running to their son as soon as they were given the all clear sign. They continued their praise and thanks to the crew. It was always rewarding to get so much gratitude but they had been through the drill many times before and considered the afternoon's events just another day on the job.

The week seemed to drag by slower than usual. Jimmy had been calling Kay every night since they parted at the marina. He wanted to be with her as much as possible and the three-hour drive seemed like the other side of the world from New Bern.

When there was no rescue in progress or training drills occupying their day, the entire crew spent their days performing maintenance on their chopper and equipment. It was a full-time enterprise. Maintenance on a chopper was legendary. Some said a helicopter required twelve hours of maintenance for one hour of flying time.

It was getting late in the day on Thursday. Jimmy and Bill were pretty much covered in grease as they lubricated the cable hoist. That piece of equipment was one that had to work every time it was needed or someone could lose their life. Buddy Jewell walked over to them.

"Hey grease monkeys, I hate to break up your party but the CO wants to see Jimmy. So, I think I'd get rid of the grease before you do your facetime with him."

"It couldn't wait? We're right in the middle of this."

"He didn't say come see him when you feel an urge to visit. He said to get your butt over there. I didn't ask questions at that point."

"Okay, okay. Start, stop, start, stop. It never gets old."

"No problem, Jim Bob, I'll save some grease for you."

"I know you will."

Jimmy went to the sink and cleaned up as best he could before heading over to the CO's office.

Commander Hewett was a few years older than most of the station's crew. He was lean and looked to be in as perfect physical condition as any of the others on the rescue crew. He'd done his time in a chopper and nobody at the station would be doing anything he'd not already been through. He always had a smile on his face and, even after all the years in the Coast Guard, he still loved coming to the station every day and being part of something he considered his calling.

"Come in, Harrison. Listen, you got a call that was run through my office 'cause they couldn't reach you on your cell phone."

"Sorry about that. So much noise in the shop, I probably just didn't hear it."

"That's fine. But it was the nursing home calling for you again and they said it was urgent for you to call them. I guess you know it's probably not good news."

"It's a call I don't want to make, but I've seen this coming for quite a while. I'll get back with them right now."

"Why don't you use my office? It's quiet and I want to go to the canteen and get a coffee anyway."

"I'd appreciate that, sir."

"Not a problem. Take your time."

Jimmy got the card for Lakeview out of his wallet and called the number.

"Hello, this is Lakeview. How may I direct your call?"

"This is James Harrison. I'm returning a call. My mother is Margaret Harrison and she's a resident there."

"Yes, sir, Mr. Harrison. I'll transfer you."

"Hello, Mr. Harrison. This is Janet. I'm the evening manager here. I hate to tell you this but I'm afraid your mother has taken a turn for the worse. I doubt she'll make it until morning. If you want to see her before she passes, you need to come now. If you can make it, when you get to the front door it'll be locked. Press the bell to the right of it and someone will let you in. I'll alert them you're coming so they'll be expecting you."

"Thanks for letting me know. I'll start heading that way in just a few minutes. I'm in Elizabeth City so it'll be about four hours before I can get changed and get down there."

"I'd encourage you to try and make it as fast and safely as you can. I'm certain her time has arrived."

"I'm headed your way."

As Jimmy walked out of the CO's office, he met him in the hallway.

"You were right, sir. They say this is her last day. I've got to go to New Bern. Can I get off?"

"Tell you what. You know how short of swimmers the whole guard is. I'm going to call headquarters and see if they can get me another one down here to fill in for you for a week or so. I know you'll have a lot of things to take care of in New Bern. I don't want you worried about what's going on here. We'll cover for you."

"Like they say, sir. No one is indispensable."

"In your case, Jimmy. It would be tough to replace you. We'll just make do till you're back. By the way, just heard from the New Bern police. They found the body of the guy who drowned taking that woman you rescued out in a dinghy. They said he still had the rope from a crab pot wrapped around his legs. That's probably why he went under. What a shame. Ruined both of their lives. They were getting married, didn't you say?"

"That's right. They were engaged. Her life will never be the same."

"We see far too much of this type of senseless accident on the water. Always tragic, but you did your part to help. Now, get out of here and drive carefully. It's going to be a late night of driving and I know you have a lot on your mind. Keep us posted back here as to what's going on."

"I will sir. And thank you for being so supportive."

"No problem, Jim. I have a Mom too."

Jimmy took a ten-second shower, threw on some clean clothes, packed a bag that would hold him for a few days and hit the road. As soon as he cleared Elizabeth City, he called Kay.

"Kay, the nursing home called and said Mom won't make it till morning. I'm on the way. You want to go out there with me to see her? I'm sure she'd want to see you. You were on her A list for potential daughters-in-law."

"Absolutely, I want to go. I'll just meet you there. It's out Neuse Boulevard before the intersection with the bypass, right?"

"That's it. On the right just before the light. If you beat me there, just ring the bell to the right of the door and they said somebody will let you in. Tell them you're there to see Margaret. I'll be there in three hours. I'm already on the way."

"See you soon."

The parking lot in front of Lakeview was mostly empty. Jimmy saw Kay's car and pulled up beside her. She immediately got out and came over to him offering a comforting hug.

"I'm sorry about your mother. You just found out today?"

"I've been expecting their call but it's still a shock when it happens. Come on in with me."

Margaret's room looked just the same as it did prior to the day's downturn. Everyone understood there was nothing more that could be done and she didn't want any heroics trying to sustain her life for a couple days or even a week. She was at peace with her time being up. She'd attended Christ Church since she was a child and had a strong faith that she would quickly be reunited with her husband and family members who had passed before her. As they entered, they could see she was sleeping to the sound of soft gospel tunes coming from a small speaker by her bed. Jimmy walked over and gently picked up her hand inside of his. She stirred and looked up at him.

"Jimmy, you made it. I was praying I'd get to see you one more time before I go to be with your Dad."

"You know I'd be here, Mom. You were always there for me. And look who I brought with me."

Kay stepped over to the bedside next to Jimmy.

"Kay. I'm so glad you came. Promise me when I'm gone, you're going to take care of my boy. Would you promise me that? Did he ask you to marry him yet? If he hasn't and I had the strength, I'd get up and turn him over my knee. You know you're the one he's supposed to be with, don't you honey?"

"We've pretty well come to that same conclusion, Mom. You can rest assured Jimmy will be well-looked out for. I'm going to make an honest man out of him."

"Thank, God! I can go to Heaven in peace knowing that everything is alright back here. I wish I could come to the wedding. I'd..."

Margaret started to choke as she talked. Unable to catch her breath, she stopped talking and laid back on the pillow and tried to swallow several times. Jimmy called the nurse. She came over to Margaret and took her pulse.

"Very faint. I think you got here just in time."

Margaret fell hard asleep never to wake again. Jimmy and Kay both stayed in the room. Jimmy pulled his chair up beside her and kept talking to her hoping she might realize he was still there. Around midnight he felt her stir. She squeezed his hand for just a couple of seconds and then her grip released. He looked at her face and immediately knew she was gone. There was no more pain and no more waiting for the end. It was a sad moment but he and Kay both felt relieved and hopeful that she was on her way to a better place. Jimmy called the nurse attendant back to the room. They took turns kissing her on the forehead and then left as the nurse pulled the sheet up over her face.

"Well, that's certainly the end of an era in my life. She was always my biggest supporter. I could do no wrong."

"Are you going to have a service of some type for her?"

"Nothing large. She wouldn't want that. I'll meet with Paul tomorrow at the church and set up a small celebration of life for just the few friends that she survived and any of my friends who'd like to come."

"Let me help you put it together. I loved your Mom and I know she thought a lot of me."

"She literally made me promise I would call you last month when we got back together. I guess she was the push I needed to get up enough guts to call you."

"Whatever it took, I just thank God we're together again."

❧

Christ Episcopal Church

Paul Canady had been Rector at Christ Church for about five years. He was young and Margaret was happy that he was putting a lot of life back into her church. More couples were starting to attend and there was always a beehive of activity flowing around the old sanctuary. Christ Church had been founded in New Bern in 1715 and in its early days, many famous patriots attended services there. It had been the center of activity in New Bern for over three hundred years. Just walking into the grand old chapel gave you a feeling of history that seemed to preserve all that had gone on there in previous generations. It was sort of a gateway to the past.

The Rector delivered a short tribute to Margaret. He was well spoken and his message came from his heart.

"These are busy and complicated times we live in. We fill our lives with many things that might bring us some contentment for a moment. But the lasting answers to all of this world's most important questions haven't changed. Just a few things really count. Family, relationships, honest work, harmony with nature and those we love and keeping these things close to us. Margaret Harrison understood this as well as anybody I ever knew. She lived a simple life. For over thirty years, she taught many of your children in elementary school right here in town. I'm not sure she ever traveled far from home and certainly didn't travel after her husband passed. She made the best of every day, loving the people who were special to her, taking care of what was important in her life and cherishing the building you're sitting in right now. We could all learn a great deal from the way she lived her life through example. I wish everyone could have spent the time with her that I did, especially in these last few years as her health failed. She never got down, always had a smile and when you asked her how she was doing, you always got the same answer. 'Things couldn't be better.' I loved Margaret Harrison and I'm sure many of you here today did as well. And now, we send her off to spend eternity with the Lord and all of her loved ones who are waiting there for her, let us not cry for her even though we miss her. She wouldn't want that. Let's celebrate the end of a life well lived. Let us pray."

Jimmy thought the sermon was perfect. Just what his mother would have wanted. There was a small gathering in the assembly hall after the service where those who had attended could share a few thoughts and offer sympathies. He was surprised at how many had attended. He put a small obituary in the newspaper and no other announcement was made. There were at least sixty people in attendance, many that Jimmy hadn't seen for a number of years. Several of Jimmy's crew made the trip from Elizabeth City. A few of the city's prominent leaders also came to pay their respects. Greg Smith from Mitchell's Hardware, a person known and loved by everyone in town came as well as Governor Pollard and her husband, Tommy. They were both longtime members of the church and close friends with Margaret. The first female Governor of North Carolina came over to Jimmy and Kay.

"Lovely service, Jimmy. And Kay Burwell. I heard you were back in town and practicing law over at Steinbeck's. Is that right?"

"Yes, Ma'am. I started there about three months ago. Right after I passed the bar."

"You let me know if I can do anything to help you. I know a lot of the members of the old 'boys club' here in town and can get things done when I need to. You stay in touch with me. Are you here with Jimmy?"

"I am."

Kay noticeably squeezed Jimmy's hand when she answered. The Governor noticed the gesture.

"I see."

"I promised Margaret, the night she passed that I'd take care of her son and it's a promise I intend to keep."

"Well, that's one ceremony I don't want to miss. You two keep me on the guest list. Jimmy, we loved your mother and will miss her a great deal. I spoke with her after I attended the award ceremony in Elizabeth City. To say she was proud of you would be a huge understatement. I know she'd be thrilled knowing you two are getting together. Now don't forget to send me an invitation."

"I promise."

Jimmy and Kay made the rounds shaking hands and thanking everyone for attending the service. It was comforting to see so many people who had been touched by her and took the time to pay their respects. As they filed out, Jimmy thanked Paul and offered to help clean up the parish hall.

"Not going to even consider it. Your mother helped make this place what it is and we're privileged to clean it up in honor of her. Now you and Kay get on out of here and let me know when I can be of any help to you. You know I do wonderful weddings?"

"We wouldn't consider doing one without you, Paul. You're our first call."

"I'm counting on that."

They headed to Union Point Park to take in the sunset and reminisce about the day. It was a chilly night but they stayed close as they sat on a bench for about half an hour talking and just holding hands.

"You know, Kay. We've both been telling people, when they asked, that we're planning on getting married."

"We have."

"It seems kind of presumptive of me to tell anyone that when I haven't really officially proposed."

"I'm glad you noticed. I know I had. Seems like a pretty big detail to overlook."

"I intend to set that right. Kay Burwell. I loved you from the moment I first laid eyes on you, dancing around a dogwood tree in that yard just down the street from my house. You were the most beautiful thing I'd ever seen. It's been over twenty years now and I still feel the same, even stronger. I don't want to spend another year without you. Not really even a day. Would you do me the great honor of marrying me and keeping me company for the rest of our lives?"

Jimmy reached in his pocket and retrieved a delicate gold

ring with what had to be one of the smallest diamonds Kay had ever seen. To her, it might as well have been the Hope Diamond. She took it from him and immediately slid it onto her ring finger.

"It's a perfect fit and that was beautifully said. I always felt you'd come to your senses one day and realize we were supposed to be together. And now you've finally done it. Jimmy Harrison, I will gladly take you as my husband and spend the rest of my life being properly adored by you. And vice versa of course. How about a Valentine's Day wedding? We could go to the Heart Ball and then start planning who to invite and where we might go for a short honeymoon. I could get off for a week. How about you?"

"I guess we could fill the icebox up on *Sugarcane* and head over to Ocracoke."

"That sounds like the exact trip I knew you'd be shooting for. If that's what you want to do, I'm there. I guess that old boat is now going to be part of our family."

"I'm glad you understand."

There was then one monumental kiss that neither wanted to end. They embraced in the cold evening air and the sun set as they watched. They both knew how they wanted the future to be. Neither had a clue as to what life had in store for them.

6

The Heart Ball – New Bern Convention Center – December 21

JIMMY HURRIED TO pick Kay up at her condo on Middle Street in the downtown historical section of New Bern. Many of the retail businesses had modern loft apartments above them and they were the most desirable address for young professionals who worked downtown. The location offered the opportunity to walk to most of the restaurants and bars that dotted the bustling tourist part of town. Hers was a small but elegant condo above a gift shop. He hadn't seen her place before, but was not surprised she wanted to live where there was some nightlife and activity. She always loved music. He tried to keep up with her a few times on the dance floor, but always felt like he was an anchor. As on most Saturday nights, local bands could be heard playing from inside the numerous clubs located on the block. He had to park his rusty old Jeep Cherokee a half block away to find parking. The crowds attending the Heart Ball at the convention center had all of downtown buzzing like a beehive. Jimmy grabbed his garment bag with his formal uniform inside, walked to Middle Street and headed up the stairwell to Kay's loft. She greeted him at the door wearing a floor length strapless blue gown with a slit halfway up the skirt. It left him nearly breathless seeing her so radiant in her formal regalia.

"You are stunning. Let me look at you. There's no doubt in my mind who'll be Scarlett O'Hara at this affair. I have to tell you; you could do so much better than me. I don't want you to, but as smart and beautiful as you are, any man would give their right arm to have a woman like you. I'm not letting you out of my sight for one minute tonight."

"That's just how I want it, Jimmy. You need to get dressed, right?"

"Got my fancy duds in the bag here."

"The bath is just down the hall. Help yourself."

The small apartment was nicely decorated. Kay really had her stuff together he thought. Perhaps when he retired in a few years they could buy a house somewhere that overlooked the river. They'd grow old together watching boats sail by when they were too old to sail on *Sugarcane*. He changed into his dress whites and went back to where Kay was waiting. It was his turn to impress.

"And you thought I looked good. You are magnificent in that uniform."

Her eyes fixated on two full rows of highly polished medals on the left side of his chest.

"What are all those medals for? You look like General Patton."

"I'll go over them sometime with you. You're required to wear them on your dress whites. Normally they're just ribbons. These hanging medals make it seem like a much bigger deal than it is."

"Why don't I believe you? What is that huge gold one in the middle?"

"That's the Coast Guard Gold Lifesaving Medal."

"It's beautiful! Is there any medal more distinguished than that one?"

"There's the Congressional Medal of Honor. I doubt I'll ever be in a situation that I could earn that one in my lifetime."

"The ones you have are impressive enough. I'm sure there's some unbelievable story attached to every one of them and I'm going to want to hear them all."

"Let's get in our chariot and head to the ball. It's just a little over a block away. Should we walk instead?"

"I don't think so. It's freezing outside and they're even calling for some precipitation, maybe even a little sleet, according to Mr. Still."

"Well, if Les said it, then it must be so."

The parking lot across from the convention center

was jammed. Jimmy parked nearby on the street running through Union Point Park. They waited for the pedestrian crossing light and then walked quickly through a light breeze toward the front door. It was hard not to notice all the luxury cars parked almost on top of each other.

"My old Jeep certainly stands out here. I'm not one to drive some run-of-the-mill Mercedes or Cadillac. You know, don't want to run with the pack."

"I love your Jeep. It will certainly go places these cars won't."

"And, I'm sure they go to places my old Jeep never will."

Jimmy's sense of humor was not lost on Kay. Her wit was every bit as sharp as his. She could mix it up with the high-end socialites or a work crew. She'd spent a lot of time around both in her life.

There was a crowd at the front entrance of the convention center. Tickets were being collected and other guests waited for friends just inside. It wasn't a night to be standing out in the chilly air. With a crowd this size, it would be easy to get lost.

Every head in the large hall turned as Jimmy and Kay made their entrance. They didn't need all the attention they were generating, but they looked more like a couple of young movie stars attending a premier than a local event in New Bern. Many in the crowd nodded and said hello to Kay as they passed. This wasn't Jimmy's crowd. He didn't have any negative feelings toward them; he just didn't see anyone he actually knew in attendance. They made their way inside the ballroom where seven hundred people would soon be gathered. It was already filling up.

The Heart Ball was the social event of the year in New Bern. It was always a sellout with the proceeds going to benefit the fight against heart disease and strokes. It was one of the few black-tie events held each year. It gave the city's business and professional elites the opportunity to dress up, press the flesh, and help a great cause to benefit the community all in the same evening. A popular regional band was brought in to entertain after a catered meal was served.

The room was set up with dozens of round tables with each patron's name engraved on a place card in front of their assigned chair. Kay and Jimmy moved through the room until they found the table with their place cards. It was to the left of the stage where the band would be playing later. Large speakers throughout the room carried light jazz at just the right volume to block out a lot of the individual chatter and shuffling about. There was already a distinguished looking couple at their table. Kay knew them well and was eager to introduce them to Jimmy.

A long married, well-known couple, Steve owned the firm where Kay worked. Steve was a little overweight with an easy smile and his wife, Elaine, was slim and had a gregarious personality. They were the epitome of southern charm and graciousness.

"Elaine and Steve, this is James Harrison. Everyone calls him Jimmy. Born and raised in New Bern. Jimmy, these are the Steinbecks, Elaine and Steve."

"Steinbeck like the writer?"

"Actually, he is a cousin. He was in the West Coast part of the family. We're originally from Cary, North Carolina. We've lived in New Bern for about twenty-five years now. I moved Elaine to the coast under the guise of practicing law here. I actually came for the fishing. So, I see you're in the Navy."

"Coast Guard, Sir. I'm stationed at Elizabeth City."

"That's great, son. I would guess, by looking at your chest, you've seen a lot of action. What sort of conflicts were you in?"

"I'm a rescue swimmer. Most of my conflicts have been with Mother Nature."

"Very impressive. I'm certainly aware of what you do. Dangerous work. How do you know my lovely and talented associate, Kay?"

Kay spoke up.

"We've been together since grade school and now we're engaged to be married on Valentine's Day but we haven't told anyone yet, except for Jimmy's mother. She passed away just a short while ago and she wanted to make sure I was going to take care of her son. I promised her I would."

Elaine responded.

"How exciting Kay! I'm flattered that we're the first to know. Is it still a secret?"

"Not really. It actually just became official, so we haven't decided when to tell people yet. We were trying to wait for just the right moment."

Steve joined in.

"If it's not a secret, then please let me break the news to our mutual friends at the table here tonight. You know everyone with the firm, Kay and I'm sure they'll want to shake this young man's hand and congratulate him on what will certainly be the best decision of his life."

"That's fine with me if Jimmy's okay with it." She turned to him, "Is that alright?"

"I would be thrilled for you to introduce me as your fiancé. After all, I was beginning to doubt it would happen myself. I mean I wanted it to, but for a while I wasn't sure we'd get back together."

Kay moved their name tags on the table several places over so they could sit beside Steve and Elaine. As other guests arrived, the Steinbecks greeted them and introduced them to Jimmy. They held back their secret about the upcoming nuptials so they could make an official announcement when everyone was seated. The last couple to arrive was a lovely young woman named Jennifer, also an attorney at Kay's firm, and her escort. He was none other than Morrison Brooks, the toothy and completely obnoxious attorney Jimmy met previously at Morgan's Tavern. It was obvious to everyone, that Morrison had already imbibed several cocktails.

"Kay, now it's apparent why we've seen so little of you these past few weeks. You work all day and then disappear until the next morning. You should've told us that Officer Jimmy here has been squiring you around town."

"Jim works in Elizabeth City so we don't get to do much

'squiring' around unless it's on weekends. I go home in the evenings and continue working so that hopefully one day I'll be a partner in Steve's firm."

Others at the table knew immediately that Morrison was jealous of Jimmy and using the moment to put him down, his normal routine. Steve spoke up.

"I think we can all see from the amount of gold on Mr. Harrison's uniform that he is already a full partner in his profession. We are grateful for your service, Jimmy, and appreciate it every time we go out on the water that men such as yourself are there willing to put your own lives at risk to come bail us out of trouble."

"I'm just part of a team, sir. Every team member is critical to the success of what we do."

"Now correct me if I'm wrong, but when it comes down to exactly who has to bail out of the chopper and into an enraged ocean to rescue people, you're the one they call on. Am I right?"

"That's pretty much what I do, but I truly don't deserve any more credit than the rest of the team though. All of our lives depend on the pilots who fly us out in every kind of condition, the crew that maintains the aircraft, and even the shore personnel maintaining critical communications. None of what I do would be possible without them. So, it would be unfair to think I was the only one doing it."

"Well said, young man. The humility of a hero. Awesome."

From that point on, Morrison became fairly quiet, at

least when it came to Kay and Jimmy. He had been one-upped, thanks to Steve. However, lines were now drawn and Morrison would never be a fan of Jimmy's.

A large crew of waitstaff brought out a delightful dinner and dessert that made the entire table grow silent while they filled their stomachs.

After dinner, more drinks soon followed. As was the custom at this event, there was an open bar so a number of guests overachieved in utilizing that service. Predictably, the noise level in the room grew exponentially as the evening progressed. When activity increased on the stage, it was apparent the band was getting prepared to start the dance part of the evening. Steve used the moment.

"My friends, I'm sure you have all enjoyed meeting Kay's friend, Jim Harrison. Quite an impressive young man. But, I'm happy to announce to you all that he is now undertaking his most daring mission. He has asked our beautiful and talented associate, Kay Burwell, to be his wife and she has accepted. Their wedding will be on Valentine's Day. So, here's a toast to you both. You are wonderful friends and we hope we'll all enjoy this festive annual event together for many years to come. Cheers!"

Everyone at the table raised their glasses in tribute. Morrison went along with the gesture and then downed his entire Jack and Seven in one overly long pour down his throat. There was no question, Morrison had been thinking of his own future plans that featured Kay and this threw a monkey wrench into all of that.

The young woman Morrison brought with him to the event was quickly growing tired of his drinking and his company. The final straw was Morrison knocking over a glass of wine onto her dress as he dropped back into his seat after the toast. The look on her face said it all.

"If you will please excuse me, I need to visit the ladies' room and see if I can get this wine stain off my dress. It's been a lovely evening."

Everyone at the table understood the point she was making. She didn't return to the table. Shortly after the toast and a round of congratulations, the band took the stage and began filling the room with a great mix of tunes from the past and present. They'd come from Raleigh and were decidedly a cut above the usual nightspot bands that worked most of the clubs in New Bern.

Jimmy and Kay took to the floor and stayed almost constantly in each other's arms enjoying the music, the ambiance, and each other. Their happiness radiated around them to everyone who glanced their way. The band started playing a song that always had Jimmy thinking about Kay. It was Beth Nielsen Chapman's emotional love song, ALL I HAVE.

"All I have is all I need
And it all comes down to you and me

How far away this world becomes
In the harbor of each other's arms...."

Being a lifelong sailor, the connotation of the person you love being a safe harbor created a mental picture for him that he never forgot. The band did a wonderful rendition of it. He shared his thoughts with Kay.

"Whenever I hear this song, I think of you. Listen to the words."

Kay loved the melody and quickly understood Jimmy's attraction to it.

"It's a beautiful song. It's us, isn't it?"

"Let's use it as our first dance at the wedding."

"That sounds perfect to me."

The rest of the evening was more special than either of them could have imagined. The band played its final song. Guests started to hug each other farewell and head out into the stormy, cold night. The Steinbecks stayed until the end with Jimmy and Kay. There was certainly a connection there that both couples appreciated. Jimmy understood fully that Steve's put-down of Morrison was a major reason for the warm reception he received from others at their table and the success of the evening.

Elaine turned to Kay.

"It's nasty out there. I need to visit the ladies' room before we head out. Want to join me?"

Steve turned to Jimmy.

"Women. Have you ever seen one go to a bathroom by themselves? It's got to be in their DNA. Look, why don't you wait for the girls while I go get the car. They'll appreciate not getting soaked walking out in the rain. Besides, it could be quite a while if I know Elaine."

"Sure. I could use the head myself."

Being some of the last to leave the convention center, the restroom was empty with one exception. An inebriated Morrison Brooks was bent over at a sink applying cold water to his face. He turned to see who had entered the room.

"Well, well, well. Look at who we have here. Everyone's favorite cub scout. I can't believe you let go of Kay long enough to take a leak."

He reached out to grab Jimmy's arm, half stumbling as he moved.

"You're drunk, Morrison. How about I help you get some coffee before you leave here. You shouldn't be driving like this."

"Always the hero, am I right? Officer Jim. Big Jim to the rescue. Stand back everybody, hero at work here."

"That's enough, Morrison."

"Oh, you ain't even got me started yet. It's really funny that you think you can just come waltzing into her life and take charge like you own her or something. She's way too good for you. You know she's going to be a big success and you come sneaking in to grab a few nuggets from the gold mine for yourself. Don't get much gold in the Coast Guard, except little shiny pieces to pin on your uniform, am I right?"

With a wild slap at Jimmy's medals, Morrison missed his mark and fell against Jimmy. He then reared back and gestured aggressively.

"Get your hands off me. I don't need any help from the likes of you. Let me show you how I deal with feisty, overgrown cub scouts who think they are big shots."

He took a full swing with his right hand, hoping to land it on Jimmy's face. With seemingly no effort, Jimmy blocked it and pulled it behind Brooks' back.

"You've had too much to drink and I've had enough of you."

He pushed the fuming lawyer to a seat on the opposite wall. A trash can fell over during the maneuver alerting an attendant helping the departing guests in the hall outside. He came into the room to see what the disturbance was.

"Any problem in here, sir?"

He looked at Jimmy standing in front of him and the disheveled Brooks leaning forward while sitting on the bench.

"This gentleman has had too much alcohol I'm afraid. He shouldn't be getting anywhere near a car in this shape."

"I'll get a cab for him, sir. This must be the gentleman I heard about from the young woman earlier tonight. Her description was on point."

"Yeah, he's feeling a little full of himself. You know how folks can get when they've had a little too much to drink. He needs to go home and sleep it off. He'll be fine tomorrow."

Brooks glared at Jimmy.

"This is far from over. You think you've got her, but we'll just see about that. You'll never be anything but an anchor around her neck. I'll see that she gets what she deserves because she deserves a helluva lot better than the likes of you."

Jimmy shook his head as he looked at the man who represented everything he disliked about people who thought of themselves as somehow more deserving than everyone else.

"I hope she thinks more of herself than believing she deserves someone like you."

Jimmy opened the door and walked back in the main hall leaving Brooks with the attendant. It was not the kind of ending he hoped the night would bring. Jimmy found the ladies at the coat check station. They rounded up their wraps from the attendant and headed out into the night air.

"Kay, thank you for bringing Jim with you tonight. It was a pleasure meeting him and we are both thrilled you two are getting married. You promised we'd be on the invitation list."

"We wouldn't dream of having it without you and Steve there."

"We are so looking forward to it. Well, we're parked right here. Where are you parked, Jim?"

"Across the street in Union Point. There weren't any spaces left when we arrived."

"Well, you two hop in the back and we'll drive you to your car. It's too cold and wet out here to be walking in this mess."

"You don't mind? The traffic is still jammed up."

"In that case, you won't be slowing us down a bit. Am I right?"

"Thank you."

As they drove, Steve noticed that some of the drops hitting the front window were bouncing. The rain was turning into sleet. Steve turned into the park.

"Which car is yours, Jimmy?"

"The blue Jeep just ahead. Kay, you stay here while I get my old rust bucket started. When it's this cold, the choke sticks and she can flood pretty easy. I have to let it sit for a few minutes and then it will usually kick over."

"Will do."

As he jogged over to the Jeep, Steve and Elaine took the time to offer their thoughts on Jimmy. Elaine gushed as she spoke.

"Kay, I can see it in your eyes when you're together. You've made the perfect choice. What a wonderful young man. He's the kind of man that built this country. Someone you can always count on."

Steve offered his assessment.

"Let me second that. What's that old saying? 'He's the kind of man every young boy wants to grow up to be and every old man wishes he'd been.' As much as the Coast Guard needs men like him, it would be great if we could find something for him to do here in town. If you ever get to talking with him about that, let me know. I've lived here and practiced for a long time now. I know a lot of business people and I'm pretty sure we could find something here that he'd enjoy, and probably make a lot more money than Uncle Sam pays him."

"I'm so glad you like him. And believe me, I sure hate saying goodbye to him every week when he heads back to work at the Coast Guard Station. I'll have to think on how to bring this up to him. I don't know how he'd feel about moving home. He loves New Bern, but he also loves the Coast Guard. It would be a tough decision to make. Of course, I'd love it."

Jimmy came back to the window, the sleet still falling sharply on his face as he spoke.

"Steve, can you drive Kay back to her place? It's only a couple of blocks. I don't want her waiting out here in the cold until I get the car started."

"Are you sure, Jimmy? I don't mind waiting with you."

"No need for both of us to freeze. Why don't you put on a pot of coffee back at your place? I'll be over there shortly and that will help me wake up for the ride home."

"Great idea. I'll do it."

As Steve and Elaine pulled up to Kay's condo, she invited them to come up.

"Why don't you come in a have one cup of coffee with Jimmy and me? Won't take but just a few minutes and it'll warm us all up."

"If you're sure we won't interrupt you two."

"Absolutely not. Now, you come on up. Besides, I want to show Elaine my little place."

"Ok, but just for one cup."

They headed up the flight of stairs to the condo. Back at Union Point, Jimmy tried a couple more times to start the Jeep before it finally fired up. He drove through the now empty park and back to Kay's place. He parked behind Steve's large silver Suburban. He thought to himself.

"No chance of missing this school bus."

By the time he climbed the stairs and went inside Kay's condo, the smell of fresh coffee was filling the room. Steve and Elaine were sipping theirs. Elaine got up.

"Let me get you cup, Jimmy. You still like it black, right?"

"Black and black. Nothing added. The more caffeine the better."

"That's easy enough. Coming right up."

Kay walked over to him.

"You're soaked."

"I have my jeans and sweatshirt in the bag. Give me a minute to change and I'll leave like I came."

"You look just fine in jeans but I have to tell you, you were the most handsome man at the ball. Nobody else was even close, unless, of course, it was Steve here."

"You don't have to flatter me, Kay. I agree with you. You two were the most beautiful couple at the ball."

Elaine offered her opinion.

"I was always a sucker for a man in a uniform. When I met Steve, he was still in the Marine Corps Reserves. He'd put on that uniform and I was ready to take him home."

Steve couldn't help but remind her.

"Baby, I was about forty-five pounds thinner back then."

Elaine slid over closer to Steve. She grabbed his arm and kissed him on the cheek.

"You're just as handsome now as you were then. You're still the same guy I married."

"Well baby, you know what they say. Once a Marine, always a Marine. Jimmy, are you still hooked on the Coast Guard? Will you stay in?"

"I can retire in a few more years. If I got out now, I'd have to start over at the bottom somewhere. Being a rescue swimmer doesn't translate well to other careers."

"I can and will help you with that if you ever decide to become a civilian. You just call and I'm on it."

"Thank you. That's comforting to hear. I would love to live in New Bern, especially now that Kay and I are getting married."

"We don't have to think about that right now, honey. I'm going to be right beside you no matter where you are and what you're doing, Doctor, Lawyer, Indian Chief…and, of course, Coast Guard rescue swimmer."

Jimmy walked over to the window and looked out at the sleet starting to leave a film on the chairs sitting on Kay's balcony.

"It's looking nasty out there. How far do you have to go, Steve?"

"We live in Brice's Creek, just on the other side of the Trent. It's only a few miles. You're the one we're worried about."

"I have to be back tomorrow no matter what. I've taken

off so much time lately with my mother's passing and all. I'll be fine. My old Jeep has four-wheel drive and it can make this trip without me. I've done it at least a thousand times."

Steve and Elaine hugged them both goodbye and headed down the steps. Jimmy stayed behind for just a moment. He walked over to Kay, wrapped his arms around her and gave her a long, deep kiss.

"This was the most wonderful evening ever. Just having you there with me. I took your hand and I wanted to scream to everyone who could hear me. She's with me. The most beautiful woman in the world is marrying me."

"Don't think I didn't feel the same when we walked in together. You with your handsome uniform on with all your medals hanging off it. You make me feel so special, unlike anything I've ever felt before. And I'm so happy that I'll be spending many years with the one person I've always loved. You better get going. The weather is getting worse, and the longer you stay, the harder it's going to be to say goodbye. I'll see you next Friday, right?"

"You can absolutely count on it."

7

ONE LAST KISS and Jimmy ran down the steps to his Jeep. The motor started easily and he pulled out onto Middle Street. He reminisced on the details of the evening repeatedly as he drove. The road had a fine covering of sleet on it but the old Jeep had four-wheel drive and handled it easily. He'd take it slow and concentrate on staying alert. He was thankful for the coffee.

The incident with Brooks in the men's room had certainly opened up a new concern. He might be just an egotistical drunk but he had money and influence. Not to mention he was around Kay all week while Jimmy was in Elizabeth City. It was clear that he'd be working against him, trying to pull Kay away from him. He thought there'd never be any chance that she'd be interested in a man like him. Still, he had a determined adversary to deal with from this point on. In some ways it was more daunting to him than sitting in the doorway of a rescue chopper heading into a dangerous storm. Mother nature hadn't selected him as her principal target. Morrison Brooks had.

He felt wide awake and able to make the trip home. Traffic was light due to the weather and the hour. He turned onto the ramp for Interstate 70 to cross the Trent River bridge. As he approached the span, the traffic began to slow to a crawl. When he drove onto the bridge, he could see two men with flashlights standing in the center of the structure directing traffic into the left lane. Several cars were parked on the road in the right-hand lane. As he approached them, he looked over to the low guard rail on the side of the bridge. There was an opening where the aluminum rail was missing for about twenty feet and several large areas of concrete under it were broken. It was instantly obvious to him what had occurred. Someone had gone off the bridge. He pulled over to the right, left the motor running and went to one of the men standing near the broken rail with a large flashlight.

"Somebody go over?"

"Yep, just happened; about a minute ago. A couple of fellas are circling back on shore and trying to get to the car. It's still floating a bit but it won't be long. Don't know how many people are inside."

"Shine the light down on the car for me."

The man focused the beam on the roof of the large silver SUV. Jimmy knew exactly who was in the car. The man looked at him only to see he was quickly taking off his shoes and removing his jacket.

"What are you doing, sir? You can't go in there. It's at least twenty feet down to the water. You'll kill yourself."

"It's what I do. I'm a rescue swimmer. If that car goes under, we'll never get to them in time. I'm going in. Shine the light on top of the car and don't turn it away."

In less than two seconds, Jimmy looked over the rail, picked a spot to the side of the now partially submerged vehicle and jumped in. The small crowd gathered around the site were astounded to see the big splash as Jimmy hit the water. As they were looking down, blue and red emergency lights on rescue vehicles pulled into the lane from where Jimmy had launched himself. Several ambulances with sirens blaring could be heard approaching the scene. Emergency workers rushing to the scene focused their lights on the water's surface.

"He's committing suicide. Water's probably forty-five degrees. Whoever's inside that car has already been down there four or five minutes. It's nuts. The guy is crazy. It happened so fast. I couldn't stop him. One second, he was standing here, the next, bam! He's overboard. I wouldn't have believed it if I hadn't seen it with my own eyes."

Jimmy knew he was the only one there with even a remote chance of saving Steve and Elaine. The velocity of the jump carried him to the bottom of the river which was only about ten feet deep at that location. As he hit the river bottom, he felt a solid impact and an undeniable snap in his leg from striking either an old piling or concrete substructure of the bridge. It was a serious blow and he knew it, but he put it to the back of his mind. He made his way quickly over to the door on the passenger side. He could see a terrified Elaine who turned and looked at him in disbelief as he tapped on her window. He tried to open the door but it was locked. He used his hand to indicate to her that she should try and unlock the door. She fought vainly as the water crested over her shoulder. Jimmy moved behind her to the rear door and was surprised to see the small knob on top of the interior part of the door showing it was unlocked. The pressure was tremendous and he had to place one knee on the side of the car as he pulled at the door with both hands. Seconds seemed to pass like minutes when the door finally broke free. Water started to flood into the car at a tremendous rate. Jimmy reached forward and unlocked Elaine's door. He had to jam himself into the front seat between the couple. He noticed Steve was not conscious and was slumped over at the wheel. Elaine was hysterical. He placed his legs on top of her lap and with everything he had, kicked open her door. Excruciating pain shot through his leg. He quickly unbuckled her seat belt and literally pushed her out of the car in front of him. He looked up to see someone yelling at him from overhead.

"Over here. We've got a ladder down to you."

A rescue worker was halfway down a long aluminum ladder that extended from the top of the bridge where everyone was looking down into the river. Several other men held tightly to the top of the ladder as a fireman eased down it to the surface of the water. Jimmy cradled Elaine's head as he took only a few strokes to get her over to the ladder. The fireman quickly dropped a rescue harness around her below her arms.

"I've got her. I'll be right back for you."

"There's a man in the car. I'm going back for him."

"Is he still alive?"

"I don't know but I'm going to find out right now."

Jimmy turned and headed back over to the open passenger door. The vehicle was now totally full and the roof was just starting to go under water. He crawled inside. Steve was lifeless. He pushed his head up and fought to unlock his seat belt. His own hands were almost frozen and it took a full minute to break him free. Steve was a large man and it took far too long to pull him out of the car by his coat. Finally, they floated to the surface. Jimmy was completely spent when he pushed Steve over to the outstretched arm of the fireman.

"Got him. You come over to the ladder and hang on. I'll get the harness to you as soon as we can get this guy up. Jeez, he's huge."

It took at least five minutes to get Steve's dead weight up to the top of the bridge. Rescue crews stood ready to load them both into ambulances and rush them to the hospital. Now, Jimmy was the only one left to save.

Jimmy surfaced about fifteen feet out from the ladder. Men above and on the ladder urged him to swim toward them. He tried in vain to use his hands and feet. He looked up and saw a montage of blue and red flashing lights, people moving in all directions and heard confused noises that meant nothing as he began to lose consciousness. He was still wide-eyed and looking up as his head slipped silently under water.

East Carolina University – Vidant Medical Center – Greenville NC

Strange recurring sounds were slowly rousing Jimmy back to consciousness. His eyes weren't open, but he was aware to some extent. There were many different sounds that his mind was weakly trying to process. Some were obvious such as carts being pushed down a hall, footsteps on tile, occasional loud bursts of sound over a loudspeaker with different names being called out. Mechanical sounds from medical equipment seemed closest to him. Some had a rhythmic beat. Other sounds were more like periodic electric hums. One particularly annoying sound had the recurring chirp of what sounded like a busy signal on a phone that never ceased.

As the all-encompassing fog began to lift and he started to fully awaken, he had a deep feeling that he had survived something profound. As he took stock of his body and his senses, his first thought was that his mouth was dry. He tried to swallow only to be deterred by a large tube. He moved a hand up to try and swat it or pull it out. Then, someone beside him grabbed his hand and pulled it gently away.

"No James, we can't remove that. It helps you breathe.

Just relax. I'll use this little bottle to squirt some water in your mouth. Just a tiny bit. There, is that better?"

Jimmy didn't answer. He was too weak to respond. He could hear that someone else walked in beside her and they started to talk to each other. They mentioned a lot of numbers and words he didn't really comprehend or even care about. He did hear another person's voice, a man. He said to the woman.

"So, he's finally awake?"

"Yes, just now. I think he's still out of it though."

Jimmy made no attempt to follow their conversation. He never opened his eyes and quickly fell back into a deep sleep.

Jimmy drifted in and out of consciousness often without any concept of time or his surroundings. He was totally unaware he'd been in a hospital bed for almost two weeks.

When he awoke around midday on the second Sunday, he began seeing several things that did not make any sense. His eyes were finally open and sending him clear images. He saw that his right leg was suspended in a sling about eighteen inches from the bed he was lying on. Startled, he realized that he was in a hospital bed and in a considerable amount of pain. He tried to sit up, but found it hard to do anything. The same voice he heard before spoke softly to him.

"They told me to call you Jimmy. I'm Gayle, the floor nurse. Doctor Finney said you'd probably be coming around soon. He took out the breathing tube this morning and you are breathing just fine on your own."

Jimmy spoke for the first time. Words seemed to be hard to pronounce. He started and stopped several times before Gayle could make any sense of them.

"Where, where am I?"

"You're in Greenville, North Carolina. You're at the University Medical Center. You were in serious condition. For several days, we didn't know if you'd make it. Doctor Finney said you were in phenomenal physical condition and that was what undoubtedly saved your life."

"What happened?"

"Jimmy, I'm going to call Doctor Finney and let him update you about what's been going on. You just lie back. He'll be coming around shortly. There's an awful lot of people who've been dropping by to see you and many others calling to see how you were doing. In particular, there's one beautiful young lady who's almost lived here these past two weeks. They've been waiting for good news about you and I'm sure that over the next couple of hours they'll all know you're making good progress. I'll be just down the hall. Press this little button right here if you need me. Like I said, Doctor Finney will have the answers you want in just a little while."

He thought over what he'd just been told.

"Several weeks? What on Earth happened to me?"

Jimmy studied the room. He was now feeling fully awake and had some serious leg injuries. He was becoming increasingly aware of pain in his extremities and numbness in his right calf and thigh. His right hand was not responding well and part of his mouth felt like he'd just come from the dentist office and was still numb. He was hooked up to an IV and his suspended leg had metal rods literally extending through the skin into it that were connected to an external brace. His biggest concern was how long he'd be in a hospital room. This didn't look like the type of injury where you left the hospital after a couple of days and maybe had some kind of brace to wear for a few weeks.

Then, one thought literally took over his mind. Where is Kay? Is she okay? Am I the only one in the hospital? Thoughts of that harrowing evening on the bridge and in the water came flooding back so fast. He started breathing hard, trying to comprehend all the details as they rushed into his mind. What about Steve and Elaine? Did everyone make it out of the water in time? He began to remember bits and pieces of the wreck on the bridge. His questions would be answered over the next few hours. Doctor Warren Finney, a specialist from the University came into the room. He smiled and his pleasant demeanor was reassuring.

"James, you're finally awake. How do you feel?"

"I'm a little concerned Doctor. You're a doctor, aren't you?"

He was still finding it difficult to pronounce his words properly. He had to concentrate to make them come out of his mouth in a coherent manner.

"Yes, I'm Warren Finney. I'm an Orthopedic Surgeon. I put your leg back together."

"How bad is it?"

"I'd like to say you'll be as good as new, James. I'm afraid that's not the case. First, your right leg is at least two inches shorter than your left. The bones were so shattered that there was little to work with. We had to remove some of the bone so we'd have a place to connect these rods you see coming out of your leg. They'll be removed as soon as the bone is strong enough to handle your weight."

"How long could that take?"

"I'd guess two to three months."

"You've got to be kidding. I have a job. I'm in the Coast Guard. I need to be back at work."

"That's just not going to be possible, James. Your unit has sent representatives here at least twice a week to check on you. They're aware of what's going on. They'll be back soon, I'm sure. Your Commander is Mr. Hewett."

"Phil."

"That's right, Phil Hewett. He said to tell you not to worry about a thing except getting better. They've made arrangements to have your job covered for whatever time this takes. I had to tell him that the truth is, you will probably never be able to be a rescue swimmer again."

"Ever? You mean my leg is that messed up?"

"It is. It's not just the bones. There's severe nerve damage. The rehabilitation team will start by working to get you to where you can stand and take a few steps on your own. It's going to take a lot of hard work and some time for you to recover. I don't want to sugarcoat this. It's not going to be an easy path forward, but you are young and fit. You'll get there, but you're going to have work your hardest and take satisfaction from small improvements. This is not the news I know you'd want to hear, but you have to know. We're going to need your maximum effort for you to get better."

"Doc, is some of this going to be...you know... permanent?"

"We don't know how much permanent damage there will be. How well you do in rehab will tell us that. And it's not just your right leg. You have damage to your right side as well. Your right arm is not responding well to touch and your speech may well be affected. If you haven't noticed yet, you're slurring your words quite a bit."

"My mouth feels numb, like at the dentist."

"That's the kind of thing I'm talking about, James. You were submerged in the water without oxygen for several minutes. There is certainly some neurological damage. Only time, healing and how hard you work at rehabilitation will tell us how much can be regained. Some of your function may be lost forever. James, I want to tell you, I've heard all about what you did to wind up here with us and it was as incredible a story as I've ever heard. If you did all this damage to your leg when you jumped in the water, I don't see how you even moved anywhere after that. The pain had to be through the roof and you were doing this remarkable rescue with just one leg and one arm. Most people would have never moved again after that jump. You're a unique person. You have an uncommon kind of bravery that most men don't have."

"I don't feel unique right now."

"The thing you need to work on the most is staying positive. I'll be here to see you every day and you can ask me anything you want. I'll always be straight with you. Now, there's someone in the lobby I know you'll be happier to see than me. I'll have the nurse come comb your hair, clean you up a little bit and then go get her for you."

"Kay? Is it Kay?"

"It is. She's practically lived here since this happened. That woman loves you more than you even know. Such a beautiful lady. You're a lucky man."

Doctor Finney left the room and directed an attendant to come help Jimmy get a little more presentable. After a quick hair brushing and a once over with an electric razor, she cranked his head up with the adjustable bed. With his leg in the sling it wasn't possible to sit up fully.

"Alright, James. That's about as pretty as I can make you. I'm going to go get your lady friend for you."

Jimmy didn't know what to think. He kept running different scenarios through his mind. Could they still have their wedding in February? How could he see her while she was working in New Bern and he was an hour away in Greenville? There were more questions than answers. He heard footsteps in the hall and then the voice he wanted to hear the most broke the silence.

"Thank you, Candace. I'll be okay from here."

The door opened wide and in front of him was the face he needed to see more than anything in the world. With tears streaming down her face, she walked over to his bedside, bent over and hugged him, sobbing hard the entire time. She could hardly speak.

"I thought I lost you. I was so scared. This was the worst two weeks of my life. All I could think of was not having you with me, all the time. It was awful. Thank God, you're back. I prayed for you all day, every day. It must have worked."

Jimmy was overcome as well. Both of their faces were wet with tears. Whether it was the time and physical stress he'd been under or just realizing what happened to him was hitting him, this was one of the most emotional moments of his life. He was unable to move his arm enough to place it around her neck.

"I'll do the hugging, baby. All you have to do is smile and tell me you love me. That's what I've been thinking about all this time. I was so scared."

"You know I love you. We're still going to get married on Valentine's Day. You'll see. I'll be walking up the aisle. Whatever it takes I'm going to do it."

"I know you will, Jimmy. I know you will."

Kay said the words but there was some doubt in her mind.

They spent a full hour mostly just looking at each other and smiling, so happy for their reunion. Kay brought a small speaker and played music with her Ipod next to Jimmy's bed. The first song she played was ALL I HAVE, their wedding song.

"I'm going to leave this with you. Your nurse, Candace,

says she'll help you use it any time. Just ask her to cut it on and tell her what you want to hear. Well, there's some other people here to see you. I don't want to hog you all to myself. Actually, I do. But they've been waiting for hours. I love you, baby. I'll try to see you every day. It'll probably be after work but you can count on me being here. We're going to get you well."

He smiled as she left.

"I love you. See you soon."

Only minutes later, more familiar faces came into the room."

"Jim Bob. How are you man? You scared the heck out of us back at the station. You know, you're not supposed to do any incredible stunts without us. We're your support team. You see, you leave us at home and this happens. How're you feeling? I have to tell you; you don't look your best. But, check this out. Some things never change."

Bill pointed to the leg in the sling.

"You're still hanging by a cable. Just like when we're working. A touch of home right here in the hospital."

"Forgive me if I don't laugh."

"You're sorta jumbling your words together a little, Jim Bob. Did you hurt your mouth?"

"Nerve damage. It'll get better."

"What did the doc tell you? How long you going to be here? We've got some Yankee swimmer from New York on loan to us right now. It ain't the same. I need for you to get well soon and get back to the station."

Jimmy knew it was a lie when he said it.

"Not too long buddy. I'll be back soon. Save my place."

"No one can take your place, Jim Bob. Nobody. You call us at the station if you need anything. I'll be here so quick you'll think I'm a magician. You promise you'll call?"

Jimmy just nodded his head. He was feeling tired and weak. His eyes closed while Bill was still in the room. Bill spoke softer to not wake him again.

"OK, Jim Bob. I'll be leaving now. Be back soon."

Jimmy was asleep in seconds.

Two weeks went by in a fog. Kay came to see Jimmy every day as promised. He'd been moved from a critical care room to another in the rehab wing of the large hospital. His leg was still in a sling but twice a day a rehab specialist would visit, remove it from the sling and help him with some specific bends and stretches while he was still lying down. Her name was Wanda and she was a very affable, middle aged, African American. By anyone's standards, she was a large and strong woman. Strong in stature and in demeanor. She was a tough taskmaster and not willing to let her patients give up or spend too much time having a pity party.

"Okay, Admiral. Time to get you in a wheelchair. You've been lying around watching soap operas for a couple of weeks now and I've been taking it easy on you. That all comes to a crashing halt today. We're going to wheel you down to my laboratory and you're going to do some pull ups right from this wheelchair. Am I scaring you?"

"I don't know, Wanda. You're pretty scary, but I think it'll take more than that."

"We'll see. A lot of people aren't scared until I get them into the mad doctor's laboratory, then it's 'take me home or get me out of here.' You gotta be tough to run with the big dogs."

"I'm pretty tough. At least I was. We'll see if I still got it."

On the way down to the rehab equipment room, they passed the door to an atrium. There were several of these in the hospital. It was an outdoor area, totally surrounded by the building. There were lush plants covering every space that wasn't a walkway. Even though it was February, it was a beautiful sunny day with temperatures in the sixties.

"Could we go outside for just a minute, Wanda. Seems like a year since I felt the sun on my face."

Wanda turned the wheelchair around on a dime and pushed Jimmy through the atrium door.

"This what you wanted?"

"Man, I've missed being outside. I wish I could go to my boat. I'm missing being on the river or even just seeing the water. The sun feels great on my face."

Wanda stayed with him for about five minutes before shattering the moment.

"Sorry, Jimmy. We've got to get going. Believe it or not, I work on a schedule and there's some other folks waiting for me to torture them today."

"Thanks, that really lifted my spirits."

They wheeled into the rehab equipment room. Wanda took Jimmy over to a low horizontal bar used to let wheelchair patients try to pull themselves up. Basically, it was wheelchair pullups.

"This is it, Admiral. Belly up to the bar. Let's see how many chin-ups you can do."

Jimmy tried to reach up to the bar and was dismayed to realize he wasn't able to lift his right arm enough to even touch the bar. The left arm was weak but able to reach up and get a hand on it. It was a traumatizing moment for him.

"I can't seem to move my arm enough to even lift it up. What do I need to do? This is really bad, Wanda. Can you make this better?"

"I'm going to try."

Wanda walked around the chair, put her hands under Jimmy's arm and helped him lift it up toward the bar. She understood immediately there was zero strength and muscle response. Nonetheless, she helped him pump it up and down around ten times.

"We'll make a drill out of this and do it every day until you can do it without me."

"Be honest with me, Wanda. Do you really think this will get better? I don't feel like I have any control over it at all. And,…"

"Yes, and what?"

"I'm supposed to be in a wedding soon and this has me worried. My leg is still in a brace and I can't use my arm. I mean I can't use them at all. Tell me the absolute truth. What do you think my chances are of ever being able to use them again? Will I ever be able to walk on my own?"

"Honey, if you want me to tell you in absolute terms, I can't. Nobody knows if you'll ever get better or have a huge breakthrough next week or next month. I'll be honest with you. Since you're asking me. I've been doing this for over twenty years and I've worked with a lot of folks. My best guess, and that's just what it is, is that your arm will remain extremely weak from here on out. Maybe some nerves will regenerate but it will never be enough to make this arm something you can work with. It just won't. Your leg, we don't know. Doc Finney says the brace may come off next week and they'll remove the rods and put you in a smaller, fiberglass one like a pro football player wears sometime. It'll help your leg take the load and let you start to move your knee some. You'll need a lift on the bottom of your right shoe to even up your legs. A couple weeks or so after that and I can give you a better opinion. Till then, we'll work with whatever we can to help the rest of your body stay strong."

"Just one more question."

"OK, give it to me."

"Do you think, in all honesty, there's a chance at all that I could go to my wedding in a about a month and walk down the aisle? Honestly?"

"Would you be OK with a crutch?"

"I'd take that."

"We'll put in two weeks of hard practice after this brace comes off and see where the good Lord takes us. I never say anything is totally impossible because where there's faith, there's always hope. I'll help you all I can."

Wanda knew he'd never walk ten feet in a month, crutches or not. There was no point in killing the dream. It was a realization he needed to come to on his own.

"You're the best, Wanda. Tough, yes. But the best."

"I'll take that as a compliment."

"It is."

The following two weeks consisted of a difficult physical therapy routine with Jimmy giving everything he had to getting stronger. Whatever functions were still working would be the best he could make them. Rehab drills were painful and frustrating, especially for someone who'd maintained his body like a finely tuned instrument for so many years. To be reduced to an invalid confined to a wheelchair was a condition he knew he couldn't live with. Whatever effort it took, he would find the strength to give it.

The last few weeks brought with them some changes that were staying front and center in his thoughts. Bill Flynn and the gang back at the station initially visited him twice a week as promised. The following week, Bill called and said they were in training and would miss the next several visits. The next week, there were no visits and no phone calls. He gave them every benefit of the doubt as he knew their job was more demanding than most people could imagine. It involved constant training and preparation. Surely, they'd be back to visit before long.

Kay had been true to her word and visited almost daily or called to tell him why she couldn't make it. She planned to visit Jimmy that afternoon, but requested a visit with

Doctor Finney ahead of it. She sat in the waiting room outside his office for a short while. She expected to wait for an hour or so as that had been her experience with most doctors over the years. She was surprised when her name was called exactly at the scheduled time. An office assistant came over to her.

"Ms. Burwell, Doctor Finney can see you now."

"Thank you."

The young woman opened the door to the doctor's office and Kay went in. She then closed the door behind her.

"Kay Burwell, how nice to see you."

"Thank you, Doctor Finney."

"I can only surmise why you requested this meeting. I'm sure you'd like a candid update on Jim."

"That's it exactly. I don't see much improvement in his right arm and even though his leg is out of the sling he doesn't seem to be able to move it much. He had this dream that he'd be well enough to get married, walk to the altar on Valentine's Day. Obviously, that's not going to happen."

"You're correct. I've been doing this for many years. I've seen a lot of cases similar to Jim's. His is particularly hard because his life and career before the accident was a physical one. Truthfully, his conditioning undoubtedly saved his life. He has made tremendous progress, but sadly, it's my opinion that he will never be physically up to that career again."

"Oh…what do you mean? I thought his recovery might be slow but there would be a full recovery at some point. What are you saying now?"

"He will recover some abilities, but not back to where he was before the accident. The plain truth is, with the serious nature of his injuries, Jim will be physically disabled from here on. He will be able to walk without a wheelchair or walker but it will be with a severe limp as one leg is considerably weaker than the other and it is a good bit shorter. He'll need to be fitted with orthopedic shoes that will help with the height differential, but they won't make his leg any stronger. His right arm has severe neurological damage that is permanent and it is paralyzed. His speech has improved some and I'm encouraged by that. With continued practice, he can more than likely get his voice and speech to the point that most people won't notice any problem with it. Just remember this. Jim will always be the same person you have known and loved for all these years, but physically he won't be able to do the things he used to do."

"This would mean his career as a Coast Guard rescue swimmer is over. I don't know what he will do to make a living since that's all he's ever wanted to do and all he's ever lived for."

"How about driving a car?"

"There are companies that make specialty cars with control features that allow a handicapped person to drive. When he reaches a plateau and can't improve any more, he might want to check into one of those. They are extremely expensive."

"How about his boat? Sailing is his passion. He's got a sailboat, not a huge boat, but he loves it more than almost anything. Will he be able to sail his boat again?"

"Realistically, I don't see how that would be possible with his mobility challenges and only one good arm. There's so much full body strength required to pull lines, not to mention maintaining his balance. Perhaps he could ride on the boat and let someone else be the captain."

"I'm willing to bet he doesn't know all this yet, does he?"

"He is becoming painfully aware of his limitations. I don't intend to be Doctor No and tell him what his boundaries are. Most of this will become clear to him without anybody ever having to explain it to him. It's best to let him try for himself and decide on his own what he can and cannot do."

By now, Kay's face was flushed and her eyes swollen with tears.

"I'm sorry, Doctor Finney. This isn't what I was expecting to hear. Our life together will be forever altered by all of this. I just don't know how we'll be able to deal with it all. It's all just so sad and depressing. It seems terribly unfair to us. Why, Jimmy? Why us? I'm absolutely crushed by this."

"I hated to be the one to tell you this, Kay. His therapists have dedicated every ounce of their energy and resources to getting Jimmy this far along."

Doctor Finney stood up, walked over to Kay and placed a hand on her shoulder.

"Well, I've got my rounds to make. Feel free to come back by or call me. If I'm not available when you call, I'll get back to you as soon as I can."

"Thank you, Doctor Finney."

Almost in a daze, and without stopping in to see Jimmy, she walked back to her car and headed home. She felt she was unable to face him with what she had just heard. She needed to clear her head and try to make sense of their situation.

≪

Kay's Parent's House

Rachel Burwell met Kay at the door.

"Kay, are you alright, dear? You sounded so depressed on the phone. I'm concerned for you. How are you this morning?"

"Not good, Mom. This has to be the worst thing that has ever happened to me. No way I saw this happening. Just when it seemed like the future was going to be wonderful, and now this."

"I know, darling. How tragic for Jimmy. Let's go sit down with a cup of coffee and talk about it. And, I have a wonderful surprise for you. Your Aunt Mildred is here. She heard about what happened to Jimmy and drove up from Charleston just to see you."

The portly Aunt Mildred came in from the kitchen with a pitcher of coffee and a tray with three cups and a few coffee rolls. She sat them on the table and embraced Kay.

"I'm so sorry, dear. My heart broke when I heard what happened. I know you are devasted. I would be too. Sit down and let's talk. How is he doing?"

"He's trying to stay positive. For him, it's the end of everything he ever wanted to do. His career, his love of sailboats. He can't even drive a car again. He'll be lucky to just be able to walk. Worst of all, I don't know what this does to us. We were getting married. I'm at my wit's end trying figure out what to do. I have a career too. I don't know how I could take care of him and work full-time. I mean, one of us would still have to make a living. It would probably ruin my chances of becoming a partner at my firm as well. That would not be a forty hour a week job. I'm just at a loss."

Rachel interrupted.

"We know dear. There's no good answer for something like this. And Jimmy, such a fine person. It's that age old saying about why do bad things happen to good people."

Mildred had always been an outspoken member of the family. She had been waiting for the opening to say what she came to say.

"Kay, let me tell you about a close friend of mine. Something similar happened to her. She married a boy she'd been in love with since just after high school. They were in their early twenties, both of them. It was 1966. We'd all just graduated high school down in Charleston and were working. She and I worked for the telephone company. That's where they first met. His name was Willard. Willard Jeffries was a handsome, hard-working young man. They were so in love, they ran away and got married. Everything was going just fine until the next spring."

"What happened?"

"Vietnam is what happened. Willard got drafted. They'd been married less than a year. He got sent overseas to fight. Just about two months before his tour of duty was to end, he got wounded. Stepped on a land mine. Didn't think he'd survive at first, but he did. They sent him to Walter Reed Medical Center to help him recover and he stayed there for almost a year. There was a ton of rehab, but a man with no legs and only one good arm can only get so much better. They finally sent him home. He and Mildred tried their hardest to make things work. She worked days at the phone company and several evenings a week cleaning houses to try and pay all the bills. Of course, there was no job he was capable of doing. She had to be out of the house most of the time working. We all tried to help. We'd go by their house and check on Willard. As time went on, everyone noticed he was starting to drink a lot. I didn't know if it was because of the pain he was in, or depression or feeling worthless as a man living off a woman. Truth is, she was working herself to death to take care of him. And when she finally did get home at night, he'd be drunk and fussing at her about everything. It was a bad situation. A really bad one. Finally, Mildred couldn't take it anymore and just left him. Didn't say a word to any of us. She just took off from home one morning and didn't come back. We later found out she'd moved to Oregon and started a new life. We heard from her a couple of times after that and before long she was just a part of our past. Willard wound up in a Veteran's home and died there just a few years after she left. It was a dreadful time for both of them. If he had just stayed with the VA and never came home, they both would have been better off."

"So, you're saying I should just forget about Jimmy? Let him figure all this out on his own? I don't know if I could do that, even if it was for the best. I love him. I guess I always have. I'd be lost without him."

"I know, Kay. But you might be even more lost with him. I'm just saying you should think about it. You're at a crossroads here and any decision you make will impact the rest of your life. The wife of a handicapped man would not be an easy one."

Kay broke down and began to cry, her chest heaving as she took deep breaths between sobs. Rachel came over to her and hugged her as she continued letting all of her emotions pour out. Aunt Mildred sat on the couch, sipping her coffee, confident she had steered her niece in the right direction.

Jimmy's main concern worried him far more than the lack of visits from his buddies at the station. Kay's visits had been daily until the past ten days. She missed over half of them. She called and each time there was a different reason that she couldn't come. There was the caseload at work, then a friend was sick. Next, her car was acting up. She promised she'd be by to visit him today and as the hours ticked by, he was worried that something else would come up. He realized it was difficult to leave after a hard day's work and make a two hour round trip to Greenville every day. Anyone would quickly tire of that. He reasoned he needed to tell her to cut her visits down to maybe one workday and one weekend trip each week. Even after all the work he'd put in trying to get better, it was now apparent the wedding would have to be put off. Maybe June would be the best time. There wouldn't be much partying beforehand but they'd still have the wedding and get on with life. By the end of the day's rehab, Wanda realized that Jimmy was not his usual positive self.

"What's going on with you, Admiral? Hemorrhoids acting up? You didn't give the machines much love today. Can't get better if you don't put out all you got."

"I'm worried. Maybe that's not the right word. Maybe concerned would be better. I'm afraid it might not be fair of me to expect Kay to continue on this journey through Hell with me. She's not visiting like she was and then today I haven't got a phone call from her telling me she can't make it or why. I don't think I'd be able to do any of this without her. I've got to know there's a future. Maybe it won't be the future we were counting on, but at least a future we can make together. Why go through all of this if it's just for me? I know you don't like to hear whining about how things are going and why even try, but I'm just about there. I need some reason to keep up all this effort."

"You know, Jimmy, when things aren't going well in my life, I try to remember just a couple of things. First, there's a lot in this world we're just not in charge of, no matter how much we want to be. Second, I don't worry about things that haven't gone wrong yet. Enough unpleasant things will happen without me dreaming them up, so I try to always just take a wait and see position before I start to worry. Besides, there's at least a little bit of good in every day, if you look for it. It's easy to only see bad things, if you don't try to find the good things. The bad ones slap you in the face. You don't have to look for them. But the good things take a little more looking. They are there."

"Thanks, Wanda. You should have been a preacher or something. You're about as good at setting the mind on a positive track as you are the body."

"One won't work without the other, Admiral. Now, let's try a few more reps here on the machine and then we'll get you back to your luxury suite."

"Right. Right."

Jimmy had lunch in his hospital room. His leg was no longer in the sling and he was encouraged to find he had some degree of movement and feeling in it. Perhaps he could it bring it back on line with Wanda's help. He'd been almost three months in the hospital now and was starting to feel more like a prisoner than a patient. Kay called to tell him she was on the way to see him. He wanted to surprise her, so he told her to meet him in the atrium in his wing of the hospital. He hoped the change might help her to see he was slowly improving. He knew she'd been discouraged seeing the man she loved reduced to a wheelchair jockey. But he was better and she would have to acknowledge that reality if he was in the chair under his own power. He wheeled himself down the hall and outside to the sunny atrium. He positioned himself facing the sun and the door. Kay soon appeared and opened the door. She paused for a minute and just looked at him. He smiled.

"Look, Ma. No hands! Got down here by myself and the leg brace is down to this sporty little number. Won't be long till I'll be walking down the aisle with the woman I love. Wanda says maybe with a crutch, but walking just the same. Come on over and give me the kiss I've been dreaming about for three days. Seems like a month since I've seen you."

Kay walked over and sat on the concrete patio bench beside Jimmy. The kiss was not forthcoming. It was obvious something was troubling her.

"Jimmy, I have to speak with you and it's going to be hard, so please just let me talk till I'm finished."

There was an undeniable dread building in him. He already felt something was seriously wrong by her solemn demeanor.

"Jimmy, I love you like no other person I've ever known. There's no denying you were the man I was supposed to marry."

"Supposed to marry?"

"Let me finish. I'm already struggling here. As much as I love you, I'm not going to be able to marry you. You are the strongest, most courageous person I've ever known. You were my perfect, beautiful man. I had always seen you as the person who'd sweep me off my feet and we'd go everywhere, do everything together. You were so handsome, so…strong. You'd take me in your arms and the rest of the world would disappear. And now, with this…I'm just not that strong. I can't do it. I've cried myself to sleep every night thinking about this moment. I know it will break your heart. It's the last thing I ever wanted to do. It's so unfair to both of us what has happened. I want you to know that I truly loved you. I still love you. I just can't marry you. I hope you'll understand one day that this is for the best and forgive me. I'll keep in touch and come by to check on you. I want you to get better, so much better. You stay strong and please try to move past us. I'm going to try. As hard as this will be…I know it's for the best. I've got to go now. I can't stay. I'll break down."

Kay bent over and kissed Jimmy on the forehead. She ran her hand down his arm and touched his fingers as she passed over his hand. She took one last long look and, with a flood of tears running down her face, she practically ran from the atrium.

He sat in his wheelchair and stared at the door for almost an hour after she left.

Just before Kay arrived, his life and attitude were in the best place he could ever imagine. Now the heavy weight of the words he just heard from her pulled him down into a well of total despair.

∽

It had been a week since Kay's confession had crushed him. A deep depression set in. He was still going to rehab every day and Wanda was now the only person he was speaking with on a daily basis. She was not only a great physical therapist, she was a counselor and a psychiatrist all in one package. Her sessions with Jimmy were the high part of his day. He'd now been in the hospital over three months. Today, he was surprised to hear that Elaine and Steve Steinbeck were coming to visit with him. With so many problems of his own, he hadn't thought about them much since the accident. He knew they survived and were in better shape than he was. When they arrived, they knocked quietly on his door.

"Come in. Is that you, Steve, Elaine?"

"It is. How are you feeling?"

"Considering all things, I guess I'm about as good as I could expect to be. How are you both doing?"

"We're pretty much on the mend. Elaine's arm was broken. I had a couple of vertebrae that were compressed but my back has always hurt so nothing much new there."

Elaine walked over to Jimmy who was sitting in a reclining chair in the room. She took his hand.

"Jimmy, there are no words to express our gratitude to you for literally saving both our lives. I'm just heartbroken that you were hurt so badly trying to help us. And now..."

Elaine broke up as she spoke.

"And now, I hear that you and Kay are no longer getting married. She told us the news a few days ago. I feel like we ruined your life. If there is any way we could ever make this up to you, you know we'd do anything. We want you to know that."

"I'll be okay. Life is still moving on. Everybody has problems. There's lots of people with problems worse than mine. Speaking of Kay, what's she doing? I mean, is she well? Is she seeing anyone else?"

There was an awkward pause. Elaine answered.

"Steve says she's really doing well at work. She will undoubtedly make partner in short order. The clients love her. Just like we all do."

Jimmy wasn't going to accept no answer as a reply to his question.

"And is she seeing anybody?"

"I really don't know about what she does after work. We don't ask."

Jimmy felt his gut tighten with that answer. He paused and looked up at the ceiling for a moment. He took a deep breath and continued.

"Steve, there is one thing I hope you'll help me with."

"Name it."

"When I leave here, perhaps in a month I need to find some kind of work. Since the bank took Momma's house, I need to work and find a small, cheap place to live. I don't know how much I can actually do yet, but I will give it my all. Anything is fine. I'm not expecting a lot from here on out. My life has taken a pretty dramatic change and I'm just going to try and make the best of it."

Elaine was still tearing up as she spoke. Steve held it together. This wasn't new territory for him. He'd seen a lot of injured marines during his time in the service.

"We'll be here for you. Through whatever happens. Please just accept our heartfelt thanks and know that we are so sorry for what has happened to you. Please forgive us for being a part of that."

"You have no reason to apologize for anything. I would have done the same for anyone in that situation. I was trained to do just what I did. It was as much a reflex as anything. Please though, let me know from time to time what Kay is up to. You don't have to tell her I asked. In fact, please don't. I don't want to interfere with her life from here on out, but I still love her and care deeply about what happens to her. I probably always will and want only the best for her. Thank you both for coming by. You made my day."

The couple said their goodbyes and left the room. As they headed toward the hospital exit, Steve reached for Elaine's hand and reflected on their visit.

"He's got more guts than anyone I've ever known. I feel terrible for him, yet there's a certain presence about him, almost an aura. I just feel there's still some great things in his future. God bless him."

Jimmy was released in May. He'd spent five months in the University Hospital. He had nothing but praise for everyone there and the help they'd given him. He was now walking with the help of a crutch for his right leg. The device was difficult to use as his right arm had almost no strength on its own. He had to literally run a strap around the arm securing it to the crutch. It wrapped around twice and was secured with Velcro as there was no way he'd ever be able to tie it with a knot. One special staff member walked with Jimmy to the door of the hospital.

"Well, Admiral. Didn't think this day would ever get here, did you?"

"I owe so much to you, Wanda. If it weren't for you, I think I would have jumped out the third-floor window. You healed a lot more of me than just my arm and leg. I'll never forget you."

Wanda had grown fond of her ward. She leaned forward and pulled Jimmy almost totally off the ground as she hugged him.

"Baby, don't you give up on yourself. There's a lot of life left inside you. And if you get down in any way, you just call Wanda and I'll drop whatever I'm doing for you. Love you, baby. Now get out of here before I bust out crying."

"Love you too. I'll be in touch. Bye."

True to his word, Steve had sent over a young staffer from his firm to drive Jimmy back to New Bern. They were directed to go back to Steve's office where he was going to give Jimmy some updates on apartments that were available and some possibilities for work.

8

Office of Steinbeck and Associates

THE OFFICE ADMINISTRATOR escorted Jimmy to Steve's office. As they walked through the hallway Jimmy scanned in every direction trying to catch a glimpse of Kay. He passed a closed door with her name on it. He listened for her voice as he passed by to no avail. Steve was standing in the doorway to his office as they approached.

"Jimmy, did we have the car there on time?"

"Yes, sir. Thank you for picking me up."

"Not a problem. Are you able to sit?"

"I can."

"Well, take a seat and let me tell you about some things I've found for you. There are several job possibilities. Remember, these places are run by friends of ours and they also know you. They have no expectations and will hire you based on the fact that they want to help you. Whatever you can do for them will be just fine. They'll work with you. One is Tom Ballance over at Captain Ratty's. Mark over at Galley Stores says he'll do the same and the one I think you might be the most interested in is Mitchell Hardware. Greg Smith, the owner, is one of the best people I know and he said he'd be honored for you to come work for him. There's a lot going on over there from stocking shelves to cutting keys. I know you'll find ways to earn what he would pay you and you'll be treated well. What do you think?"

"Mitchell's is my top choice, hands down. I'll go speak with Greg first thing in the morning. Any luck with a place to live?"

"That's not so easy. Most places want a lot more information than you might want to give them. Income, credit report, two months' rent up front and a security deposit. I don't mind helping out with the money but I don't know what they'll think about your income and ability to work and pay rent. A friend of mine runs the subsidized apartments over at Trent Court. I'm sure that's not a place you ever thought about living, but it may be your only choice. At least in the short term, until you can get established back here in town. There's absolutely no maintenance required; the city takes care of the buildings and grounds."

"Steve, I'm not picky at all and I want to be totally self-sufficient. I don't want people worrying about how I'm going to make it. I'll be fine."

"I'll get somebody to drive you over there. I'll tell him

you're coming and to wait for you. He said there were a few vacancies so maybe you can get over there tonight. Do you have any furniture?"

"A few old pieces that were in my mother's house. I have them in storage here in town. It's enough to get started."

"Well, let's get going and if you need help with anything, give me a call. I'm here all day, every day."

"Steve, thank you for everything. I promise you this is all I need. I'm not going to be a burden on you or anyone."

"You'll never be a burden to me or Elaine."

The Director of subsidized housing met briefly with Jimmy. It was plain to see that he'd been briefed by Steve as to what the situation was. He already had a unit picked out for him and asked for nothing more than a signature. No application or background check. It was more or less say 'hello' and get a cheap apartment.

Jimmy knew only too well that Trent Court was one of two low income housing projects run by the city and were generally considered to be the most crime-ridden districts in the entire area, for good reason.

Steve's driver waited outside in the car as he had been briefed that this meeting wouldn't take thirty minutes. He drove Jimmy the short distance from downtown onto Eden Street which ran behind Tryon Palace. He always thought it ironic that the most famous place in the entire area, the colonial Governor's Palace, sat immediately beside such a downtrodden housing project. The city planted some greenspace and built a tourist parking lot in the small area separating the two places but it couldn't begin to hide a project as large and stark looking as Trent Court.

The sun was quickly setting as they entered the project. As Jimmy expected, the street corners had several young men and an occasional woman hanging out with no particular activity underway. There were chairs outside a number of front doors where people with few prospects could while away the time chewing the fat with a cold drink or a smoke. It was primarily a minority neighborhood and a dark four door sedan with two white men in it caught the attention of those on the street corners and sitting outside. To them it was just more city spies sent to keep an eye on what the residents were up to. Ninety- nine percent of New Bern's residents who didn't live in the project avoided it like the plague and would go out of their way to not drive through it. Jimmy knew the history, but also understood he was in no position to be choosy. At least he'd have a place of his own and he'd make the best of it. The driver helped Jimmy carry a couple of bags, virtually his only personal possessions, to the door of his apartment. He used the key the Director had given him and entered the first-floor unit. He'd specifically chosen this unit for Jimmy with no steps and located on the end of the building closest to downtown.

"I feel like everybody here is watching us."

"Good guess, Jim. To say we stand out a little bit would be an understatement."

"Yeah, I look like a refugee from a prisoner of war camp

and you look like a city detective. They probably think I'm in the witness protection program."

"I don't think the Feds will be bringing witnesses from crimes here to keep them safe."

"Probably not. Well, I'm in. Let's see if the lights work."

The lights illuminated a small, dingy apartment with navy blue tile on the floor. It needed paint everywhere and had the smell of a place abandoned fifty years earlier. He noticed a garbage can at the end of the kitchen counter that needed emptying and a closer look indicated that most of the smell started there. Jimmy would clean it up immediately and try to make the place livable.

"Thanks for the lift. I guess I've got it from here. I see one twin bed in the bedroom and I've got a couple of blankets in my bag. If the shower works, I'm golden."

"If you need a ride anywhere, anytime, Mr. Steinbeck told me I was to drop whatever I was doing and come get you. So, you know that's always an option."

"I'm going to try not to call. I should be able to handle everything I've got to do on my own. But I do appreciate the offer more than I can tell you. Thanks again.

"No problem."

The young man left and Jimmy surveyed his new home. It was tiny with a single bedroom and bath. The fixtures were out of the 50's and had as much rust as chrome on them. He turned the knob and both hot and cold water sputtered out of the faucet. The bathtub looked like someone roasted an animal of some sort in it and forgot to clean up afterwards.

Jimmy walked over to one of three small metal chairs at the Formica covered kitchen table and sat down. Thinking back over the past year, it was difficult to not be bitter about the journey his life was on. He'd done nothing wrong and tried his best to make a positive impact on the world. And yet, here he was, reduced to a handicapped young man with dismal prospects, not much better than a street person. The unfairness of it all was more than he could bear this evening. He opened his bag, retrieved an old army blanket and spread it out on the bed. He thought to himself, it feels like someone is already lying in it. It has so many lumps in the mattress. Kinda like a soft spot on a dirt floor. Why am I surprised? It's just where I am. I'll figure it out tomorrow.

Jimmy knew he was not able to drive a car. His right arm and leg were almost dead weight. The only vehicle he'd be able to use would have to be custom built for a handicapped person and cost a fortune. It was out of the question. He did have one vehicle that came to mind and he'd start a search for it in the morning. That would be job one. Get some wheels.

❧

Prather's Cycle Shop

"Good morning. Prather's Cycle Shop."

"Hi, I'm looking for something kinda unique and I wondered if you might know where I could find one."

"I'll do my best. What are you looking for?"

"Have you ever seen a bike that looks like a huge tricycle? It's sorta like a three-wheeled beach cruiser. I have a leg problem and can't keep a two-wheeler up right. I need something to ride about a half a mile to work in downtown New Bern. And, to make the search a little more difficult, I don't have much money."

"We don't carry anything like that at our shop, but I'll see what I can find and keep an eye out for you. Give me your number and if anything turns up, I'll call you."

"I would really appreciate it. You could say I'm desperate right now."

"I understand. Give me your name and number."

Jimmy gave him his number and then his name.

"You're Jimmy Harrison? Who went to New Bern High School?"

"Yes, that's me."

"I was in school with you. We used to shoot the bull in homeroom. I'm Rick McRae."

"Roadrunner Rick? Star of the track team?"

"The same. What on earth happened to your leg?"

"I was involved in a wreck on Trent River bridge last year. I had a lot of injuries and the big ones to my arm and leg won't be getting much better. I'm gonna have to get around on a bike from here on out."

"Tell you what. Stay put and I'll call you back. I need to talk with the boss man and see what we can find. He has a lot more sources than me and might be able to get you a lead on an old one we can fix up. You don't mind if it has a few scratches on it, do you?"

"If it didn't, it probably would soon enough with me trying to ride it. Any help would be appreciated."

Within five minutes the phone rang.

"Is that you, Jimmy?"

"The same."

"Buddy, I've got some great news for you. I spoke to the owner and he remembered what happened on the bridge. I didn't know it was you who saved those people. What an unbelievable story. Anyway, you've got a new beach trike headed your way."

"Like I told you, I don't have much cash. I was thinking I could spend about a hundred bucks on something. I don't mind used."

"The boss is pretty hard-headed and he said he's not taking a penny from you."

"Nothing?"

"Just tell me where you want it delivered. It'll be tomorrow cause he's having it delivered from the warehouse in Wilmington this afternoon. I'll get it assembled, lubed up and bring it to you myself."

Jimmy was overcome at this small gesture and could barely contain himself to speak.

"I just don't know what to say. I wasn't looking for a gift."

"Consider it the bike shop's reimbursement to you

for services already rendered to the city. I'll see you in the morning."

"I'll be here. Apartment 111 on Eden Street in Trent Court"

❧

When the sun came up, Jimmy walked outside to see the neighborhood. He'd never studied it before. Just like everyone else in town, he had always tried to avoid it. It didn't offend him but the word was, don't drive through there unless you're looking for trouble. He had several friends back in school on the football team who lived there, but he never gave much thought to what they must have been dealing with back at home. He certainly was gaining a new appreciation of what it took to come home here every day.

"You must be the new neighbor."

Jimmy turned to see two elderly ladies sitting on an old green metal glider on their front porch patio. It looked like an antique that you could have seen on the front porch of many houses down south in the fifties. The women were both black and offered big smiles as they slid back and forth on the old moving couch. They sported hand-held fans and kept them moving in front of their faces slowly, generating a breeze as they spoke.

"Good morning, ladies. I'm Jimmy Harrison. I just moved in last night. Don't even have my stuff here yet."

"In that case, you probably ain't had no coffee or nothing to eat this morning. Am I right?"

"Why…yes, I mean no. I don't have any food inside yet."

"Well, darlin', you come take my side of the glider here with Miss Beatrice and I'll go fetch you a cup of coffee. And how about a country ham biscuit? By the way, I'm Joyce Hart. What do you want in your coffee?"

"Just black, nothing else."

"Ok, now you tell Beatrice about yourself while I fix this up for you."

Jimmy walked over to the metal glider, sat down beside the old lady and told her about himself. Remarkably, she remembered Margaret.

"Yes, darlin'. I knew your Momma real well. I worked at Lakeview for almost twenty years. Still work there some weekends to fill in for folks that are sick or on vacation. I remember your Momma told me she had one child, a boy. So that's you. You're Margaret's boy."

"I'm what's left of him."

"I'm a little surprised to see that you have some physical problems. I thought she told me you were in the military."

"I was. I was in the Coast Guard, but I got hurt and they had to discharge me."

"Well, I'm sorry. But I tell you what, Jimmy. It's okay to call you Jimmy?"

"I'll be hurt if you don't."

"Jimmy, you're going to do just fine here. Me and Joyce, our kids are all grown up and moved away to the big cities, Raleigh and Atlanta. So, we need somebody to look out for and especially to cook for. We know each other's recipes so well it ain't no fun to cook for just ourselves. We'll enjoy having you over for meals a lot. You can count on that."

"Wow, that would be real nice. I thought I might have trouble here, you know, meeting people."

"Honey, there's good and bad people everywhere you go. We got plenty of both right here in Trent Court. Just so happens you moved into a building right beside two of the nicest and prettiest ones."

Beatrice laughed out loud at her description of herself and Joyce.

"And, God knows we do love to cook and eat."

Perfectly on cue, Joyce came out with a metal tray covered with food. She then retrieved a chair identical to the one in Jimmy's new apartment and sat down alongside the others. Jimmy dove into the food like a lion bending over his downed gazelle on the Serengeti.

His encounter with these two women had brightened his entire day. By the time he finished his biscuit and a second cup of coffee, he felt like he'd known them all his life. They were good-hearted country people, just like his family. As they sat and talked, a pickup truck with a Prather's Cycle Shop logo on the side pulled up in front. Rick McRae was driving. He hopped out with his ever-present smile and walked over to where Jimmy and the ladies were sitting.

"Good morning everybody. Special delivery of Jimmy's new set of wheels."

Had he been able to, Jimmy would have run to the truck. As it was, he slowly shuffled out to the curb. He was no longer walking with the crutch. Even though he could stand and walk, it appeared that he was pretty much dragging his right foot as he moved. He held his right arm tight up against his chest. He'd done everything he could to increase his ability to move but had come to the realization that this was probably as good as things were going to get for him. He finally made it to the back of the truck where Rick was pulling out the trike.

"Caribbean blue, the color I always wanted on my Corvette."

"You had a Corvette?"

"No. I always wanted one. Not going to happen now. But, I do have a vehicle with the color I wanted. Rick, this is a really cool bike."

"Mr. Prather spared nothing. Basket, oversized tires, even a horn. You'll have the only bike in town that Corvette owners hoped they'd have one day."

"You reckon?"

"I do. Let's adjust the seat to your height and make sure you can ride this thing."

Rick stayed for over an hour making adjustments on the new bike. When he was confident everything was set up the best possible, he reached out to shake Jimmy's hand. As Jimmy stuck out his hand, he was a little shocked when Rick stepped forward and gave him a guy hug. They were never the best of friends in school, so this show of compassion was a surprise. Rick stepped back.

"If there were a set of keys to the bike, I guess I'd give

them to you now like a game show host. Instead, I'm just gonna say it was great to see you again, Jimmy. If you have any problems with this bike, you call the shop and I'll come right over. What are you going to be doing for work?"

"I'm going to take my new ride into town this morning and start trying to find a job. I want to work. I need to work. This bike is going to make it possible to get there. Tell Mr. Prather I am the most appreciative customer he ever had."

"Believe me, he's happier about this than you are. Okay, it's back to the shop. Ladies, take care of my man, here."

The ladies both beamed.

"You got it, darlin'."

Jimmy thanked Beatrice and Joyce profusely and they made him promise to always check with them before dinner to make certain he was eating well.

He then slipped on a clean shirt, a light jacket, the helmet that Rick brought and started peddling into town. He quickly discovered that he was, for the most part, peddling with only his left leg. With a little practice, he had the bike moving at a respectable pace. He headed out from Trent Court on Eden Street. He rode along the banks of the Trent River less than a mile from where his life was forever changed on the bridge. There was a crabber in a small workboat collecting his crab pots trying to earn a meager living from the sea. He passed between the Stingray Café and the front of the North Carolina History Center onto Front Street taking a left on Craven. Less than a block away,

Mitchell Hardware sat in the same spot for over a hundred years. The inside had changed very little in that time with its wide-planked heart pine floors and high tin ceilings. The store was stocked to the brim with items not found in most hardware stores today. There were displays of items sold in the store when it originally opened, everything from horse-drawn plows to a baby coffin. Tourists visiting New Bern couldn't consider leaving without visiting Mitchell's.

The owner and full-time manager was Greg Smith. Widely-known and well-loved by everyone in town, he had a perpetual smile and a pleasant greeting for everyone who entered. Many people in town testified they'd never seen him in a bad mood. He had a knack for remembering all his regular customers' names and quite often tourists would come back to town after leaving for over a year. He'd call them by name and ask them how things were going back at home, remembering what city and state they were from. Jimmy was also a fan of Greg's and had known him his entire life. Steve said he'd already mentioned hiring him to Greg and he seemed willing to give it a shot. From Jimmy's point of view that would be the perfect situation. It was a place he enjoyed, was familiar with, and offered the endless opportunity to meet a lot of interesting people both locals and visitors.

"Good morning, Jimmy! I've been expecting you to come by. When do you want to start work?"

"That was quick. No interview? No criminal background check? How did I get hired so easily?"

"Look, Steve told me your situation. I've got a lot of small tasks that have to be done here all the time. There's always a ton of stock to be priced and put on the shelves, small packages to be unloaded and occasionally delivered close by to other businesses in the historic district. I'm not going to ask you to do anything you can't physically handle. You'll be a great addition when it comes to knowing everybody in town and also greeting the tons of visitors we get. I'll pay you fair. You don't have to work Sundays. And if you need time off to do some personal errands during the week, just let me know. I'm looking forward to getting to know you better. So, when do you want to start?"

"I can stay right now. Would that work?"

"Sure will. Come on into the office. You'll need to fill out some paperwork, social security number, stuff like that. Then we'll get you started."

Within an hour, Jimmy was pricing small items and placing them on display shelves. The group who worked at the store were all helpful and a pleasure to be around. Everyone enjoyed working there and it was more like a family than a group of employees. The day flew by. When the store closed at six o'clock, Greg came over to Jimmy.

"Time to go home, Jimmy. We close weekdays through Thursday at five-thirty; Fridays and Saturdays at six. Once in a while, we'll work late taking in freight or stocking shelves if we're super busy but for the most part, we leave on time. We'll see you in the morning at six forty-five. We open the doors at seven. I notice you're riding a bike. If it's raining or storming, call me on my cell phone and I'll drop by your place and pick you up."

"You know where I'm living?"

"Steve gave me the full update. No secrets at Mitchell's."

"Okay, I'll see you in the morning. And Greg…"

"Yes sir."

"I really enjoyed the day. Thank you for giving me a chance."

"Isn't that what friends are for?"

"I never knew how much till now."

"That's a good thing. See you in the morning."

9

JIMMY STARTED HIS bike ride home. Being spring, the sun was setting later and there was plenty of light on the ride back to Trent Court. In the winter, it wouldn't be light this late and he'd have to take extra care to not get run over. Perhaps some extra lights on the bike would be in order. He continued re-tracing the same route home that he'd taken in the morning. As he pulled into the yard in front of his apartment, there was a group of young men in their late teens and early twenties gathered on the corner. It looked like a group not up to any worthwhile enterprise. Jimmy was cautious as he passed. He acknowledged them.

"Hey guys. Nice day."

Nobody spoke back or even nodded. An icy collective stare was the best they offered. He continued on another fifty yards to his apartment. He was hoping Beatrice or Joyce might be out front, but quickly saw there was no one there. That's when the harassment started.

"Hey cracker. What you doing riding that shiny new tricycle through our street? This here is a private street and you ain't got no business being here."

"I live here now. This is my apartment right here."

"I don't believe you. They ain't sending no cripple white boy to live in the Court. Ain't happening. You're going to have to peddle that kid's bike right on out of here before somebody falls on you."

The group started gesturing in a hostile manner at him. It was a collective effort and he understood fully that he'd been chosen to be their afternoon's entertainment.

"Guys, you can see I'm not able to argue with anybody. It's all I can do to ride this bike. How about just letting me go into my apartment and I won't come back outside at all. You'll have the whole street to yourselves."

"We ain't worried about no street. We're worried about little fruitcakes like you moving in on us. We don't want to get it started. Next thing you know, the whole street will just be a freak show. So, you need to just turn that thing around and get outta here, now."

The oldest and largest of the group was a menacing looking character with dreadlocks down to his shoulders wearing baggy pants, a wife-beater tee shirt and untied high-dollar sneakers. He had a major chip on his shoulder and had decided that Jimmy was a fair target for his aggression. He walked over behind him and started pushing his back, trying to get him pedaling the bike away from the apartment.

"Move it, cracker. I ain't asking you. I'm telling you. Get going, now."

He kept pushing harder and harder. Before the accident Jimmy wouldn't have tolerated this sort of abuse from anyone. Taking off this guy's head would have been a walk in the park. But, that was then; this was now. He couldn't hold his own against a twelve-year-old today. He refused to peddle the bike. The shoves got harder each time and by the fifth shove, the bike flipped over and Jimmy splayed out into the grass. The group gathered around him and the leader began pushing him along the ground with his foot.

"For a one-legged dog, you sure got a lot of attitude, cracker. You're getting ready to learn some lessons this evening."

A young black boy rode up on his bike. He was much younger than the rest of the group. He went over to Beatrice's apartment and knocked on her door. She opened the door and seeing what was taking place, walked over to the gang, the young boy with her. His name was DeVaughn but everyone called him Dee. Beatrice and Joyce knew him well. He'd certainly been by their place many times for a slice of cake or pie. Those were not the kind of treats he would get at home.

"You boys ought to be ashamed of yourselves. Out here beating on somebody who's got one good leg and one good arm. You think this makes you tough guys? You're just a bunch of worthless bums. I know some of you and I know who your Mommas are too. You want them to hear about this? I don't think so. And you, Marcus. You do nothing around here but cause trouble. Every time something bad happens, or goes wrong, somebody gets hurt or something gets broken, you ain't never far away. You need a good butt-whipping, boy."

Marcus was not intimidated at all by Beatrice. He answered to nobody.

"Hey old lady, if you don't want some of the trouble happening at your house, you better turn around and run yourself back into it. You don't want no part of me."

A lot of screaming was going back and forth. The commotion was not uncommon on the street and one of the residents wasted no time in calling the police. Within minutes, the blue flashing lights appeared and two squad cars pulled up to the corner simultaneously. They never came to this area with less than two units. Trouble was born in Trent Court and they knew it. A large deputy sheriff walked over to the group. He was overweight with a lot of equipment hanging off his service belt. His hand rested on the grip of his .357 caliber revolver. He'd been to many scenes like this on Trent Court. His patience didn't last long with this gang.

"Well, Marcus. I see you can't stay out of trouble for two days. Wasn't it just last Saturday I hauled you in for vandalism?"

Marcus just gave an insolent stare at Sergeant Moeller. He was no more intimidated by the deputy than the deputy was of him. He offered no words.

"You know, Mr. Gangster, that the Court has special laws dealing with how people treat the handicapped. Judges don't look favorably at punks picking on somebody who can't fight back. To tell you the truth, I don't either. I've already had a belly full of you recently and I'd like nothing better than to haul you downtown and put enough charges against you that you'd stay in the county lockup at least a month till your day in court. I promise you won't feel nearly as tough with the group living accommodations in the county jail as you do here. They'd love to have somebody with pretty little dreadlocks like yours to spend the night with. You want to come with me or do you want to just go about your business and let the rest of these children go back to their homes? I need an answer now."

Again, Marcus said nothing; stared at the Deputy and finally turned and walked away. As he walked, he turned back once, looked straight at Jimmy who was still on the ground and pointed a finger at him to let him know he'd see him again, soon. Sergeant Moeller went over to Jimmy. He and Dee helped him stand up. Dee righted his bike.

"You alright, son?"

"Yeah. Just wounded my pride. I'm getting used to it."

"Hey, I know you. You're that Harrison guy that saved those folks on the Trent River Bridge last year. I was on the scene. I didn't think you'd make it. I guess that's why you've got a bum leg now, am I right?"

"You are. You know what they say about no good deed."

"I know what you did. I saw it with my own two eyes. Look, that punk, Marcus, will be back."

"I'm sure."

"Don't get involved with him, challenge him or even get on his side of the street. But, if he does anything, all you need to do is call and I'm the one responsible for this area. I'll be here in less than five minutes. You call, you hear?"

"I do. You can count on it."

The officer turned to Beatrice and Dee.

"Beatrice, thank you for standing up for this young man. Get him to tell you what he did for a career sometime. You'll be surprised."

"Was he a cop?"

"No, a Coast Guard Rescue Swimmer. He'd go out in a hurricane and bring in people whose boat sank way out in the ocean. He got hurt on a rescue. Get him to tell you about it."

"And Dee. You're the best, son. You stay away from Marcus and his group. They're trouble and they'll all either wind up dead or in prison. You're a lot smarter than they are."

"I will. You know my mother, don't you?"

"I do. Cecille."

"Then you know why I don't want to get in no trouble. She'd be worse than jail."

Everyone laughed and the officers went back to their squad cars. In a minute, the street was quiet. Jimmy was in his apartment, as were Beatrice and Joyce. Dee took off home on his bike.

⬦

Life in New Bern – Summer 2012

The days seem to pass quickly. Jimmy had settled into a routine. It was nothing he'd ever wished for, but it was what his life had become. He was mature enough to understand just where he was and determined to try and carve out some type of life he could tolerate. There were no other viable options that he could find.

Most mornings he'd arrive early at Mitchells. Greg would often bring in doughnuts for his crew and there was always fresh coffee in the office. He and Greg would talk while they finished off their first cup. Most of the time, it was about what needed to be done at the store that day or the coming week. Sometimes it would get a little more personal. Greg wanted to make certain that Jimmy had the things he needed to live and that he was not in any danger at Trent Court. He understood the difficulties of living there and knew Jimmy would make an easy target for anyone cruel enough to go after him. He didn't want it to seem like he was prying into his personal life, but did want him to know that he'd be there for him if he needed help of any type.

On Sundays, Jimmy had become a regular again at Christ Episcopal Church. Because his mother loved it and he always went there as a child, he felt a particular comfort and sense of home there. Paul, the Rector, always seemed eager to talk with him, as did Governor Pollard, if she was back in town from her office in Raleigh. She and her husband saved Jimmy a seat on the pew next to them every week for the worship service. He'd known the Governor for years, even received a Coast Guard Award from her, but never had a close relationship until now.

He was slowly building a new family around him. The fact that many of the city's leaders were in this unlikely group that supported him was even more remarkable. He saw in them the strength and quality of his small hometown. They saw in him an outstanding young man with a difficult life, through no fault of his own. New Bern was a town full of tradition, character and compassion. A description that was well deserved.

After church this particular Sunday, he hurried back to his apartment. He was particularly excited, as his old friend and fellow Guardsman, Bill Flynn, had called and said he'd be coming by for a visit. As Jimmy turned into Trent Court, he could see that Marcus and a few other thugs were on the street directly in front of his apartment. Marcus had acquired an old Chevrolet Impala. It was rusty, smoked like a furnace when he accelerated, and made more racket than a Harley Davidson every time he drove off. Of course, he'd put in speakers that would have worked great for a block party. When he parked, he cranked them up to the maximum output. Everyone in the project was disturbed by the racket, but with Marcus's growing reputation for unprovoked violence, no one would cross him. The word in the neighborhood was that he was now dealing in drugs and working with some of the established gangs in town. This was obviously his career path. The thugs couldn't restrain themselves as he pedaled past them.

"Hey peg leg. You ain't learned to ride a two-wheeler yet? If you were any punier, you'd have to be pushed in a stroller. Yeah, your Momma would have to take you to town."

The entire group laughed at Marcus' attempt at humor. It was degrading, but Jimmy was used to it by now. As long as they didn't harm him physically, he'd just ignore it. There was a problem today. Bill was coming and he didn't want him to be harassed by this collection of idiots. He got the old business card off the counter and called the police department. As promised, in only minutes, Sergeant Moeller pulled up in a squad car. He went straight to the gang and got in Marcus' face.

"What's the problem, officer?"

Marcus spoke with a sneer and with no attempt to hide his disdain for the law.

"Violation of numerous city ordinances."

"Such as."

"Disturbing the peace, excessive noise, unlawful assembly on city property. I'm sure there's at least four or five more I could come up with. What I need for you to do is simple. Move your friends here, and your noise machine over to Lawson's Landing or someplace that you won't be disturbing everyone in the neighborhood. Let's get moving."

"Did the little peg leg faggot call you? I guarantee you he did. That little cracker. This won't happen no more. I'll see to that."

"You make one move toward him, say anything threatening or even look at him wrong and I'll make your life totally miserable, you creep. Just like you make everyone around here miserable. Don't cross me, Marcus. I'm serious like a heart attack. There's nothing about you that I like, even a little. Nothing would make me and the rest of the decent people around here happier than to see you cross the line and wind up right where you belong, in that State Prison. So if you don't want to go there today, don't want to give me a reason to take you in."

Without further words, Marcus and the four thugs piled into the rust bucket lowrider and headed out of the neighborhood, but not in the direction of Lawson's Landing. Wherever he was headed, Sergeant Moeller knew he'd be taking trouble with him. He watched until they were out of sight, looked over to where Jimmy was standing behind his screen door and smiled. He turned and got back in the squad car.

An hour later, Bill Flynn came to the door.

"Jim Bob, you home, son?"

"Come on in, Bill. Grab a chair. Can I get you something to drink?"

"You wouldn't have a cold beer in the fridge, would you?"

"You realize I knew you were coming and you still ask a question like that? Of course, I have a six-pack. Been icing it down all day."

He grabbed two beers from the ice box, handing one to Bill and keeping one for himself. He hadn't had one since the night of the accident. But this was a special occasion.

"So, Jim Bob. How's everything going? You said you were working at a hardware store here. You liking it?"

"Nothing will ever compare to working with you and the crew at the station. That was the high point of my life. It can't be replaced. I know that and I'm just trying to move on, make the best of things. How's everybody back there?"

"Well, let's see. Phil finally got married. Buddy got transferred to Kodiak and I just re-upped. I moved up the ladder a little and got Chief."

"Congratulations, Bill. So, that will get you to twenty, won't it?"

"Yep. My retirement is pretty well guaranteed now. Just a few more years and I'll come down here and bother you full-time."

"You don't have a permanent lady?"

"I'm married to the Coast Guard. You know what that means. How 'bout you? Did you ever hook back up with what's her name?"

"You mean Kay?"

"Yeah, that's right. Kay. What's going on there?"

"She'll always be the love of my life, but she's moved on. I guess the thought of having to live with somebody who can't even drive a car was just a little too much to deal with. I think she's got another guy, some slick lawyer downtown. No way I can compete anymore."

"Well, if you ask me, she's the one who's missing out here."

"Kind of you to say that, but I understand. It just wasn't meant to be. So, are you headed back to the station tonight? You could crash here with me if you want. We can finish off the six-pack and you can sleep over there on my high-end orthopedic couch."

Jimmy pointed to the old fabric couch with mismatched throw pillows and blanket thrown over it to hide a few tears in the cushions. He really hoped Bill would stay as he wanted to talk more with him about the Guard and the great times they had working together.

"Your accommodations are first class, but I've got a big day tomorrow with four rookies starting. I'll be playing the part of the old seaman who'll show them how to climb the ratlines."

Jimmy was already dreading Bill shoving off for another six months with no contact.

"I hope you won't wait so long before you come back again. I love to talk with you about the guys and what everyone's doing."

"You can count on it. I'll…"

Bill was interrupted mid-sentence as the screen door swung open hitting the wall with an unfriendly smash. They both turned to see Marcus entering the room.

"What do you want, Marcus? You're not supposed to come around here. You've been told."

"Your buddy, Officer Moeller, is downtown at a wreck. I'm upset that you brought him to the Court to harass me earlier today. I guess I haven't explained clearly enough to you how I want you to behave living here in my hood. Trent Court belongs to me. Not to you, not the police, not nobody else."

Marcus started to move toward Jimmy. Two more of his gang stood just inside the doorway watching to prevent any exit from the apartment. Bill, who was momentarily frozen by the surprise forced entry into to Jimmy's apartment, moved between Jimmy and Marcus.

"What do you think you're going to do, cracker? I will mess you up bad. Put yourself back on the couch while I explain to peg leg what he needs to do to live here, or really to just live."

With virtually no hesitation, Bill jammed his forefinger into Marcus' chest as he spoke. Bill not only had six inches of height over Marcus, when he stood up, it was more than apparent that he also had a good fifty pounds more of rock-hard muscle on his frame. It was immediately obvious that fear was not in his vocabulary and his aggressive side was a lot more intense than what Marcus expected.

"I'm going to tell you how you're going to live, punk. You're never coming here again for any reason. You're not going to speak to my good friend, Jimmy, or interfere with anything he does. If you do, I'll be back and bring a few of my friends with me that make me look small and nice. It'll be the worst day of your life. See, punk I'm not Officer Moeller and I don't follow any rules of the Court. I'll take your head off and make your two stupid friends over there eat it. Do you need for me to show you how it works? I can give you your first lesson right now."

Using just one finger, Bill's prodding had pushed Marcus

halfway across the room. Marcus reached into the back pocket of his jeans hanging halfway down his legs.

"OK, white boy. You wanted some of me? I'm ready for you to teach me my first lesson. I'm probably going to have to cut you short though."

Marcus aggressively flung the blade open on a long switchblade knife as he spoke. Calmly, and to Marcus's amazement, Bill moved closer to him.

"You're an absolute moron, you know that? Bringing a knife to a gunfight."

Bill opened up his light blue jacket and Marcus could clearly see the forty-five-caliber service revolver.

"I've got about four medals from the Coast Guard that say I'm really good with this thing. Want to see if they know what they're talking about?"

Marcus started backing toward the door. Bill followed closely.

"If you come back here, ever again I'll return to pay you a visit. If anything happens to my friend, I'm just going to assume you were responsible. The only things left of you around here will be your stench and a bad memory. Don't fool with me, boy."

Marcus and company came to the realization this was not somebody they wanted to have to deal with tonight. Cursing as they scrambled to his beat-up Chevy, they revved it up and screeched down the street leaving a cloud of black smoke behind them. By now, Jimmy was smiling.

"Way to go, Bill. You know what I was thinking the whole time?"

"What?"

"They thought you were going to show them how bad you are and I'm thinking, jeez Bill's loving this. They ought to see him if they really get him fired up. Want another beer?"

"OK, a last one for the road and then I've got to get going."

Jimmy laughed out loud at a thought.

"What's so funny?"

"Marcus is such an idiot. He thought somebody who jumps out of helicopters miles out in the ocean during a hurricane for a living would be scared of him. Give me a break."

"Actually, Jim Bob. I never did that. You were the only one of our crew dumb enough to do something like that. We were just the half-baked idiots who took you out there."

The two men reminisced for another half hour before Bill dropped his empty can in the trash. He gave Jimmy a hug and headed out to his car. He was despondent as he drove away. Seeing how Jimmy now had to live and how far from where he'd been was extremely depressing. He didn't know how often he would be able to bring himself to see Jimmy this way.

10

September 2012

JOYCE AND BEATRICE practically adopted Jimmy. He brought out their maternal side. Most every Sunday found them all together for a home-cooked dinner at the ladies' apartment.

"Honestly, Joyce. This is the best meatloaf I've ever tasted. I don't how you cook things that have so much flavor. I've eaten a lot of meatloaf in my life, but none ever tasted this good. What's your secret?"

"Well, first, you've got to use lard when you cook most everything. A lot of folks have sworn off lard because they want to live to be a hundred and some of the cooking shows keep telling them that stuff is bad for you. It'll make you fat and clog your arteries. Know what I say? I say who wants to live to be a hundred if you have to eat stuff that don't taste good every day. I want food that tastes good and if I only live to be ninety-five, then so be it."

Joyce smiled over at Beatrice.

"And, there's a few other secrets my Momma taught me that I don't share. Family secrets."

"Whatever those secrets are, you sure know how to cook. Now, do you mind if I get a little bit nosey with you two?"

"I don't think you can ask no questions we haven't heard before. Don't mean I'm gonna answer them, but go ahead. Try me."

"Have either of you ever been married? I don't ever see any men around here."

"And you won't, darlin'. Yes, we've both been married. Beatrice had a fine husband. Tell him about George.'

Beatrice paused for a minute and gathered her thoughts. As she spoke, it was apparent these were memories which were special to her.

"My man, my husband, George Whitehead Wilson was his name. He was one big, handsome hunk of a man. We were married when I was nineteen and he was twenty-two. He joined the Marines. I always worried about him cause that can be a dangerous job. He fought in Vietnam, three different tours. When that was over and they brought the men home, I thought to myself, thank God he's home safe with me now. Then, a few years later, happy years while we were home together, they sent him over to Lebanon. He was in the barracks in Beirut the morning they bombed it. Killed over two hundred Marines. He was one of them. I just got a visit that day from two soldiers telling me he was gone. There wasn't even a real war going on over there; just a bunch of terrorists running around trying to kill people. It took me years to get over it. To tell the truth, I never got over losing that man. I still miss him every day. Always will, I guess. Finally, I called Joyce, who had already lost her man and said, sister, we need to live together. I don't like being alone all the time. There won't be another man for me."

Beatrice turned and looked out the window so the tears welling up in her eyes would have a chance to stop. Joyce took her turn.

"Jimmy, you sure do ask hard questions. My man was Estes Hart. He was a handsome devil. He was a slick talker, too. When we were young, he took me dancing all over the place with him. He could dance, sing and God, he'd tell me things that just had my heart racing all the time. Loved him right off. He had problems though. He never had a father. His mother wasn't worth two cents and he was raised by aunts and uncles who really didn't care much about him. He never got an education or found a decent way to make a living. When we got together, he tried anything he could to make enough money to take care of us. It was almost impossible. The jobs a black man with no education could get were the worst. He worked on road paving crews, the city sanitation department and even tried to enlist. Army wouldn't have him 'cause he couldn't pass the written tests. He couldn't hardly read. But he was always good to me. No matter how bad things were, he was always good to me.

We had the power and water shut off at our place so many times I can't even begin to count them. He was embarrassed that here he'd taken a wife and couldn't find no way to take care of her. Children were out of the question. I wasn't even going to think about bringing nobody else into the world when we couldn't even feed ourselves. No sir. Then things seemed to get better for a while. I felt safe, so we had a child. She lives in Atlanta now, but that's another story. Anyway, Estes would come home with a handful of cash, give me some to spend and we'd go out for dinner to a nice restaurant. He'd tell me he was on his way and that things were going to be getting better from then on out. And then, one night I waited up for him till two in the morning. He never came home. Instead, a Deputy Sherriff came by and told me they'd arrested him with several other men. They was selling dope; had been doing that all the time he was bringing home money. There had been some sort of altercation with a bunch of no-counts that sold them the drugs and somebody fired shots. One of them got killed. Estes couldn't afford a decent lawyer and he wound up having to plead guilty. He was sentenced to forty-five years. I visited him every couple of weeks for years. He finally told me to forget him and get on with my life. He said I should get a divorce and find another man. I didn't want another man. He quit letting me see him at the prison. He wouldn't answer my letters. I finally got a letter from the prison about five years back telling me he was dead. Died of cancer in jail. What a waste.

We never even got a divorce. I guess I'm still married to a man I haven't seen in over twenty years; a dead man."

"Those are two sad stories, ladies. My life doesn't seem any more tragic than yours. I do know there's nothing harder than not being able to see somebody you love. Especially when they're still alive and just don't want to see you anymore."

"Is that your sad story, Jimmy?"

"Unfortunately, yes. After I got hurt, she didn't think our life together would ever work so she broke up with me. We were supposed to be getting married last Valentine's Day. She still lives here in town. Our paths don't really cross. It would probably be a lot harder if they did. Still, she stays on my mind all the time."

"I know, honey. If you really love somebody, I mean really love them, you never fall out of love with them. You might even hate them, don't want to see them or be around them, but guess what? You're always going to love them. That's just a fact of life."

After all the sad story sharing, Joyce brought out a freshly baked carrot cake.

"There's nothing better to pick up somebody's mood than a piece of homemade carrot cake. Again, my Momma's secret recipe. You taste it Jimmy and tell me it's not the best cake you ever tasted."

Jimmy took up the challenge.

"You're right, Joyce. Your Momma should have run a restaurant. If all these secret recipes were hers, she's the best cook I ever heard of. I don't normally eat this much, but I think I could do with one more piece if there's enough."

"Honey, there's all you want."

The rest of the evening went by all too quickly and it seemed like only an hour or two before it was the next morning and Jimmy was back on his way to the hardware store.

Jimmy had taken a keen interest in the seed department in the store. Seeds were easy to handle, and, for him, interesting to talk about. There were flowers, grass, bird and crop seeds. They were located in the front of the store in a section that would have looked perfect when the store first opened in the late eighteen hundreds. He also enjoyed the fact that being beside one of the two main entrances everyone passed by him. There was always interesting conversation about the community and gossip about the citizenry. In this one spot, if you listened, you could keep up with everything that was happening from the weather to who was getting married or divorced. Jimmy had taken to wearing bib overalls much like a turn of the century farmer would have worn. They were perfect for him. They were easy to put on and take off, sort of baggy and with only undershorts and a tee shirt, he was ready to go. Put a straw hat on his head and he was the perfect image of a farmer selling seeds. He was also becoming knowledgeable about his product. Before long a lot of customers started coming in and asking for the garden guy or the seed guru. Greg and the other employees started referring any questions about gardening to him. It was a real source of pride for him, something he'd had little of the past year. He felt beneficial to the store and not just a recipient of Greg's good nature and charity. Jimmy also developed another skill. Perhaps it came from looking out the door of the chopper into an endless sea trying to find a tiny spot floating on the water hoping to be rescued. He had the ability to focus on small details. One of those details was whether or not a potential customer in the store might be a shoplifter. They didn't venture into Mitchell's that often, but he had an uncanny ability to pick them out of the crowd of shoppers. It might have been just the look on their face, or perhaps an unnatural way of looking around the store. Whatever it was, it was something that caught Jimmy's attention immediately. From a distance he'd follow them around the store. He'd take note of anything they might pick up and not put back. Occasionally, they'd already have a shopping bag with them from another store and swiftly drop the stolen items into it thinking nobody would ever challenge what seemed to be, a legitimate purchase. This particular morning brought with it one of the cleverest approaches to stealing he'd seen. A young couple, perhaps in their late twenties, entered pushing a baby carriage. The young brunette woman handled the carriage and the bearded young man with her had a small golden retriever puppy on a leash. They were all smiles and the perfect picture of a big city couple on retreat at the coast. The woman gushed to her man as she entered.

"What a wonderfully charming place. It looks just like an antique store. And the stuff on the walls, oh my goodness, it looks more like a museum. Come here, Ben. You've got to see this."

She motioned him over to numerous items one at a time covering almost the entire store. Other customers would come over to them.

"What a beautiful little baby girl. All in pink. She's just precious. And you also have a little golden retriever puppy. That's so sweet, they can grow up together."

"Thank you. That's exactly what we were thinking. I mean, some people said things like a puppy and a baby are too much at the same time. Like, you know...they'll wear you out. And I'd say to them, like, nonsense. Like, we love having both of them around all the time. It's like, the best."

The repetitive use of the word 'like' put them immediately in a category of people that Jimmy didn't 'like'. It struck him as shallow and mindless dialogue used constantly by shallow and mindless people. He suspected them from the start. As they walked, people gathered around the baby carriage and the man would back away slightly from the group and pick up products from a shelf or display cabinet. He'd hold them by his side and as the woman started to move forward, he'd bend over the carriage as if to check on the baby. He'd reach inside the carriage and stuff the items under the baby's pillow. Jimmy watched this scenario repeat itself numerous times as they made their rounds of the store. The young woman picked up a small souvenir emblem of New Bern mounted on a magnetic refrigerator button.

"This is so cute, Ben. Let's get one of these to remember this charming town."

"If you want one, go ahead and get it."

Jimmy quickly pointed out the couple to Greg in a manner such that he knew exactly what Jimmy was trying to tell him. Jimmy then moved over behind the cash register to handle the transaction. The young woman waited her turn in line. As the customer in front of her left, she stepped forward, opened her purse and took out two singles. Her escort stood behind her holding onto the baby carriage and puppy as she tried to pay for the item.

"That was one fifty plus tax, right young man?"

"Not exactly. From my count it's about a hundred and fifty."

"What are you talking about?"

"I'm speaking of the things your boyfriend there put in the carriage."

"You're accusing my husband of stealing from your store? That's totally ridiculous."

"Hey, if I'm wrong, I'm sorry. Wouldn't be the first time I made a mistake."

Greg stepped between the man and the carriage and gently lifted the pillow under the baby's head. The woman screamed at him the entire time. He smiled and ignored her protests.

"Get away from that carriage right this minute. I'm going to call the cops on you."

Jimmy smiled as he replied to that statement.

"No need to ma'am. I just called them for you. Bet you they'll be here in less than two minutes. They always keep a couple on cycle patrol downtown. You know, Ma'am, the shame of it all is that anything you needed bad enough to steal, Greg Smith would have given it to you."

The woman suddenly grew silent and started looking toward the door. Her supposed husband left her, the baby and the puppy as he briskly stepped toward the same entrance. As he pulled on the door to make good his escape, a young New Bern officer stepped directly into the open doorway. The man stopped and retreated back into the store.

After having the woman remove the baby from the carriage, the officers found about a hundred and fifty dollars' worth of unpurchased goods, just as Jimmy suspected. The officers called for a squad car and soon the entire entourage, woman, man, puppy and baby girl were all headed over to the police station.

Greg went over to Jimmy and put an arm over his shoulder.

"How in the world did you figure out what they were up to?"

"I think I have a gift, Greg. It's totally instinct. Just glad I could stop them before they made good on their escape. I feel kinda like a street cop. Maybe I should have been a detective."

"No doubt you would have a made a great one."

Over a period of six months, Jimmy nabbed no less than a dozen thieves attempting to steal. Greg had to wonder how much stock he'd lost before Jimmy started working there. It must have been a considerable amount.

As the summer came to an end, the tourists visiting New Bern thinned accordingly. The store always did a good business year-round, but there was a noticeable drop as the kids started back to school. It allowed a little more time to spend with each customer and engage in conversation. Jimmy took full advantage. One morning a young woman of about thirty-five approached him. He noticed her immediately. She was tall and slender with blonde hair piled on top of her head. She looked somewhat familiar, but he couldn't quite place her. He knew he'd seen her somewhere previously. She was engaging, with a ready smile and pleasant demeanor.

"Good morning. You must be Jimmy."

"I am."

"My name is Virginia Goode. I was told that you know almost everything there is to know about a garden. Is that right?"

"I'm sure it's not everything, but I know quite a bit about a few things, especially the seeds."

"How interesting. I love gardening. I have flowers all around my house. Some of them are doing great, especially the mums. They seem to love the weather here."

"Yes ma'am. That's the reason New Bern has the Mum-Fest every year."

"Of course. But there are several plants I love that I can't seem to get to grow well. I buy starter plants, not usually seeds, and plant them with fertilizer mixed into potting soil.

I couldn't believe it, but over half of them died on me. I can't figure it out."

"It could be lots of things, but if I had to guess it's probably some problem with the soil or the drainage. Lots of sand around here and if the drainage is wrong, they could be either too dry or too wet. I'd have to look at the plants and the soil in the flower beds to be sure."

"You're a treasure. Could I talk you into coming over to my place on your day off and taking a peek at my garden? I'd be happy to feed you dinner as my way of saying thanks."

Jimmy was sensing an interest in him that went beyond gardening. Normally, he'd never go to a customer's house to look at their plants, but he found this woman attractive. He decided to take a chance.

"I guess I could drop over after church on Sunday. I usually eat Sunday lunch at a friend's house, but I could come over around three and see what you've got going on."

"That would be terrific. I live at 219 New Street. I'm in the first block off the river. My place is over two hundred years old. I'd love to show it to you. You're from New Bern, aren't you? I think I remember somebody telling me that."

"Why, yes I am."

She was definitely interested in him if she had been talking about him with someone.

"I can't tell you how excited I am that I could talk you into coming over. I'll see you Sunday."

"I'll be there."

With virtually no interest in him by a woman in almost

a year, this one piqued his interest. His mood picked up considerably. Several of the crew working in the store commented that he seemed to be in really great spirits, to which he replied, "I love this time of year. A little chill in the air and the mums in bloom. Life is good."

∽

On Sunday, Jimmy had lunch at Joyce and Beatrice's as it had become almost a ritual. Joyce noticed he was a little more animated than usual.

"This fried chicken is to die for, Joyce. I feel like I'm going to explode."

"Well, save some room 'cause I baked an apple pie and I've got some butter pecan ice cream to go on top of it too."

"You're killing me, Joyce. You know I can't say no to that. I do have to hurry up though. I've got to be downtown around three."

"Ah ha! I knew you were up to something. What's her name?"

"What makes you think it's a woman?"

"Sixty-five years of studying men. I can read some men like a book."

"You got me. She's a woman who came into the store and wanted to know some stuff about her plants and why they keep dying on her. She lives over on New Street and wanted me to come by her house and take a look."

"Oh, she's good. What do you think, Beatrice?"

"Uhm, huh! Good alright. Got this young man heading

over to her place to look at some dead flowers on his day off. She's a smart one alright. And New Street? That's money row over there, Jimmy. She might be just the ticket you need to move uptown."

Joyce started singing a line from a favorite television show and snapping her fingers.

"Now he's moving on up...."

"You two cut it out. I'm just going to look at her dead bushes. That's it."

"Ok, Jimmy. Just remember who told you first."

"If you're right, I'll...I'll come back tomorrow evening after work and eat all the rest of this pie."

"You're on. Now be about your business."

11

JIMMY PEDALED ANXIOUSLY the mile and half to Virginia Goode's home. The bicycle ride from Trent Court to New Street was the longest he'd been on since getting the bike. It was not an issue today as his adrenalin was pumping. He thought Virginia was pretty and smart. It was hard to believe she might find him interesting enough to spend time with. It certainly couldn't be his appearance, he thought. It would take a special woman to look past such dramatic physical issues as Jimmy had. He made the turn onto New Street, one of the premier streets in the residential historic district.

New Bern had many blocks of homes that were still intact after two hundred years. Most of these homes had been totally restored inside and out. The most fashionable and expensive areas in town were comprised of these architectural masterpieces. Virginia either came from money or won the lottery. It was a huge wood-framed home built in the late 1700s. It was impeccably maintained and the lawn reflected the work of a dedicated homeowner. As he approached her front porch, he saw her sitting in a wicker rocking chair obviously on the lookout for him.

"Over here, Jimmy. Just pull your bike up in the lawn. Won't hurt a thing. What an interesting bike. It looks like a huge tricycle."

"It was a gift from Mr. Prather who owns the bike shop here in town. It's been a lifesaver for me. Couldn't get to work or really anywhere without it."

Jimmy walked over to Virginia. He felt nervous.

"Where are these plants you're having problems with?"

"Just over here."

She took him around the corner of the house to a flower bed where almost nothing was doing well.

"I already see the problem. Shade. Between these huge live oaks and your house, this area gets no sunlight. There are some plants that could thrive here, but not the ones you're trying to grow. Now that I know what the problem is, I can recommend some plants to you that will do nicely here. Just come back by the store this week. I'll even set some aside for you or order you some specially if you want me to."

"Would you? That would be wonderful. Now, come on in and let me fix you a cold glass of iced tea. You like iced tea?"

"Yes, I was raised on it. It is sweet tea, isn't it?"

"You know it is."

Virginia opened the screen door and held it open while Jimmy entered. She was considerate of the fact that he lacked agility. The hallway had random width heart pine floors and numerous pieces of antique furniture. Entering the splendid old home was like stepping back in time.

"Come on in the parlor. I love saying that. New homes never have parlors. But when this home was built, every fine home had a parlor where guests would be entertained. And oh, let me introduce you to my sister. This is Norah. She's two years younger than me and a heck of a lot smarter."

Across the room sat a young woman. She was trying her best to smile and she feebly held out her hand to greet him. She was sitting in a wheelchair and Jimmy recognized her immediately as the woman he'd seen leaving the church.

He then remembered where he'd seen Virginia. She was the woman pushing the wheelchair that morning. Now he understood her interest in him. She was hoping he might take an interest in her sister, even if it was just as a friend. Someone to talk with other than herself. Norah's arm was almost too weak to extend. Jimmy quickly took her hand.

"Great to meet you, Norah. I'm Jim Harrison."

"I know you, Jimmy. I was in a couple of classes in school with you. You probably don't remember me. I wasn't in a wheelchair back then. Muscular Dystrophy has finally robbed me of almost my entire body. Back then, I wore leg braces but could still walk. My friends, as few as there were, just called me Nor."

"I do remember you. You sat in the row beside me in homeroom. Gosh, you were super quiet."

"I was shy. Young people, for the most part, stay pretty far away from anyone who's different, especially someone who's handicapped. You certainly didn't have any problems making friends back then. I remember all the girls thought you were so cute and they all wanted to date you. But you had the same girlfriend all the way through high school, didn't you?"

"I did, Kay Burwell."

"Whatever happened to her?"

"She still lives in New Bern. She's a lawyer now. Doing really well."

"You're not together?"

"Not anymore. We split up after my accident. I think my being suddenly handicapped scared her off."

"I'm sorry. Nobody will ever understand that more than I do. So, how are you doing now?"

"It was tough at first, but I'm learning to deal with a lot of things I always took for granted before this happened. People have no idea what it's like waking up every morning and looking at somebody in the mirror that isn't at all who you are, or at least were. I feel like I've got anchors chained to me everywhere I go. Even the simplest task seems to take an exhausting effort now. I have a whole different respect for anyone dealing with severe physical challenges. You for instance; I now have a better understanding of how hard every day must be for you."

"It is hard. Really hard. I'm so blessed to have a sister like Ginny. She's the angel on my shoulder. Without her, I'd have to be in some sort of home where they take care of you. She does all the cooking, helps me get dressed and goes on lots of long walks with me. She pushes my chair all the way down to Union Point every couple of days. I can't use my arms enough to turn the wheels. Pretty sad, aren't I?"

Jimmy looked at her face as he spoke. Her face still appeared as it would have before she was stricken with this horrible illness. Her smile was warm and readily offered to him.

"Norah. I think anyone who met you and talked with you would appreciate you for a lot of reasons other than how well you can walk or play tennis."

She laughed. Jimmy shared small talk with her for at least an hour. She opened up to him quickly. She must have felt, with his own health issues, she could relate to him much more easily than with most people. Jimmy took his time and sincerely tried to find out a little about her interests. In many ways, it made his life look a lot easier.

"You know, Jimmy…the thing I think I miss out on the most is dancing. There's nothing I'd love more than to get out on a dance floor and waltz the whole night away. It just seems it would be like floating on air. My legs would move effortlessly with the music and I'd twirl till I was so dizzy that I couldn't stand up. That would be a perfect night for me. I don't know, maybe it's just a fantasy I have that keeps me going. When I lay down at night, I can see it so clearly.

I almost feel like it's actually happening, like a true out of body experience. Pretty silly, right?"

"Everybody has things they want or would like to do. Things they'll never get to do. It just seems a little unfair that many people want to travel to Europe or own a mansion on the ocean. You want something so simple that for most people that they don't even have to think about being able to do it. I don't know why life has to be like this, but here we are. You want to go to a dance, and I want to be able to take my sailboat back out on the river. You know the old saying, don't you?"

"Which one?"

"If you don't have a dream, you can't have a dream come true. I think I heard that in a song a long time ago."

"It's a good thought. I wish you could get on your boat again. And, I'd like to go dancing, just once. That would hold me for a long time."

"Well, it's getting a little late in the day. I've really enjoyed talking with you, Norah. I hope you'll let me come back over and see you again."

"It would mean more to me than you'll ever know. Promise me you will."

"Count on it."

Virginia returned to the room and sat on the couch listening for the last few minutes. She had given them most of the afternoon to themselves so they could talk without inhibitions.

"I guess I better get back on my bike and start heading

home. It'll take me an hour to make the trip. Norah, you are a delight to talk to. I enjoyed spending some time with you."

"I don't want to put any pressure on you, but remember your promise to come see me again some time."

"I promise you, I will be back. Virginia won't have to buy any seeds to get me to come over."

"What kind of seeds? I don't get it."

"I'll explain it to you later. I will tell you this. Your sister loves you more than you even know."

Virginia smiled as Jimmy said goodbye. He held the front porch railing and made his way back to his bike. After his ritual of getting on the bike with only one good leg and arm, he started pedaling down the street. He was disappointed that Virginia had no interest in him for herself at all. But she loved her sister and was grasping at straws trying to find someone who might be sympathetic enough to her to at least visit and bring a smile, even if it was just once in a while. He determined right then he'd be that person. He knew only a little of what she'd been going through her entire life. If he could brighten up just one day now and then, he'd do it.

MumFest – Saturday Morning

Greg asked Jimmy to man an outside display for MumFest on Saturday morning. This was a three-day festival beginning on Friday and lasting through Sunday afternoon. It was, by far, the biggest community event of the year bringing in thousands of tourists. Several blocks of the historical downtown section would be closed off to traffic. With pedestrian traffic only, it meant that booths and display tents could be set up on the street in front of all the shops. Mitchell's was emphasizing plants and seeds this year. Jimmy had enlisted Dee's help and he was enjoying the festivities immensely.

"You get paid for this, Jimmy?"

"Well Dee, not much."

"I'd do this every weekend just for fun."

"I enjoy it a lot myself. It's fun to be a part of all the activity. I like to ask people where they're from. It's surprising how far folks traveled to come to MumFest. There's normally a few from out of the country. Even when I was in the Coast Guard, I'd try to get over here at least one of the days the festival was running. It's just fun to see all the displays. And now, you and I are running one. Pretty cool, huh?"

"Yes, sir. I'm liking it. A lot."

A voice called out from the street.

"Jimmy. Over here."

A golf cart pulled over in front of Mitchell's where Jimmy and Dee were seated by a table. It was Virginia at the wheel and Norah beside her, a seat belt helping her to sit up straight.

"Good morning, guys! So, you're the spokesman for Mitchell's this morning?"

"Apparently. They obviously don't know what they're asking for."

"I know better than that. Who's this young man help-ing you?"

"This is Dee. He's a buddy of mine. He lives just a few apartments down from me at Trent Court. We hang out together quite a bit. I'm teaching him how to sell plants to the city slickers."

"Well, Dee, it's nice to meet you. This is my sister, Norah. Are you getting off for lunch, Jimmy?"

"Actually, I only have to work until lunch today. I'll be free in about twenty minutes, why?"

"Norah and I want to invite you and Dee to come with us to Sting Ray Café for a seafood lunch. What do you say? And before you answer, it's all on me. I won't discuss that any further. Are you in?"

Jimmy looked at Dee who was already smiling from ear to ear. He almost never got to eat at a restaurant. It wouldn't work with their meager budget. And seafood? He was ready to go. The ladies waited until their shift was over and every-one piled into the golf cart. Jimmy looked it over.

"I like this. Do you use it a lot?"

"Used to. I had it built specially for Norah. It has all the controls on the steering wheel and dash. Originally, she could drive it and went all over town with it. Since her arm has gotten so weak, she can't safely drive it anymore. But we got special permission to drive it through here even though the streets are closed to cars."

"This is nice. I might look into one of these after I save up a little bit."

"It's even got side curtains so you can use it in the winter. You want to drive it? Here, switch seats with me and give it a try."

He didn't wait for her to ask again. He got behind the wheel and, within seconds, had the controls figured out. They took off down East Front Street to the Stingray Café located directly across the street from the North Carolina History Center.

Stingray's had always been a favorite of Jimmy's. It was far from fancy. It more closely resembled a catfish house you might find along the coast of Louisiana or Florida. There were lots of fish nets, buoys, and mounted fish on the knotty pine-planked wall. Workmen and locals kept the place full even in the off-season. The seafood was always fresh, mostly caught by Ed, the owner, and his son. They also owned the small seafood market directly beside it, another unpretentious business. You could actually go into the market, pick out a fish and the restaurant next door would cook it fresh for you. With all the tourists in town for MumFest, they felt lucky to be able to get a table today.

Virginia knew Ed. He saw the group enter, motioned to a waitress and pointed at them. She had a table cleaned and ready for them in just a couple of minutes. They sat down and picked up their menus. Jimmy didn't need a menu. He could already taste what he had in mind.

"I love this place. Been coming here for years. It's mainly fried seafood but, to tell you the truth, I'm not much into broiled fish. Give me some breading and, of course, if you don't have hushpuppies fresh out of the grease, it ain't my kind of place. I'm gonna have a shrimp basket, apple sauce and sweet tea."

Dee went for the clam chowder and crab cakes. The girls decided to split a seafood platter. It was large and had three different types of seafood on it.

"I don't really eat all that much," Norah explained as she put a small smear of butter on a hushpuppy. "Ginny and I almost always split. As much sitting as I do, I don't burn a lot of calories so it doesn't take much to make me feel full. Don't get me wrong, though, I love seafood."

They continued talking, laughing and eating until the most of lunch crowd had departed. They were the last table still seated. Ed came over to them.

"Virginia, Norah, you can all stay here as long as you want. The staff will be cleaning the other tables up if that won't bother you. They'll be getting the place ready for dinner. I was happy to see you back. It's been quite a while. Who are your friends here?"

Jimmy reached out his left hand to shake with the owner.

"I'm Jim Harrison. I've eaten here a lot over the years, just never got to meet you. I love your place though. This young man is Dee. We're neighbors. We live just around the corner."

"Trent Court?"

"Yes, the building closest to here. After this great meal, I'm going to make it a point to get back here as often as I can."

"Love to have you."

They told stories and laughed until their faces hurt. Virginia finally had to break up the affair.

"I hate to bring this meeting to a close, but I'm on the Altar Guild for the church and I have to be over there sometime this afternoon to get things set up for church in the morning. This was so much fun. I'd love to get together like this at least once a month."

"I'm in. How about you, Dee?"

"Unless I have to pay. We don't have money to eat out." Virginia replied.

"You're money's no good here, Dee. You eat with us; it's always on the house."

"That case, I'm here."

They piled back into the golf cart and Virginia drove the group back to Mitchell's. Jimmy and Dee both left their bikes there earlier and needed to ride them back to Trent Court. Across the street from the store, a caricature artist had set up a booth. Norah commented when she noticed him.

"Look, that man is drawing cartoon pictures of people. Can we go see how he does it?

Jimmy replied.

"Anything you want to do is fine with me."

They drove the cart across the street and watched as the artist completed charcoal renderings of an elderly couple.

"He's really good."

The man heard her comments and quickly realized she was handicapped and unable to walk over to the chairs where the couple had been sitting to have a drawing made. When he finished their piece, he walked over to Norah.

"I could easily do one of you and your friends here sitting in the cart. Ten dollars and fifteen minutes."

"I don't know. Jimmy, what do you think?"

Virginia answered for them.

"Of course, they want one. Dee and I will stand to the side and you can draw Norah and Jimmy in the front seat."

She could tell by the smile on Norah's face that was exactly what she hoped would happen. The artist moved his easel and bench over to the front of the cart. He chatted with them as he made deft strokes on the charcoal pad.

"I hope you don't mind; I'm taking a few liberties with this to add a little flavor."

"Help yourself. The only way my face could make this any better would be if I moved it out of here and let you draw just Norah. Now, she has a beautiful face."

"She truly does."

As promised, the work was completed in just under fifteen minutes. The creator smiled at his work; picked it up from the easel and walked it over to the cart. He turned it so that Norah and Jimmy could see what he'd done. It was an excellent caricature of them both. There was nothing in it that indicated that either of them had a handicap. However, he'd decorated the cart in such a fashion that it appeared they were sitting in a vintage, 1957 Thunderbird convertible. Norah gushed when she saw it.

"Oh my gosh. It's my dream date. The one I never got to go on. What do you think, Jimmy?"

He looked at the illustration and then to the artist.

"You are good. It's a cool portrait. Thank you."

Virginia reached for her purse and pulled out a twenty-dollar bill. The man symbolically put his hands behind his back.

"No Ma'am. This one's on the house. I enjoy seeing folks smile. This young lady just made my day."

Norah looked to the artist.

"And you made my year. Thank you so much!"

They collectively decided to take the cart further down on Craven Street. They would take a quick look at what else might be happening. The intersection of Pollock and Craven, in front of City Hall, had music blaring from speakers on each corner. They cautiously eased forward in the cart. When the crowd saw they were unable to approach on foot, they graciously moved aside to let the cart closer so they could see what was going on. Norah peered through the crowd.

"They're dancing! Wearing fifties poodle skirts and beehive hairdos. They're great. I love this. If there's anything I'd like to be able to do, it's this. Moving to the music would be a thrill. And I love music from this period. I think they call it 'doo-wop' music. Did you ever dance, Jimmy?"

"I went to a couple of dances at school, but never really knew how to dance. I just moved to the rhythm as best I could. I'm sure I made a fool of myself, but nobody seemed to care. Let's just say that I can probably dance just as well now as I did back then."

"I'm sure you were great."

"If you want to think that, go ahead."

After watching several dances, they drove the cart back to the parking lot behind Mitchell's. As they hopped out, Norah spoke up.

"Jimmy, I just want to let you know how much I've enjoyed today. And your phone calls. I look forward to them so much. It's the high point of my week. Please come by and see me when you can."

"I've tried to call because sometimes it's not easy to ride that far. I'm having some problems with my leg. But, that aside, I'll do my best. Either by phone or in person, I'll be in touch."

Virginia looked over to Jimmy.

"Thank you. This meant a lot."

"I enjoyed it as well. Thanks again for lunch and for coming by to get us. See you again soon."

"I hope so."

The girls rode off in the cart. It had been a fun afternoon and a great break for him and Dee. It was always sad to see Norah and know what she must be going through. And yet, she always had a smile on her face. It couldn't be easy.

12

JIMMY WAS STARTING to have some health problems. On Monday when he awoke, he noticed that his right leg was sore, swollen and red. He figured he must have pushed it a little too hard over the weekend. He was up and down a lot at MumFest. Undaunted, he put on a shirt, his trademark overalls and headed to work. With the leg so painful, it was far more difficult than usual to make the short trek to Mitchell's. By the time he arrived, he was sweating profusely and the pain was noticeable on his face. Greg came over to him.

"Jim, what's wrong? You don't look well at all."

"I'm not sure. My leg really hurts."

"Let me take a look, if that's alright."

"Sure."

Jimmy rolled up his pants leg. Having to bend over and use both hands to accomplish it proved to be more than he was capable of. He stood up and leaned against the back-room wall.

"Sorry, you'll have to give me a little bit of help. Pretty embarrassing."

"Not a problem. I'll get it for you. Let's see what we have going on."

Greg was startled to see the leg was bright red and swollen so dramatically that the skin seemed to shine.

"Jimmy, I'm afraid we need to get you over to the hospital. This looks bad. I'm not a doctor, of course, but I can see this looks infected. Tell you what, let me get David to watch the store for me and I'll drive you over to the emergency room. It could be nothing serious, but I don't think we can take that chance. You alright with that?"

"I guess so. I don't need anything else to go wrong. I'm at my limit with problems if you know what I mean."

"That's exactly why we need to go now, before it gets any worse."

Greg let the staff know he and Jimmy would be out of the store the rest of the afternoon. He brought his car around to the front and helped Jimmy get in the back seat.

"Stretch your leg out Jimmy. I know it's got to be killing you. Won't take long to get over to the emergency room. Hopefully, they can give you something to get the swelling down and ease the pain. You think something might have bitten you? I mean, a spider or a fire ant, something like that?"

"Not that I'm aware of. It was just swollen when I woke up. I think I might have pushed it too hard yesterday. I rode my bike a couple of miles. That's the most I've ever done. It was pretty tiring. Other than that, I don't know what it could be."

The hospital emergency room was packed as usual. Greg got Jimmy a seat and went over to the registration desk.

"Good morning, Greg. How are things at the store?"

"Just fine, Nancy. Thank you for asking. Listen, one of my employees is Jimmy Harrison. He's sitting over there on the last row by the door. He has a lot of physical problems and now his right leg looks like an overripe melon. Any way you could expedite getting him in to see somebody? He's in a lot of pain. He's not up to this."

"Let me see what I can do."

Nancy got up and walked to the treatment room located behind the administrative area. Like most people in town, she'd shopped at Mitchell's countless times and been the recipient of a warm smile and personal greeting from Greg on every visit. It was time to repay the kindness if possible. After less than ten minutes, Jimmy's name was called. He limped over to the counter. Nancy noticed he could barely stand and had an attendant bring a wheelchair over to him. Greg went with him back into the treatment area. A young resident physician met them immediately.

"You're Greg Smith from Mitchell's aren't you?"

"I am."

"What's the problem with your friend here?"

"This is Jim Harrison. He works with me. He has a number of problems with his right arm and leg but this morning when he came to work, he was in a lot of pain and his right leg is as red and swollen as a ripe tomato."

"Let's take a look."

The doctor knew immediately what the problem was.

"Cellulitis. It can be painful and it's nothing to fool around with. Untreated, it can be deadly. Normally, I'd prescribe an oral antibiotic and rest for a few days. That usually helps it to clear up. People with other serious conditions such as immune system disorders, diabetes or other illnesses, are more susceptible and at a higher risk of complications; some of which are serious. Since Jim has other medical issues, I'm going to admit him to the hospital, get him on intravenous antibiotics and watch him carefully. If all goes well, then we can have him back to work later in the week. How does that sound, Jim?"

"Not really what I was hoping for but I'll do whatever I have to. I certainly want to get better."

"This is what you need to do."

Greg already presumed this would be the outcome.

"I'll wait with you, Jim and get you tucked into a room. Then, I guess you're going to need a few things from your place. I'll be glad to go there, pick them up and bring them back to you."

"I won't need much, toothbrush, razor, two more pairs of boxers, socks and maybe a couple of boating magazines?"

"You got it."

"Here's a key to my dump. Don't expect much. If you

have any problem, there's two ladies who live next to me, Joyce and Beatrice. They'll help you with anything."

Within the hour, Jimmy was in a room and Greg headed out to his apartment. Jimmy had an IV hooked up and a remote control in his hand for the television. He determined he'd just watch old movies until he was discharged. It was hard for him to not flashback to the months he'd spent in the hospital and rehab after the accident. He appreciated hospitals and doctors but he was already itching to be well and back to work.

The evening went by quickly. The pain meds had kicked in and he was resting comfortably. Around 8 p.m., another doctor came in to talk with him.

"Good evening, Jim. I'm Arnold Meyers. I'm an Internal Medicine Specialist. I've looked over your chart. I think we can get you squared away in a couple of days. But, I've got to tell you that people who have compromised immune systems or underlying health issues tend to have recurrences of cellulitis. It's probably going to be something that could flare up with you for the rest of your life. There's no way to guarantee that it won't. You have to be careful all the time. An open scratch on your leg gets a little dirt in it and cellulitis could easily come back. It's a blood infection and, in certain circumstances, can be serious, even fatal. I'm not trying to scare you. I just want you to know what it is and want you to be particularly on guard for it. If your legs ever look like this again, you need to head back to the emergency room immediately. No waiting around with it. The quicker you get treatment the better. Do you have any questions I can answer for you?"

"What's the chances of getting that Tom Hanks movie Castaway on the tube here?"

"I'm afraid that's a question for your night nurse. She'll be by shortly. You keep that sense of humor and you're going to be fine."

"Thanks Doc. When you've had as many health problems as I've had, you get pretty used to bad news. I'm okay with it."

Greg came by a short while later with the requested items.

"Okay, buddy. You do what they tell you here and I'll be by every day to check on you. Get well so you can get back to the store. I'm sure there will be lots of fall gardening questions coming up and, with you gone, we're in trouble. Take care. See you soon."

"Greg."

"Yes?"

"You've been awfully good to me and I just want you to know that I appreciate it more than you know."

"Thanks. You're more than welcome, Jimmy. You have done so much for other people all your life and are deserving of what anyone can do to help you. I'll be back tomorrow."

As the television played in the background, Jimmy's thoughts centered around his life the past nine months. Everything he enjoyed, all his best friends, his career, and even the love of his life had all disappeared. He thought to himself that jumping out of a helicopter into the ocean in the middle of a hurricane was not nearly as frightening or traumatic as heading into what he'd been experiencing. Given the choice, he would take a hurricane any day. But this is where he was and his choices were limited. He'd have to take life one day at a time on its terms.

He was discharged after three days and sent home with a prescription for antibiotics. He didn't return to work until Saturday.

It was good to be back at a place where he felt like an integral part of the life there. The crew left notes for him from folks who needed answers on gardening issues. That prospect alone got his day off to a good start.

By midday he was catching up and went to the back workroom to eat a sandwich that Joyce made for him. It was turkey on rye with mustard. She knew it was his favorite and took great delight in the fact that such a small gesture could bring someone so much satisfaction. He savored every bite. Almost done with lunch, he heard a familiar voice coming from the front of the store. He looked forward from the back room toward the counter where Dave was waiting on a customer. Even from a distance, he knew instantly that it was Kay.

He set his sandwich down and quietly eased forward between two rows in the fastener section. They extended upwards about seven feet and were fairly tight together making his eavesdropping impossible for Kay to notice.

"I'm looking for a cooking gift for a friend. She loves the old timey iron skillets to make cornbread and several folks said you had those here. I doubt anywhere else in town would have them."

"We have several varieties. They're just over there behind you to your left with all the cooking supplies."

"I don't have a clue what I should buy. Can you just pick one out for me? I'm really not a cook. If she wants to exchange it for another model that would be alright, wouldn't it?"

"Of course. Just keep the receipt and we'll be glad to let her bring it back. Here, this is a basic and traditional skillet. I think your friend will be more than pleased with it. Need anything else?"

"I was thinking about taking a couple of mums back to the office. They are so pretty this time of year. I saw some out front, didn't I?"

"You did. And we have an expert on them right here in the store. I'll try to get him to help you."

"I don't want to be a problem. Any two will work."

"No problem. Our garden guru is Jim Harrison. He knows all about them. I'll get him to help you. He's in the back of the store."

"Are you talking about Jimmy Harrison from New Bern?"

"Yes, you know him."

Kay paused and stammered.

"I used to, a long time ago. I didn't know he worked here. Tell you what. I'll pass on them today. I'm starting to run late getting back to the office. I'll come by another time."

"You sure?"

"I am. Thanks for your help."

"No problem."

Jimmy heard the entire conversation. To think she didn't want to see him brought up so much hurt, it was indescribable. At least he could have looked her in the face and had a short talk with her, even if it was just about mums. How could she so easily turn away from him? He walked slowly back to the workroom. He stared off into space as he tried to empty his mind and slow down the pain inside. It was as difficult a moment as he had been through in his life.

Seeing Kay and hearing her voice refreshed her constant presence in his thoughts. Over the next few days, he remained distracted. Greg mentioned to him that he seemed deep in thought.

"Just preoccupied with trying to get over this cellulitis issue. Keeping a close watch on my leg to make sure it's getting better. So far, the antibiotics seem to be working but the doctor told me to keep watch constantly 'cause I can't be too careful. Guess it's got me a little worried about it coming back."

"I understand. Anytime your leg starts hurting and you need to get off your feet, you just tell me you need to go home and that'll be fine with me. I want you well and handling all our gardening customers. I mean, did you see how many of them came by the store to talk with you while you were in the hospital."

"I did. I've called them all back. It was really nice to feel needed and missed."

"I mean it now. You take care of yourself."

Jimmy couldn't get Kay out of his mind. He wished he'd never seen her again. The futileness of it all, his endless days without her were more than he could bear.

After a week of trying to figure out what he should do to stop his mind from descending into total despair, he came up with a plan. He'd be outside of Kay's office as she left work. If he could just get her attention for a minute, he'd tell her all the things he was thinking and that he understood they would never marry. But hopefully they could still stay in touch. He could see her from time to time if she would let him. He determined that tomorrow, after work, would be the day.

Jimmy stood on Pollock Street in front of the law firm where Kay worked. As the sun started going down, it began to sprinkle. He never liked this time of year when the sun went down by five thirty. It was depressing. People started leaving the office in small groups and even a few by themselves. It wasn't a place where people worked fixed hours. Sometimes when they were involved in a big case, it meant working late into the night. For the most part, everyone's hours were different from day to day. He waited under the awning of a nearby business with his eyes keenly fixed her office building. After an hour or so, he saw her standing at the door as if waiting for the rain to slow down a bit. When that didn't happen, she opened the door and started out. Jimmy began to walk toward her. What he had to say wouldn't take long and the rain would be the perfect reason to make it a brief and less awkward conversation. He just wanted a minute of her time. Before he could get to her, Morrison Brooks pulled up to the curb in front of the building in his black Mercedes and briskly walked toward her with a large umbrella. He held it over her with his right hand and put his left arm around her waist pulling her tightly toward him. He kissed her firmly on the lips. As they separated, she said while smiling.

"Stop it, Morrison. Everybody in the office will see us. Can't you at least wait till we get to the car?"

"Probably not. Besides, they all know we're getting married soon. I would hope they'd be happy for us. Come on now, let's get out of this rain."

He walked her over to his car, opened the passenger door making sure no rain fell on her during the process. He walked back to the driver's side, lowered the umbrella, stuck it in the back seat and got in. As he started to pull out of the parking space, Kay looked toward Jimmy. He could tell she saw him clearly and turned her head away as if saying I don't want you to be in my life. Once again, it was excruciating.

Jimmy rode home in the rain. He didn't care how wet he got as it started to rain harder. By the time he reached his apartment, he was completely soaked. He walked over to the refrigerator and retrieved one of the remaining beers he'd bought for Bill Flynn. If he ever needed a beer, this was the night. He finished off the two that remained. He hadn't had this much to drink since he went out with the crew back in Elizabeth City. He felt a little bit lightheaded but it did help him to fall asleep, wet clothes and all.

It rained hard throughout the night. Jimmy tossed and turned in a restless sleep punctuated with flashbacks of happier days. By dawn, the rain had passed.

He realized he had fallen asleep with wet clothes on. He found a dry set and got dressed for work. He went through his daily ritual like a robot and remained deep in thought throughout the morning. He couldn't help but wonder what was left for him that was worth living for. He hadn't let his mind go in that direction through all of his trials; but this morning, he was weighing his options, omitting no possibility.

Two days later, he was still not his usual upbeat self. He was quiet at the store, but it was a busy time of year and everyone was up to their ears with customers and incoming stock needing to be priced and displayed. No one seemed aware that he was keeping to himself and his thoughts. About one in the afternoon, Greg yelled out.

"Jimmy, special delivery."

Startled, he walked over to Greg who handed him an envelope.

"You've got mail."

Jimmy took the stationery size envelope and retreated to a spot behind the seed counter and opened it. He read slowly.

Dear Jimmy, I saw you outside of my office the other night and I was so surprised. Please forgive me for not stopping, but I was with Morrison. It would have been an awkward moment for all of us. I know your life has been difficult and I feel like the most horrible person ever for not being there to help you through it. I think I have some sort of character weakness that couldn't accept what happened to you, the man I was in love with and who I was planning to marry. I hope one day you can forgive me for that. I just don't have the kind of courage to have handled such a dramatic change in my life. You were the strong, vibrant man who would make my life everything it wasn't. We'd attack life together, see the world and experience all it offered. When the accident happened, all that changed. I felt like it was unfair to me, as well as you, because it stole from me every dream I ever had. I washed the past from my mind and determined what we had back then could never be again. Morrison was there all the time when I was in despair and grieving. He brought me the security I needed and before long, we were together as a couple. I can't change any of this. I will always remember us the way we were before any of this happened. There will always be a special place in my heart for you, but I think it's best if we don't see each other, even as friends. I hope you understand where I'm coming from. I wish you nothing but happiness, Jimmy. I know you are tough and you are a survivor and that you will come out of this stronger than ever.

Warmest Regards,

Kay

Jimmy now understood nothing further was possible between them; not even a friendship. There were too many painful memories for her. And she was marrying that elitist attorney. He didn't see how she could possibly be attracted to such a stuffed shirt, but if he made her happy, then so be it.

Now, he had to figure out what he could do with whatever was left of his life. He tried to pick himself up as best he could. He poured himself into work and most evenings, Greg would have to make him leave.

He didn't want to be alone with his thoughts back in his apartment at night. There were some places in his mind that he didn't want to visit. Work was the distraction he used.

Throughout the next month, he had several more bouts with his leg. It would get red and swell up, but now he knew what he was dealing with. A quick visit to the doctor's office, a new prescription for antibiotics, and it would clear up. He realized its recurrence was not a good sign and, most likely, an indication that his general health was slowly declining. His bike was getting harder to ride and the trip to and from work was becoming a hardship. Still he kept his problems to himself as much as possible.

Wednesday morning, December 5th was a cold day for New Bern. Everyone at Mitchell's was trying to stay inside. The cold really got to Jimmy that day especially. Riding to work on the bike was becoming almost impossible. He didn't know how much longer he'd be able to continue.

Around ten a.m., with no customers in the store, Greg came to the counter and shouted.

"Ok, everybody. Come on up front here. Team meeting."

This was not a usual occurrence and everyone was curious as to what Greg had on his mind. When everyone had gathered up front, he explained.

"Jimmy has been working here with us for about six months and we all think the world of him. We'd hate to lose him. However, it's becoming obvious to me and to some of you that riding his bike has gotten to be a little too much for him. If he couldn't ride his bike to work, he wouldn't be able to work with us. So, that being said, I didn't want to have to fire him for being late and pay unemployment to him. The only answer I could come up with was this. Since today is Jimmy's birthday...that's right Jimmy, you put it down on your employee information form...we're going to take this time to eat some carrot cake, drink a little fruit punch and...drum roll please.."

Dave pounded a drum roll on the counter.

"For this auspicious occasion we, your friends and fellow Mitchellites, want to present you with a special present. Two ladies who worked at the store came up beside Jimmy and each grabbed an arm. He was confused. He didn't need help to stand. Then they started escorting him to the sidewalk out front. He was surprised beyond all expectations to see Bill Flynn, Phil Hewett and Chuck Hutaff standing there and beside them, Virginia Goode. Behind them was the most unusual, yet striking, looking golf cart he'd ever seen. Sitting on the passenger side, dressed with a heavy coat was Norah.

"This golf cart, if you can still call it that, is a gift for you from all of us, and especially from Norah Goode."

Jimmy walked over to the cart and bent over to hug Norah.

"It's beautiful. But who on Earth did this paint job?"

The cart had been painted a bright white with a diagonal orange stripe around the nose. It had been designed to mimic the paint detail of a U.S. Coast Guard chopper.

"Holy cow! It's even got our number on it."

A custom lettering job included everything from Coast Guard logos to Capt. Jim Harrison in script on both sides. He was speechless. Greg walked over to him.

"It's got a full enclosure and new batteries. Charge it up every night and you've got an easy ride to work."

Two of the employees pushed it inside from the front of the store. Several customers followed them in but stood by and watched as Jimmy walked over and sat down by Norah on his new ride.

"I don't know what to say. You guys are too much. You sure you want to do this?"

As the previous owner, Norah responded.

"It's exactly what we want to do. I can't use it anymore unless somebody else is driving. Maybe this will get you to come over and take me for a ride sometime?"

"That's a promise. Thank you all so much."

Greg continued

"You add a lot to this place and we want you to be here as long as you can handle it. This should extend that a good ten or fifteen years. And it's all enclosed. You can ride in the rain. And look, turn signals and headlights. But, no speeding. I'm not coming down to the jailhouse and bailing you out."

"You won't have to worry about that. What will it do, ten miles an hour?"

"At least. So, hold it down on the curves. Okay everybody, let's eat some cake."

Jimmy, his friends and the Mitchell's staff kept the party atmosphere going all afternoon. As customers came in, they offered them fruit punch and a slice of birthday cake. For everyone present, it was a wonderful day.

Jimmy developed a plan for his day off that was totally impossible without the cart. On Sunday after lunch with Joyce and Beatrice, he would take his cart over to the marina and see his boat. He hoped it was still floating.

Sunday was a spectacular day. Joyce and Beatrice overfed him as usual. Their Sunday ritual together was an event he looked forward to all week. Not only was the food phenomenal, they told him some of the most interesting stories about New Bern he'd ever heard.

Growing up as an African-American in New Bern was an entirely different experience than growing up as a white person though they lived just a few miles apart. New Bern had been a predominantly black town up until the 1950s. The section of town known as James City, was the first freedmen's town in the United States. Those were towns where freed and even runaway slaves could live without worry of being pursued by any authorities. There was a rich and varied black history in town that he found remarkable and he took a keen interest in the stories they told.

Jimmy mentioned to Joyce that he'd never met Dee's mother, Cecille, so they immediately invited her and Dee over for lunch. She was a large woman, a great smile and outgoing personality.

"I've heard a lot about you, Jimmy. And Joyce, thank you and Beatrice for asking me and Dee to come over. I've seen you both around here for quite a few years, but you know how it is here. I keep to myself 'cause you never know what's going on in the next apartment. Ain't really any of my business anyway. Besides, between working two jobs and taking care of Dee, there's not much time to do anything else."

"We're all happy you could come over. And Dee, he's practically living over here since Jimmy moved in. He's a fine young man. Always so polite. Don't find that much anymore with young people. You've done a wonderful job raising him."

"I'm real proud of him. Growing up with no father and living where we do, it ain't been easy. So many bad examples around. Jimmy's been nice enough to let him come over after school on days when I have to work late. It feels good to know he's gonna be looked after when I'm not here. I thank you for that, Jimmy."

"I enjoy Dee's company. He's a story a minute. He keeps me up on everything that's going on in the world."

Dee was working on his third piece of Joyce's fried chicken in no time.

"This is the best fried chicken I've ever had. Momma's is real good too, but she doesn't get home early enough to fry chicken so we don't have it much."

Joyce had to correct that assertion.

"Dee, I'm sure your Momma's chicken is every bit as good as mine. You're just very hungry this afternoon."

"Well, it is good."

Cecille looked over at Jimmy.

"I guess this will come as no surprise to you, but Dee here says as soon as he finishes high school, he wants to join the Coast Guard and become a rescue swimmer like you. Now, seems to me that's a pretty dangerous occupation."

"He hasn't told me that yet. He's asked a lot of questions, but I didn't know he was seriously thinking about it. It's a great organization. I don't think you could be with a much better bunch of guys. They always have each other's back. In our line of work, you counted on it. As far as dangerous, yes, being in the search and rescue group has some built-in danger as you can imagine. But the reward of plucking somebody out of the ocean after their ship has gone down, is tremendous. I got so much satisfaction out of it. I never got injured, other than a broken finger or a scrape the whole time I was in. It wasn't until I was on my own time that I got hurt. If my crew had been there with me, I doubt it would have happened. The training Dee would get is the best in the world, and they'll pay for a college education after high school if he wants to keep going."

Dee countered.

"When I finish high school, I don't think I want to keep going to school. I want to jump out of helicopters into the ocean and save people. Now that sounds exciting."

"It can be, Dee. But school is important. I'll bet after you've been out of it for a while, you'll be itching to get some more education and that's when the Guard will be there to help. You keep thinking about what you want to do with your life. You've got plenty of time left. You don't have to make all those decisions right now. You think that chicken is good, just wait till you get a slice of Beatrice's homemade apple pie. You can't have three pieces of that."

"Well, I'll just get one big piece."

Beatrice asked Cecille a few questions about Dee's father.

"He never met his father. I was young when I got pregnant with Dee. His dad was young, too. We talked a lot about what we'd do when we got a little older. We were going to get married and move to Washington, D.C. His name was Gabriel, like in the Bible. Everyone called him Gabe. I was seventeen and he was a year older. When I found out I was pregnant I think it scared the bejesus out of him. He kept saying…'it's going to be okay. I'm going to get a job, save up some money and move us to D.C. where my uncle has a car lot. He's willing to help me get started working on car motors and such.'

Well, I think that when his parents found out he'd gotten a girl pregnant, they shipped him right straight off to live with that uncle. Never seen him or heard from him again. I've been right here in Trent Court for all fourteen years with Dee. It hurt a lot at first, but now I know I was blessed. I've got as fine a son as a woman could hope for. And when he gets out of school and starts work, he says he's going to take care of me for a change. I don't want him to worry about me, but that what he says he's going to do."

"I'm sure he will, Cecille. He's a smart kid with a good heart, and…a great example at home."

The evening passed with everyone talking about their years in Trent Court. There had been a lot of New Bern history that passed through its streets. Even the great Hall of Fame basketball player, Walt Bellamy, had lived there. A street several blocks away was named after him.

Joyce said she had few regrets as well.

"I've told Jimmy about how Beatrice and I wound up living here. There have been times that I'd see folks in the rich part of town living in those fancy homes with three new expensive cars out front and I'd think that I had gotten short-changed somehow. But, when I look around me right now and see you folks here with us, I can't help but feel that some of those other folks might not have as many people that think something of them. Count your blessings. That's what my mother always said and you know, just about everything she ever told me was right. That was one smart woman."

"Well, we better be going. Got to go back to the house and wash some clothes, so my boy here has clean clothes to wear tomorrow. Dee has school in the morning and I have to be at work at the cleaners by eight a.m. Now Jimmy, tomorrow evening after I get done with my day job, I have to go down to the Country Biscuit and help clean up, get the place ready for breakfast. I'll be home around eight. Can Dee hang out with you at your place till then? I'll come by and pick him up on the way home."

"No problem at all, Cecille. Dee adds a lot of company to an otherwise quiet and dark little apartment."

"I know what you're talking about. I know when I get home every night that he'll be there and it gives me something to look forward to all day. Well, good night folks. Thank you, Joyce and Beatrice, for a wonderful afternoon and a delicious lunch. I hope I can have you all over to my place one day soon when I'm not working."

"We'll look forward to it. See you soon."

13

JIMMY WAS IN his new golf cart and on the road to the marina by three p.m. Since the cart would only go up to twelve miles per hour, he stayed close to the right side of the road. Approximately two miles of the trip was on U.S. Highway 70 East where the speed limit was fifty-five, but nearly everyone drove at least seventy. He forced traffic to slow down considerably as he crossed the Trent River bridge. More than one horn blared aggressively at him as he traveled across the span.

He came upon the spot where Steve and Elaine's car jumped over the rail and he'd gone in after them. Other than some concrete repair that looked a little cleaner than the surrounding area, you'd never guess anything occurred there.

About a half mile past the bridge, he turned right onto the service road that went to the marina. When the sailboat masts started to come into view, he got a comforting feeling in the pit of his stomach. To him, a marina was the best place to spend time. He pulled the cart into the boatyard, edging it as close as he could get to his finger pier. As he walked out to his boat, he passed Edgar who owned the yard.

"Hey there, Jimmy. I was beginning to think you'd moved away from the area. I've adjusted the lines on your boat about a hundred times since you were here last. How are you doing?"

"I won't lie, Edgar. I've had a lot of problems, mostly health problems. My old legs are giving me trouble and you can see my arm hasn't gotten any better. But I am working full time over at Mitchell Hardware and I really enjoy that."

"That's a great place. Greg Smith is a prince, isn't he?"

"I never knew a better guy. He's been wonderful to me. He and the rest of the folks who work there bought this golf cart for me. All I had before was a three-wheel bicycle. That's why I couldn't get over here. Of course, today, I felt like I was taking my life in my own hands driving it over the bridge to get here. It's amazing how many people are in such a hurry that slowing them down for just ten seconds, has them ready to shoot somebody."

"Tell me about it. I don't even like to get on the highway anymore. Truth be told, they're probably headed to the store to get a six-pack or some cigarettes, nothing worth speeding over. But, they're all in a mad rush. Liked it better thirty years ago. Used to be able to put the top down on my old convertible and have a relaxing drive somewhere for fun. If you try that today, you're relieved just to find you made your destination without getting run over or shot by somebody with a bad case of the road rage."

"That's the gospel truth."

"Jimmy, there's something I have to talk to you about."

"I know right where you're going, Edgar. I haven't paid you any slip rent in a long time."

"I wouldn't mention it to you. Didn't want to anyway, but I've carried it for you about a year. I'm not looking for you to pay me the back rent, but could you start paying some in the future? It's the cheapest slip on the dock. Other folks would pay me three hundred a month for it. I'll still only charge you two hundred but I need to get a little something 'cause I've got bills to pay myself."

"I know Edgar. I've felt awful about it. There just wasn't anything I could do. I still don't make much, but I'll try to start paying you next month if that's okay with you. Kim Glenn over at The Boathouse asked me if I needed a little part-time work to go along with my regular job and I told her it might be a good idea to help me catch up. I don't know what it would pay but she wants me to come in late Sundays and clean the place up. I think I might do that to help pay my slip rent here."

The Boathouse was a giftshop in the historical district. It was a favorite shop of Jimmy's as it carried every sort of nautical memorabilia. His absolute favorite items were models of old sailing ships.

"You know how much I love *Sugarcane*, and even though

I'm not sure I could get into her by myself, it would kill me to have to get rid of her."

"Jimmy, nobody loves boats more than me. I understand totally where you're coming from. Look, I'll continue to work with you. If you can't pay me on time or even come to the boat, give me a call and let me know what's going on."

"I will absolutely do that."

"Since you mentioned it, can I give you a hand getting aboard?"

"I hate to ask you but it might be a big help."

Edgar helped Jimmy aboard. It was apparent he needed help.

"That sure clears up any ideas I had of taking her sailing by myself, doesn't it?"

"You let me know when you want to go out and I'll try to break free and go with you."

"You sail? I thought you were a power boat guy."

"I grew up sailing a Penguin dinghy right here on the Trent. Learned how to work on motors to make a living. Haven't been in years but you might get me hooked on it again."

"It's a date, then. Some afternoon when it's really nice I'll give you a call and we'll go out for a couple of hours. I'd really enjoy that."

"Sounds good, Jimmy. I've got to get back to the shop. Give me a couple of blasts on your air horn and I'll come down and help you off."

Jimmy sat on the boat for a full hour. He didn't really

do anything other than peer down into the small cabin and stare out onto the water. He had to admit, the sea was the thing he missed the most. He loved every inch of the Neuse River and Pamlico Sound. They were his backyard. He loved all of the moods Mother Ocean threw at him. He'd seen her at her best and at her worst. He'd been out there bringing people in from wrecked or sunken boats for years. He'd experienced conditions that would scare the hardiest of souls. He loved the sea and the thought he'd never be out there again was a lot to stomach.

He stayed until the evening air started to chill. He picked up the small air horn and tapped the top twice. In a couple of minutes, Edgar responded as promised. He helped Jimmy out and walked with him back down the dock. In all truthfulness, he was afraid to let Jimmy even walk down the dock by himself. It was disheartening for him as he'd known Jimmy for years. It killed him to see the condition he was in. He thought that misfortune had spent an undue amount of time on him.

As they reached the shore, Jimmy turned back one more time and took a long look at *Sugarcane*. Besides his last look at Kay, this was about as hard a moment as he'd ever experienced.

"Thanks for everything, Edgar. I'll try to catch up on my rent next month and I'll sure call you if I can make it one afternoon to go out."

"Count on it, Jimmy. I'll see you soon, buddy."

Jimmy got back in his cart, and steeled himself up to

face the traffic on the way home. As he started to drive off, he pondered to himself.

"This seems more dangerous than being a rescue swimmer. I think my odds were better on the chopper."

⋙

Christmas at Christ Church was always a special occasion. Being over three hundred years old, the church site had become a bedrock of the town and a historic spot that nearly every tourist visited. Inside its arched sanctuary was a display case that contained a prayer book, a Bible and a silver communion set given to the church in 1752 by King George II. The parish priest took it to his home and hid it when the Union forces occupied New Bern during the Civil War. He didn't want the historic treasures to become a spoil of the war. The Bible was an exceedingly rare version called the Vinegar Bible because of a typesetting error when it was printed. The word 'vinegar' was accidentally used instead of 'vineyard'. These were cherished items at Christ Church and the communion set was used at least once a month for the parishioners at communion.

Being Christmastime, Governor Pollard was back home from the capital in Raleigh. Politically, the nation was in an uproar and it was a relief for her to be in her hometown where little ever changed. She saw Jimmy enter the Chapel by himself and she motioned for him to come sit with her and her husband, Tommy. She never tried to draw attention to herself and, for the most part, the congregation was accustomed to her worshipping with them and treated her the same as anyone else. She knew Jimmy's history and was sympathetic toward him but never let her concerns for his well-being become obvious. He realized she'd never asked him to sit with them before his accident so he was touched that she went out of her way to show her concern now. Nonetheless, he was honored by her friendship and always accepted her overtures. When the service ended, she asked him.

"Jimmy, we would be delighted to have you come home and have dinner with us this evening. You don't have any family in town anymore since Margaret passed, right?"

"That's right. I would love to go but I hope you will give me a raincheck. I want to hang around here for a little while and see if I can speak with Paul. I have a few things I need to run by him. But, please ask me again."

"Absolutely, Jimmy. Next time I'm home, we'll give you a call."

"And, I'll be there. See you next trip."

Jimmy waited until the line at the door shaking hands and greeting the well-loved priest thinned down and he positioned himself as the last in line.

"Good morning, Jim. How are you this Christmas?"

"To be honest with you, I've got a few issues I really need to talk with you about. I need some answers to a few things I thought you could help me with. Would you be able to talk with me for a little while?"

"I've got two things I have to do first, but if you'll go

wait in my office, I'll join you there shortly. Will that work? Might be ten or fifteen minutes."

"I'll be waiting for you. Take your time. I know this is short notice and I really don't have any other place to be. If you need an hour, take it."

"Thanks, Jim. I'll see you shortly."

About forty-five minutes later, Paul entered his office where Jimmy was waiting.

"Well, Jim. Wonderful group today, wasn't it?"

"Yes sir. Holidays always bring people out. I'm betting the attendance here is always the biggest at Christmas."

"Christmas and Easter. My two favorite times of year as well. Now, what's on your mind today? What can I help you with?"

"It's a little hard for me to talk with people about my problems. That's why I'm here to see you. I guess you've dealt with just about every situation anyone could have. This will probably seem like small potatoes to you. I'm just having trouble dealing with things myself."

"How so, Jim?"

"You know, since my mother passed, it's just me. Before I got hurt, Kay Burwell and I were going to get married. We spoke with you about conducting the wedding."

"You did."

"After I got hurt, she decided she couldn't marry me. I understand. I'm not blaming her or anything. It's just that it's been really difficult. It's the hardest thing I've ever had to deal with. She was the only woman I ever had any idea of being married to since I was a kid. We went together all through high school. When she went away to college and I joined the Coast Guard, I figured it was over. We saw each other again a little over a year ago and it was like we were never apart. It was the most wonderful time of my life. Then, the accident happened and I'm no longer the man I was. I mean, what woman would want me the way I am now? Like I said, I don't fault her at all. It's something nobody had any control over. It just happened. Really, really bad luck. Now, I'm stuck with a body that can hardly do anything, not even drive a car. I'll never have any prospects of earning a decent living and Doctor Finney says to expect a lot more health problems as I get older because of this. To say the least, I'm depressed. I don't know what to do, where to turn. I'm religious. You know, I've always come to church here. It seems like there has to be some kind of purpose or plan for me. It's just that I can't see it. I don't see any way forward at all. What should I do? Kay's got a new man in her life and they're going to get married. He'll never love her like I do. No one could. It's going to kill me. I know it is. But, if he makes her happy, then, that's what I want for her. But, what will I do?"

"I have great concern for you, Jim. Life has dealt you some hard blows. I could say your faith is being tested but nobody wants to hear that. You want to know what road to take from here. Right now, there doesn't even seem to be a path for you, much less a road. Now is not the time to lose your faith. Right now is when you need it the most.

When I was young and things didn't go well for me, and we've all had problems, my Mom would say 'Paul, when life hands you lemons, make some lemonade'. I don't think that applies when life drops a truckload of lemons on top of you. You've certainly led an interesting life, full of challenges and you were always up to them. As a rescue swimmer, you laid your life on the line regularly to save someone else. That's addressed clearly in the Bible. In John 15, it says 'Greater love hath no man than this, that a man lay down his life for his friends.' And to think that you were willing to do this for many people. I'm sure most of them were strangers. That's a special calling. Don't think for a moment that God is unaware of what you've done."

"Then why is all this happening to me? I feel like he's punishing me for something. I don't even know what I've done wrong to deserve all this."

"Jim, I can't pretend to understand why this is happening. I know you've heard the age-old question 'why do bad things happen to good people?' Sayings like that are here because you're not the first nor the last person who had serious struggles like this. A thought comes to my mind right now and if it's all right I'll share it with you. I really don't know if it applies or not, but it certainly seems like it might fit in here somewhere. In his famous novel, A TALE OF TWO CITIES, the writer, Charles Dickens, depicted a character named Sydney Carton. He took the place of a man who was about to be executed on the guillotine. He was in love with a woman who loved the man he replaced.

It's the ultimate gift. When you bowed out of her life and set Kay free to marry another man, no matter how much you loved her, you have done the exact same thing. When you sat on the open door of a helicopter and decided to jump into the swirling ocean, you were making that same decision. It's one you've made before. I don't know where all this will take you but, rest assured there is a plan for you. As Sydney Carton stood in line waiting for his turn on the guillotine, he said, 'it is a far, far better rest that I go to than I have ever known'. He was actually finding peace and fulfillment through a tremendous permanent sacrifice. I can only hope you'll be able to reach that moment yourself where you'll feel like you did the absolute best thing for her that only you could do. It's the things we do for others that bring us the most satisfaction in this life. I don't know if any of this helps you, but I'm always here and always ready to talk with you about anything. If you need to talk, call me."

"Thanks, Paul. I don't know how all this makes me feel right now, but I'm going to think about the things you said and see if I can bring myself around to feeling better about some of this. I'll see you next week."

"The Lord be with you, Jim."

Christmas was uneventful. Several nights he was able to go downtown and see all the stores decorated with ornaments and lights. One night, he rode in with Joyce and Beatrice, another with Virginia and Norah. He thought New Bern had to be one of the most beautiful towns in America. If he had to be in his present situation, he couldn't think of anywhere else that he would rather face it. There was not only beauty and grace, there were a large number of wonderful people who'd gone out of their way to offer help and comfort to him.

Virginia parked her car in Trent Court in front of Jimmy's apartment to drop him off. Jimmy had been seated in the back with Norah. Any time she could be with Jimmy, she cherished. There was no romantic interest there, at least from him. She, nonetheless, absorbed every word he offered.

"Don't linger around here, Virginia. New Volvos don't park here often. You could easily attract some unwanted attention."

"There's one more thing I wanted to mention to you."

"Yes, Ma'am."

"I have a small gift here that I want to give to you."

"Really? You don't need to do that."

"I have to confess. I have an ulterior motive."

"Go ahead."

"I just happen to have two tickets here to go see Mama Mia at The Athens theatre on Pollock Street. It's a musical. They're for tomorrow night. The songs and dancing are incredible and I know a certain young lady who would kill to go see it with you."

"Stop it, Ginny!"

Norah was a little embarrassed by her sister's boldness on her behalf.

"How about it, Jimmy? It would be the best Christmas present you ever gave anyone."

"No thinking necessary. I'm in. Are you coming with us?"

"No. I just have two tickets. I'll drive you both there and come pick you up. I'll park on the street out front. They'll have someone come out and help Norah get in her wheelchair. After it's over, just wait inside till the crowd leaves and they'll bring you back out to the car. I just know you'll both love it."

"Consider it a date."

As they drove off, Norah told her sister.

"I know the help and all the things you do for me have kept you from having your own marriage and a family. Don't think I'm unaware of how good you are to me. Without you, I'd be in some kind of nursing home. And then you do things like this. I would love you no matter what but, when you do these things, it just makes me want to hug you forever. I don't deserve a sister like you."

"Deserving has nothing to do with love. To my mind, love is something that stands alone, all by itself. If you were totally well and danced on Broadway, I wouldn't be any prouder of you or love you one bit more. When I do things for you, it's just like I'm doing them for myself."

"I just wanted to say thank you. For everything."

"You are forever welcome."

At seven p.m. the next evening, Virginia pulled slowly in front of The Athens theatre. A staff member who'd been expecting her walked quickly to the back of the car as she opened the rear door from inside. The young man expanded the folded wheelchair and pushed it over to the rear passenger door. Virginia stepped out and walked over to help him get Norah's seat belts opened. Jimmy had enough trouble getting himself out of the vehicle. The attendant pushed Norah inside the theatre with Jimmy close behind. They had thoughtfully saved the end seats by the aisle on a middle row. The rest of the audience was already seated. Jimmy took the end seat of the row and the staffer parked her wheelchair to the side of the aisle right up against Jimmy's seat.

"These seats are wonderful. I can see the entire stage. They're just getting ready to start."

Live productions at the small theatre were always well done and greatly supported by the community. There was general agreement that the shows there were as well done as they would be in a major city. The cast members were all volunteers, but some of them had successful careers performing and had been acting in these community shows for many years.

The lights dimmed and a small, live orchestra began to play the introduction. Jimmy enjoyed music and had always been a movie fan. He'd never been to a live production. As the show progressed, he spent as much time watching Norah and her reactions as he did to the show.

She understood they would never be more than friends. He wanted to do anything he could to help this lovely young woman have a shot at happiness even if it came in small bits and pieces. It was heartwarming to see her moving her head and hands in time with the music. He understood how much she would love to be on the stage dancing with the cast.

When the show ended, the audience gave the cast a standing ovation. Jimmy had to admit he was impressed with how professional it was. Once again, New Bern surprised him. The young man who helped them get inside stood just behind their row until the audience departed. He slowly pushed Norah's chair up the inclined aisle to the theatre's front doors. Virginia timed her approach to coincide with the last audience members leaving the entrance. She pulled up once again to the front doors. In just a few moments, they were all back in the car and headed to Trent Court. As she stopped to let Jimmy out, Norah thanked him.

"Jimmy, I know that dancing and singing are not your greatest loves. I'm certain you'd rather watch an action adventure movie. But you'll never know how much tonight meant to me. I will remember this night forever."

He leaned over to where Norah sat and, much to her dismay, kissed her on the forehead.

"Norah, thank you for giving me the opportunity to do something that was appreciated so much. You just gave me a wonderful Christmas gift. You and Virginia. Thank you both for your thoughtfulness. Not just tonight but every day. You're both wonderful and I love you both. I'll see you again soon. Good night."

Jimmy walked up to the front door, opened it with his left hand. It was awkward action with just one hand but he continued until the door was open. He turned and gave them a wave.

Jimmy moved inside his apartment and locked the door. As usual, it was dark, chilly and empty. He realized, more than ever, that the only things in his life that had any real importance were the people he was around every day. They were the only things that gave his life meaning anymore.

After Christmas, New Year's was the next big event. There were parties throughout the city and a fireworks display over the water that the town sponsored. Individual offices and organizations joined in the festivities and a general aura of optimism filled the town. For Jimmy, it would be just another evening. Greg came to speak with him late that afternoon.

"Jimmy, would you like to ride with us to see the fireworks tonight? It looks like it's going to be a cold but beautiful evening. We'll park near Lawson's Landing and you won't even have to get out of the car. It's much too cold to be standing outside. We'd love to have you with us."

"If it was around seven or even eight p.m. I could do it, but there's no way I can stay up until midnight to watch them and not get into bed before one. Thanks for including me, though. You guys go have a good time. You can tell me all about it in the morning. In fact, if you want to get away early, I'll close up the store and lock up before I leave. I know the rituals to make sure it's closed up tight."

"Jimmy, I know you do. I've never let anybody else do it, but it would be good to know you could handle it. So, yes. I'll take you up on your offer."

"Consider it done."

It made Jimmy proud that Greg trusted him with the keys to the store and handling all the security that protected his livelihood. He'd take extra care to make sure it was done perfectly. At exactly six p.m., he locked all the doors, cut off the lights and set the security alarms. He double and triple checked everything until he was a hundred percent confident everything was done correctly.

He got in his cart and took South Front Street to Eden Street. He saw a barge out on the river where a crew was setting up the fireworks display launch pad. He wished he could stay up and see it, but he knew it would be more than he was physically up to. He continued home and watched a little television. He loved the old classics and, occasionally, an episode of Perry Mason or The Andy Griffith show. They brought back memories of a much simpler and happier time to his mind. He fell asleep on the couch. It had been a long day and he was exhausted.

After several hours on the couch in a coma-like sleep, he was awakened by television coverage of the Times Square festivities in New York City. He counted down the last ten seconds with the announcer. He cut the television off and got ready to hit the sack. Just as he was ready to lie down, he heard loud explosions going off celebrating the New Year. He walked over to the front door and looked out over the

Trent River. There was a display going on and quite a few of his neighbors had pulled their lawn chairs out in front of their apartments to watch what was happening as well. All in all, it was a great display. One of the best he had ever seen.

He started back into his apartment. Just before he got the door open, he heard tires screeching and then an impact of some kind. He knew it had to be a collision. It sounded like it was just around the corner so he began walking to where the noise came from. As he turned the corner onto Eden Street, he saw a car sitting over top of the curb. In front of it, he saw the front tire of a bicycle. With all the speed he could muster, he went over to the scene.

"Oh Lord, it's Dee. Dee, Dee, can you hear me? Dee, please speak to me."

The young boy opened his eyes and quietly mouthed the words.

"Jimmy, I want Momma. Can you get Momma? I…."

The words never finished coming out of his mouth. Jimmy lowered the boy's head. He had seen death many times in his career. He knew Dee was gone.

He walked over to the car and opened the driver's door. Inside was something that shocked him even more.

"Morrison, Morrison. Wake up. Do you hear me?"

He smacked him sharply on the side of his face. The smell of alcohol was strong in the car.

"Morrison, you've got to wake up."

Obviously intoxicated, he woke up in a panic.

"Wh-What happened? I must have fallen asleep at the wheel."

He could see smoke coming from the front of his car.

"Morrison, you need to get out of here."

"Why? It's just a fender bender."

"Morrison, you're drunk and you've hit someone. There's a young boy on a bike under your fender. He's dead."

He slowly realized he was involved in an accident and remembered he'd been drinking.

"A DUI would be bad though. You're not serious? I've killed somebody?"

"Serious as a heart attack. Look, get out of here right now. You were never here. You left your car running to get it warmed up. Go back to where the car was parked and call the police. Say that your car has been taken, stolen, whatever. Other than that, you don't know anything. I'll tell the cops I was cold and saw the opportunity to get in a warm car and I drove it home. I've got it handled here. This will ruin Kay's life and yours too. I don't want that. Promise me you'll do what I say. Promise me."

"Okay, okay, I promise."

They both heard people talking and heading their way to see what had occurred.

"Get out of here, Morrison. Now. And stay sober! No more alcohol…ever!"

The lawyer disappeared into the night. Jimmy went back to where Dee lay dead. The bicycle was still on top of him and the Mercedes' right front tire was resting on the bike and both of Dee's legs. Jimmy was only slightly relieved that Dee had not suffered for long.

As people approached, they saw Jimmy kneeling beside him.

"What the hell happened?"

"I borrowed a car and had a little trouble making the turn. I lost control and hit Dee. I'm so sorry. I thought I could handle the car. He was one of my best friends."

Joyce and Beatrice were quickly on the scene.

"Oh God, it's Dee. Jimmy, what happened?"

Jimmy retold the story again. In less than five minutes, there were blue lights everywhere. Jimmy stayed beside Dee and stuck to his story.

Deputy Moeller came over to Jimmy.

"Jimmy, you say you were driving this car?"

"Yes, sir."

"You don't have a car, do you?"

"No, sir. I don't."

"How did you get this one?"

"I walked down to Lawson's Landing to watch the fireworks. It was a longer walk than I thought it was going to be. I was freezing by the time it was over. As I was trying to walk home, my hands and feet were going numb. I saw this car running in a parking lot. I looked and there was nobody in it. I don't know why I did it. I just got in it and was going to drive it back to Trent Court. It's only a couple blocks. I thought I'd park it down the street a little ways and nobody would be the wiser. I had trouble making the turn and hit Dee. I didn't even see him. It happened so fast. I can't believe it. I wouldn't have hurt Dee for anything. He was a good friend. I don't how I'll face his mother."

"I just checked and the car was reported stolen a short while ago. It belongs to a lawyer downtown. I can't make this go away, son. I've got no choice except to take you to the jail and book you. You'll go before a Magistrate to see what kind of bail they'll give you. If you can't make bail, you'll have to stay in jail until your trial and that could take quite a few months. You're going to need to get you a lawyer, Jimmy. Just a word of advice, don't say anything to anyone without a lawyer. This is serious and right now you're in a lot of trouble. They're probably going to have to charge you with theft of a vehicle and at a minimum, manslaughter. The District Attorney could raise that charge to negligent homicide or even second-degree murder. I don't know what they'll do, but all of those are serious charges. Remember what I told you. Ask for an attorney and don't volunteer anything without one present. I don't want to do this either, but I'm going to have to cuff you and take you in. Let's go to my car and I'll cuff you there. No need to make a spectacle out of it here."

Jimmy followed the deputy to his car. For the first time in his life, he had a pair of handcuffs placed on his wrists and the officer actually had to help him step up into the back of the squad car. That fact alone started to make the deputy question, in his own mind, how he could possibly have been driving the Mercedes. But Jimmy had confessed, under no duress, so it was his duty to take him in. He reminded Jimmy of his Miranda rights. People at a higher pay grade than his would have to figure this all out.

Jimmy's mind was reeling with the possible repercussions of what he'd done. And then, there was the most terrible scream he'd ever heard.

"Oh, God! Not Dee! Not my baby. Oh…Dee…."

And then came uncontrolled screaming and crying. It was heartbreaking and almost beyond what Jimmy was able to stand. What could he possibly tell her? How could he ever explain this?

Jimmy hung his head and remained silent in the squad car as he was driven to the city lockup. The jail was basically a holding area used until a prisoner was bound over for trial. If convicted, they'd be moved to a more substantial facility designed for long-term convicts.

Jimmy was taken before a Magistrate who restated the same charges as Deputy Moeller. His bond was set at two hundred thousand dollars since a death was involved. Jimmy figured the bond might as well be ten million. Anything over a hundred dollars was above his ability to pay. He was facing the fact that he'd likely remain in custody until the trial.

With the charges he was facing and the fact that he confessed, there was no doubt in his mind that he was staring at spending many years in prison. Even with that prospect, he was still satisfied with what he'd done.

To his mind, his life had been over for a while now.

Kay still had her life and he'd do anything to make certain it had happiness attached to it. Morrison Brooks was no friend of Jimmy's. His going to prison wouldn't bother him in the least were it not for the fact that Kay loved him and was planning their wedding. He didn't want to see her have a second wedding cancelled due to some catastrophe she had no control over. This is what he had to do for her. He actually felt a great comfort knowing he had the chance to do this. It gave his life a new purpose. In the long run, it was no different than risking his life to save someone from certain death at sea. He was taking that chance again, but, at least this time, it was for someone he loved.

The Magistrate asked Jimmy if he'd been read his rights. He answered that he had. Deputy Moeller then escorted him to a processing office where he was fingerprinted, photographed and issued an orange jumpsuit. He disrobed and his belongings were placed in a bag for safe keeping. They'd be returned to him at such time as he was released from jail. The deputy then took him to a holding cell where he'd remain until he could be assigned to a more permanent, smaller cell he would share with another inmate.

"Jimmy, you're entitled to make a call if there's somebody in particular you want to tell where you are and what's going on so they can come bail you out."

"I don't know anybody well enough to have them sign a two hundred grand bond guarantee for me. I wouldn't ask that of my own family and I don't have any family that's alive. So, I guess I might as well make myself comfortable."

The holding cell had three other men in it already. They were also waiting to be moved to a permanent cell after being processed. They were a rough looking bunch of guys. The cell reeked of stale cigarettes and sweat. The men were talking with each other and every other word was a slur or a curse. He tried to sit as far away from them as possible. Compared to them, he was a shell of a man. With a gimp leg and withered arm, they all knew instantly he was no threat. The dirtiest looking of the three men called out to him.

"Hey boy, you got some smokes on you?"

"No. I don't smoke."

"What are you in here for? I know it ain't for child support. No self-respecting woman would get within a hundred feet of a dwarf like you. What'd you get nabbed for?"

"I stole a car. Then ran into a kid on a bike. He's dead."

"Damn, son. For such a tiny thing, you sure found you some big trouble. You're going to be in the big house for that one. You're probably looking at ten to fifteen years even with time off for being a model prisoner. Hard time, my friend. Come on over here where I don't have to yell at ya."

Jimmy made no attempt to move.

"Are you deaf, too? I said, come over here."

"Got a bad leg and it's hurting since the wreck. I'll be staying right here. No offense."

The burly redneck walked over to Jimmy.

"No offense taken. I'll just help you along."

He picked Jimmy up by his shirt and with only his right hand dragged him over to where he'd been sitting.

"There, that's better. All you had to do was ask. I'm Earl. I've been in this exact lockup so many times I qualify for all their frequent visitor discounts."

He laughed at his own humor.

"I think they're gonna throw the book at me this time. Failure to pay taxes. They don't like that stuff. Actually, they said I was selling untaxed alcohol. The cops and the Court look real hard at that. It's not that they care if anybody is an alcoholic. Couldn't care less about that. To them liquor isn't immoral, but somebody other than them selling it, now that's immoral. Seems funny to me. They talk about all the vices and how they're so bad for people. Then, they sell them with no competition. What about illegal gambling? They hate that 'cause they didn't make no money off it. Then the lottery came along, where they make all the money and they act like it's just the most fun, greatest thing you could possibly do. They want us to not do what they do, but to do what they tell us to do. What a bunch of hypocrites. My thought is that nothing good ever comes from the government. It's my second or third time getting picked up for it so I'm probably looking at twenty myself. So, you and me will probably get to know each other really well."

Jimmy still volunteered nothing. He stared at the cell door as if he wasn't hearing a thing Earl was saying. The old man was starting to get upset with him as he didn't like the idea of being ignored.

"You need to loosen up a little bit, son. I'm trying to be friendly with you. I make a great friend but a really bad enemy. The way I see it, you're one or the other. Which one will it be? Friend or foe?"

"I just want to be left alone. I've just killed somebody and I'm looking at dying in prison. That's enough for one night. I don't feel like talking."

"Have it your way. But, don't come looking for me when you run into trouble in here. Oh, and you can count on running into trouble here. That's just about all that's here, trouble. Lots and lots of trouble. Suit yourself, though."

The prisoner left Jimmy alone with his thoughts. He didn't want anybody else involved in this, especially one of his friends. This was his idea and so far, it was working just the way he thought it would. He sat on the hard metal bench and leaned back against the block wall. He periodically dozed off as it was late. The fireworks were over by twelve thirty, so he figured it had to be after two a.m. by now. He eventually stretched out on the bench and fell into a deep sleep until the loud clanking of cell doors disturbed him. He opened his eyes and saw that the sun was up and two guards were talking outside the holding cell. One held a clipboard and the other was studying it with him.

"Earl, get up. You're moving out to the city farm today. You'll be there till the trial. Harrison, you too. Let's go. Van's waiting outside."

Jimmy moved as fast as he could. It wasn't fast enough to keep from getting yelled at.

"Come on, gimpy. Get your butt in gear. The van has the motor running."

The guard escorted Jimmy and Earl to the prison transport van. There were already four other prisoners inside. The front row was empty so Jimmy sat down and Earl beside him. It only took a second to realize that Earl had a lot more smells going on than stale cigarettes. He probably hadn't bathed in days. Jimmy liked clean places and clean people. He hoped the county farm wouldn't be a collection of people who never bathed.

The ride out to the prison farm took about thirty minutes, but it seemed like four hours. As the van pulled through a reinforced gate, a heavily armed guard intensely watched the activity from his tower position. There were several rows of chain link fencing, each row topped off with razor wire. None of that was an issue for Jimmy. He'd have trouble just walking the perimeter of the prison notwithstanding any fences.

The men were offloaded and led into another processing room. The first thing he noticed was a lot of yelling between inmates, the guards at them and vice versa. There were obviously bucketloads of testosterone, frustration and pent-up anger. It would be easy to get hurt here.

After two hours of processing, Jimmy was escorted to a cell which would be his home until he posted bail or went to trial, perhaps months.

Bail wasn't possible. He had no money and he hadn't taken the opportunity to even call anyone. To him, his problems were of his own making and he didn't want to bring anyone he knew into this mess.

When Earl was placed in the same cell, Jimmy thought to himself.

"Of course, I should have seen this coming".

"Looks like we're gonna be spending some time together whether you want to converse with me or not."

"I guess so."

"Why don't we start over? Days can get pretty long and boring in here if you don't talk with nobody. I'm Earl Watson. I'm from Trenton, North Carolina. Born and raised there and ain't never been able to get away. When I get work, it's usually repairing tractors and things like that. To tell you the truth, I've only been in the tank here two times before. Once when I was a kid for beating the snot out of my worthless stepfather and another time because they said I stole a truck. Didn't do that, but once they get your name in the books, anything comes along they're more than ready to believe you did it. My buddy stole the truck and when he thought it might be getting too hot to drive, he lent it to me. I thought it belonged to him. Next thing I know, I was right back in here for eighteen months. Yeah, I know the drill here. So, what's your story?"

"I stole a car. A Mercedes. I was walking home one night and I was nearly freezing. It was New Year's Eve. I went to see the fireworks in New Bern, down at Lawson's Landing. I just saw this car running with nobody in it, so I hopped inside intending to drive it home. On the way, a young kid popped out in front of me out of nowhere on a bicycle. I hit him. Killed him. I knew him. I'm glad I'm in here. Anybody who'd do something that dumb and dangerous needs to be in prison."

Jimmy had now repeated the fabricated story enough times that it almost seemed like the truth.

"If you don't mind me saying so, you sure don't look like no criminal to me. I can't even imagine you being able to drive a car."

"I had trouble doing it. I guess that's why I didn't see the kid. Anyway, I'm here and I guess this will probably be the end of the road for me. Deputy said I could get fifteen to twenty years out of this. Bad as my health is, I guess I'll probably die in here. No problem. Haven't been having that good a time of it on the outside to tell you the truth. This prison can't be much worse than the one I've been living in on the outside. We'll see."

"Sounds like you've had a tough time. I think we'll get along fine."

14

Governor's Mansion – Raleigh, North Carolina

AROUND TEN THAT morning, Becky Pollard was at her desk in the Governor's Mansion. Her secretary tapped on her closed door.

"Governor?"

"Yes?"

"Your husband is on line two."

"Thanks, I've got it."

She picked up the receiver.

"Hey, Tommy. What's up?"

"I was just speaking with the city editor for the Sun Journal back in New Bern."

"Go on."

"She was telling me there was a wreck after the fireworks at Lawson's Landing. She said the police report indicated a black Mercedes was stolen and driven back toward Trent Court."

"Nothing new there."

"That's not all. The guy driving the car veered off the road and hit a fourteen-year-old kid on a bicycle and killed him."

"That's terrible. Did they catch whoever stole the car?"

"Yes. You're not going to believe this. They said it was Jimmy Harrison."

"Margaret's son?"

"Yes. Unbelievable."

"That's exactly the words I would have used. I'll find out what's going on there. Thanks for the call, Tommy. If you hear anything else on this, please give me a call. I'll get back with you after I know something."

The Governor immediately called her secretary in to her office.

"Get the District Attorney for New Bern on the phone."

"Morning, Governor Pollard. What can I help you with this early in the day?"

"I've just been informed of an event in New Bern that has really disturbed me."

"What is it?"

"The editor at the Sun Journal told Tommy that Jimmy Harrison is charged with stealing a car and running over a kid from Trent Court last night after the fireworks. Is that true?"

"I'm afraid so, ma'am. It's pretty much an open and shut

case. Cops found him at the car, no other suspects in the area and he immediately confessed."

"I wasn't there when this happened, but I do know Jimmy Harrison. I knew his mother and I've known him his whole life. He sits with us in church every Sunday when we're home. I can tell you, as sure I'm sitting here, he would never steal a car, let alone run over anyone. You need to look into this a lot deeper. Can you handle this for me?"

"Yes, ma'am. I will get with the Chief and we'll go over all of this with a fine-tooth comb. I appreciate you calling me and giving me your thoughts."

"I appreciate that. I will be following this case closely. Keep me posted with any developments."

"Yes, ma'am. It will be done."

❧

Craven County Correctional Institute

In the prison, every day at noon, there was a bell identical to what Jimmy used to hear in high school. It was lunch time. Cell doors opened and the inmates marched single file toward a large cafeteria at the end of the cell blocks.

Jimmy followed Earl. He figured he'd know where they were supposed to go and how things worked. Other than a little hygiene issue, he seemed half decent. Trenton was only a few miles outside of New Bern. They probably knew some of the same people.

There was a short line of men along the stainless-steel racks that held food trays. As the men shuffled by, the workers scooped the food into different sections of the trays. There was some sort of meat with gravy, mashed potatoes, peas and carrots, a slice of plain white bread. With the exception of eating Sundays with Joyce and Beatrice, it was better fare than he was getting at home.

As they looked for a seat, a few of the men recognized and spoke to Earl.

"Lifers. They were here when I first got here fifteen years back. Not a bad group, if you don't cross them. Prison has its own set of rules and people who enforce them. Just don't get on anybody's bad side. Don't need enemies in a prison. They don't have anything left to lose, so they'll hurt you. You shouldn't have any problems. Besides you already got one friend here."

"I do? Who?"

"Me, of course. You haven't pissed me off yet."

"That's good to know, Earl. Same to you."

They finished their meal, got up and emptied their trays into the large trash cans at the door leaving the room.

As Jimmy bent over to scrape the remains off his tray into the can, he felt a firm push from behind that almost knocked him into the trash. Startled, he turned to see Marcus from Trent Court standing there with a mean smirk on his face.

"Well, if it ain't the dwarf from the hood. Peg leg himself.

Deputy Moeller always said he'd wind up here and that prophecy had come to pass.

"It's going to be just great having you in here with me. A touch of home. There's a lot of things I've been wanting to talk to you about. In here, it's just going to be you and me, peg leg. This is good. Something I'll have fun with."

Earl, a large, imposing figure of a man, stepped between Marcus and Jimmy.

"Touch him one more time, and you'll answer to me. That won't be any fun, trust me."

"You're making a big mistake, old man. This is between me and peg leg here. We got history."

"Mess with him again and you won't have any history, got me?"

"I said, Got me? I haven't heard you yet. You got me?"

"Yeah, I got you."

Marcus leered over at Jimmy with a look that said, this ain't over yet. He turned and walked away in the company of a couple of other punks. One of them looked familiar to Jimmy. He was probably from Trent Court as well.

Earl extended a hand to Jimmy and pulled him up.

"Didn't take you long to make an enemy in here. What kind of gangster have I got for a cellmate?"

"He's a troublemaker from back where I live. I've never done anything to him. He just likes to pick at me 'cause he knows I can't do much to defend myself."

"He's the kind that will hurt you if he gets the chance. You better not get too far away from me."

"I appreciate it. I don't want any trouble from anybody anywhere."

✦

Later that day – Mitchell Hardware

Greg approached Dave.

"Heard anything from Jimmy? He said he was going to turn in early last night and wouldn't go watch the fireworks with us. He must not be feeling well. Think I'll ride over to his place and see if he's okay."

Greg pulled up in front of Jimmy's apartment. He got no answer when he knocked on the door. He was surprised to find the door wasn't locked. He pushed it open and looked around the small and tidy room. It was hard to imagine someone as smart as Jimmy having to live such a meager existence. It was hard to not feel sympathy for someone who was dealing with so much. He walked back out and pulled the door behind him. Someone called out to him. It was Joyce.

"Mister, you looking for Jimmy?"

"I am. I'm Greg from Mitchell Hardware. Jimmy works with me. Don't know where he is, do you?"

"I sure do. He's in jail. There was young boy on a bike hit and killed here last night. They said Jimmy was driving the car. Said he stole it. The police found him sitting by it when they got there. He told 'em right off he done it. Said he got cold at the fireworks and took a car that was running with nobody in it. I know Jimmy. Know him well. He didn't no more steal that car and kill Dee than I did. I don't know what made him say that. But they didn't have no choice but to take him in. Can you check on him?"

"Dee? His friend, Dee? Dee is dead?"

"That's right."

"You can count on it. I don't believe it either. He told me he wasn't even going to the fireworks because I asked him to go with us and he said he didn't feel like it. I don't know what's going on here but I'll tell you this, I will find out. Thanks for the information. What's your name?"

"I'm Joyce. Me and my sister, Beatrice, live right here next door to Jimmy. We are close as he has to family. Fix him Sunday supper every week. If we can do anything to help Jimmy, we will. Please do what you can. He's a good man."

"I'm on it right now."

Greg called the District Attorney's office. He knew him personally. He confirmed what Joyce had said.

"We booked him in last night around two a.m. This morning, they hauled him over to the county prison. He's been booked for auto theft and vehicular homicide. They're serious charges, Greg. You say you know him?"

"He works with me at the store. Let me assure you, there's absolutely no way he did any of this. I doubt it's even possible that he could drive a car. Have you seen him?"

"No. What's his problem?"

"His right arm and leg are almost useless. Remember that wreck on the bridge last year after the Heart Ball?"

"You mean when the Steinbecks went over the railing?"

"Exactly. Jimmy was the Coast Guard rescue swimmer who jumped in and saved both of them. Left him almost dead. He's paralyzed now. Coast Guard had to retire him and now he's working for me at the store. There is no way he could've done this."

"But why would he confess to this if he didn't do it? He signed a written confession."

"Your guess is as good as mine, but I will get to the bottom of it today. I'm going to call Steve Steinbeck. I'll get back with you as soon as I know something new. What's his bail?"

"Hold on and I'll look it up. Here it is. Two hundred grand. I'd release him to your custody if you'll sign for him. And by the way, apparently Governor Pollard is on his side as well. She called me first thing this morning asking me to find out what's going on. So, you're the second person to call me about him already today. From my point of view, it would be great if you'd stand for his bail. God knows if anything happened to him in prison, I'd never hear the end of it."

"I'll see you this afternoon."

Greg walked into the office of Steinbeck and Associates. Steve was waiting in the lobby.

"What's this about Jimmy?"

"You heard about the wreck over at Trent Court last night?"

"I heard something on local TV this morning. Didn't pay it much attention until I learned Jimmy Harrison was charged. What in the heck happened?"

Greg relayed the night's events to Steve. He got up and walked back into the lobby and told the receptionist.

"Hold all my calls and take messages for the rest of the day. I'm headed to the District Attorney's office. You know, I got a call this morning from Dan Rivers over at their firm. Said somebody stole Morrison Brook's Mercedes and crashed it. You don't think that's related to this do you?"

"I'll make a couple of calls while you drive over to the DA's office."

A few minutes of phone calls cleared up the details.

"It was Morrison's car alright. He said he left it to warm up outside his office after the fireworks. He had joined some friends back there for a get-together. Had a few cocktails, went outside and his car was gone. He called it into the cops and thirty minutes later they called back and told him they found it at the scene of the crash. I wouldn't have a problem with any of this if I didn't know Jimmy so well. Anyone who knows him would never believe him stealing anything. That's not in his DNA. It's also too coincidental that Jimmy and Morrison know each other. And it's not what you'd call a friendship."

"We'll keep asking questions until we understand what's going on here. I'm not about to let him spend another night in jail."

Steve and Greg went to meet with the D.A. As they entered his office, he walked over to them.

"Like I told Greg earlier, you're not the only person who's friends with Mr. Harrison. I got a call from Governor

Pollard personally. She said there was absolutely no way he did this and she wanted him released on his own signature today. I'll tell you what, the word on this has gotten around the entire community quicker than a brush fire. What do you say we take a ride out to the prison and see what's going on there?"

"Let's go."

One of the prison guards came to Jimmy's cell.

"Harrison? You, James Harrison?"

"Yes, sir."

"Call for you. Follow me."

"Do you know who it is?"

"Nope. Follow me. You'll find out soon enough."

Jimmy was led down the hall to a deputy station just outside of the electronically controlled bars. The phone was sitting receiver down on the desk.

"Hello. This is Jimmy Harrison."

"Hey, Jimmy. This is Becky."

"Governor?"

"Yes. Listen. I don't know what all has happened here that you are in that facility right now and apparently the DA isn't up to speed either. I just want you to know that I consider you a close friend and I'm not going to let you sit there in jail until this is all straightened out. The DA says you just need to change your plea to not guilty and sign a personal release guarantee and they'll let you out until the trial. Hopefully all the charges will be dropped before then, and you won't have to worry about any of this again."

"Mrs. Pollard, Governor; you know I think the world of you and realize how busy you must be. I'm honored that you'd go to all this trouble for me. But the problem is, I'm guilty. I stole the car and accidentally ran over the young boy. It was an accident, but I did it. I was too cold to walk home and just wasn't thinking clear. I can't say I didn't do it 'cause I did."

"I hear what you're saying, Jimmy, but I don't believe you. That's just not you. I don't understand why you're doing what you're doing, but why don't you sign the papers and we can get this straightened out while you are not sitting in jail waiting for a trial?"

"I can't sign it. I won't do it. I thank you for trying to help me, but I have to take responsibility. Thank you. Governor. Good-bye."

He put the phone back on the hook. The die was cast.

The electronic door was opened and Jimmy started walking back to his cell. As he passed by the laundry door, a voice called out to him from just inside. He walked over to the door, cracked it open and looked in. A strong, aggressive arm pulled him into the room.

The District Attorney, Steve and Greg arrived at the jail. After a brief conversation with the Warden, they waited in the lobby for someone to go get Jimmy. Their intent was to take him home with them within the hour. Greg looked at Steve.

"When do you think was the last time the Governor called personally to get someone out of here?"

"Probably never."

"That should be about all it would take to get out of here. This place depresses me. Just seeing it should be enough to make law-abiding citizens out of anyone. We should bring everybody out here on their fifteenth birthday and give them a tour. There'd be a lot less crime if young kids knew just what was waiting for them if they got into a lot of trouble."

"No argument from me."

The deputy started down the concrete hallway to Jimmy's cell. As he approached, he saw that Earl was alone in the cell.

"Where's Harrison? He's got company."

"Not here. They came to get him for a phone call a while back. Never returned. You haven't lost him, have you?"

"He can't be far."

The officer started back down the hallway. As he passed the laundry room, he noticed the door was cracked. As he pushed it open, he could hear groaning and then saw Jimmy sprawled out on the floor. His head was on the hard tile and there was a bright red puddle of blood under it. He walked over, raised his head and saw that he'd suffered some severe blows to his face. He wasn't totally conscious. He only responded with more groans. The officer used his hand-held radio.

"This is Browning. Inmate down on block three laundry

room. Need a medic here now. Better send a stretcher too. He's not mobile and needs to go to the clinic pronto. Maybe even the hospital."

An officer entered the lobby where Steve and Greg were waiting.

"There's been a problem."

"What kind of problem?"

"Harrison has been injured. They're taking him to the prison clinic right now."

"Tell you what, we're going to follow you to the clinic. Lead on."

"I can't do that without the Warden's permission."

"We'll stand right here with you while you call him. Tell him you're with Greg Smith, Steve Steinbeck and the District Attorney. I'm betting you'll probably get that permission."

He did as Steve requested.

"Okay, gentlemen. Follow me. Sorry about that. I didn't recognize any of you and I have to follow the rules or lose my job."

"We understand completely. You did the right thing."

As they entered the clinic, they saw Jimmy lying on a blood-soaked stretcher.

"What happened to him?"

"It looks like another inmate roughed him up."

"More like someone tried to kill him. Any idea who or why?"

"We'll find out pretty quick. There's video cameras all over the place. They're checking them right now I'm sure."

"You know, this young man is a close friend of Mr. Steinbeck, Greg Smith here and Governor Pollard. She's already called my office this morning and told me to make sure he was out of here this afternoon. When I have to call her office and tell her what's happened now, it's not going to be a pleasant conversation, I'm sure. How's he doing?"

"He's banged up pretty bad. I think we're going to need to send him over to the hospital for X-rays to make sure nothing's broken."

"Okay, get an ambulance over here right now and we'll follow it to the hospital. And one more thing."

"Yes, sir."

"I want you to tell the Warden that I'll be calling him back in the morning and I want a name."

"A name?"

"That's right. I want to hear that you found out who did this and that he's been charged with attempted murder. I'm sure the Governor will agree with me. Don't let me down. I'm already in a bad mood over this. It wouldn't be good to upset me or the Governor any more. You understand?"

"Yes, sir. I assure you we'll be on this until we have our man."

"Good. Now let's get that ambulance over here."

Jimmy came to while he was still in the ambulance.

"Where are we going?"

"The hospital. You got beaten up pretty bad. They're going to check you out thoroughly. Make sure you're going to be alright. We'll be there pretty quick."

"I'm okay. You can turn around and take me back to the jail."

"Not going to happen."

"Why not?"

"There's a lot of important people waiting to hear you're okay and out of the jail."

"What people?"

"Just some big shot attorneys, the guy who owns Mitchell Hardware, the head guy from Christ Church and the Governor. Is that enough? You just lay back and quiet down. If you want to go back to jail, take it up with them. I'm not getting in the middle of this for nothin'."

Jimmy laid back down. When the ambulance arrived at the Emergency Room entrance, Greg, Steve and Paul were waiting for him. As they wheeled him in, they approached the stretcher.

"Jimmy, you're going to be alright. You're not going back to jail. You're going to stay with me and Elaine, at least until all this is figured out."

"I don't want to be a pain, but this really isn't your problem. I stole the car and I should be in prison. Really. You don't need to be involved."

"Your problems actually are my problems. Now, you need to just be quiet about this and let's get this checkup over with. If they release you tonight, you're going home with me. End of story."

∽

Morrison Brooks was with Kay at her apartment.

"Morrison, you called me this morning and told me somebody stole your car on New Year's Eve after the fireworks. I heard this afternoon at my office that Jimmy Harrison was arrested for stealing a car and hitting some young boy with it. The child died. Was that your car?"

"Yes. I just found out a little while ago that it was Jim Harrison as well. I mean, I don't understand why he would steal a car. The detective told me that Jimmy said he was freezing cold. I had left my car running and it was warm. Obviously, we're not friends but I would have gladly given him a ride home considering how nasty it was outside. Freezing cold."

"I'm sorry, Morrison, but somebody else had to be involved in this. For one thing, I don't believe Jimmy could even drive a car. He'd have to use only his left arm and leg. He can barely walk. They said he lives at Trent Court. It's hard to believe he's been staying there. What a rough place. I have to believe he's fallen in with some thug over there and was taken advantage of. He would never steal anything. That's just not who he is. This is so upsetting. I'm going to call the Court and see if there's anything I can do."

"You're too upset, Kay. Let me do it for you. It was my car he stole. I'm not going to press any charges against him. I shouldn't have left it unlocked and running. I'll makes some calls and see what can be done. I'll get back with you after I speak with the D.A."

"Please do, Morrison. Granted, we're not together any

more, but I've known Jimmy all his life and I don't want to see anything bad happen to him. He's certainly not a criminal."

Morrison was starting to feel trapped by the situation. His career and his upcoming wedding were both on the line. If he owned up to what actually happened, he'd not only have to acknowledge driving drunk and accidentally running over the boy, he'd also be confessing to a cover-up. It was a no-win situation with no way out. He determined he'd keep silent and see how it played out. If Jimmy really wanted to take the blame for this, then he'd stick with his story to the end, even if there were a lot of doubters.

⁓

Jimmy stayed overnight with Steve and Elaine. He was still banged up from the beating Marcus subjected him to in jail.

Before officers could check the video footage to see who had attacked Jimmy, Marcus was found severely beaten up in the inmate bathroom next to the cafeteria. Earl made certain he had a run in with Marcus that left him hurting a lot more than Jimmy was at the moment.

Jimmy was so grateful for how Earl looked out for him. He asked Steve to place a call on his behalf the day after his release.

The next morning as Earl was sleeping like a rock in his bunk, he was awakened by a banging on the bars to his cell.

"Time to get up, Sleeping Beauty. You've been sprung."

"Sprung? Who sprung me?"

"Don't know, but it sure got done in a hurry. The Warden wants to speak with you before you leave. Pack up anything you want from your cell and we'll go get the clothes and stuff from the personal item depository. You'll want to clean up a little, I would hope, and then we'll go to the Warden's office."

"Darn right! I sure want to look my best when I meet with the Warden. Don't want to make a bad impression on him."

Forty-five minutes later, Earl had completed a quick shower, a once over with a razor and walked with the guard to the Warden's office. He carried his personal items in a small plastic bag. The guard knocked on the office door.

"Yes?"

"Jennings, sir. Here with Earl Watson."

"Bring him in."

The office was wood paneled with an ornate desk in the center. There were pictures of Governor Pollard and the District Attorney on the wall behind his desk. Earl thought it was all a little pretentious to be in a county farm prison. The Warden motioned for Earl to have a seat.

"Earl, I'm Dave Schroder, the Warden here. I want you to know that no witnesses have come forth against you. The officers, who arrested you, testified they have no way to prove that liquor found on the ground beside your truck was manufactured by or belonged specifically to you. I, of course, have my own theory as to what was going on there and your degree of involvement. But, as the saying goes, what you think you know and what you can prove, are two different things."

Earl shook his head in agreement as the Warden continued.

"Your case was expedited this morning after some interesting phone calls to my office. It seems that your cellmate, who suffered a beating this past week, has friends in high places. He apparently felt you had, in some way helped him and is repaying that favor. To my way of thinking, you owe him big time. You'd more than likely, spend quite a while here waiting for your trial and perhaps the arresting officers might not have been so unsure of their evidence. Either way, you're free to go. But, with your track record, you'll more than likely, be back to visit with us again. I would encourage you to think twice before you undertake any activities that might run you afoul of the authorities. The chances of you being locked up again with someone like your past roomie and getting this kind of treatment again are pretty slim. Simply put, stay out of trouble."

"I'm a new man, Warden. I promise you. I'll never be a guest of yours again."

The guard led Earl to the prison's inmate discharge station and opened up the twelve-foot-high chain link gate leading out to the street. A prison van waited curbside for Earl. The entire episode had a profound impact on Earl and motivated him to take his life in a totally different direction from that day forward.

❧

Late in the day, two New Bern detectives showed up at the Steinbeck's home to interview Jimmy.

"So you're Jim Harrison, known to pretty much everybody in town as Jimmy?"

"That's me."

"I'm Detective Brad Pearson and this is my partner, Detective Wilson Brown. We've been assigned your case. We've read the report, visited the scene of the wreck and heard the tape of your testimony. And, by the way, you certainly have a large following here in town. I don't think I've ever fielded so many calls about one case in my twelve years on the force. You're the only one who ever warranted a call from the State's Attorney General. Apparently, the Governor is fond of you too."

"I'm certainly flattered that so many people want to help me. I never realized I had that many friends."

"You should be thankful. There's a lot of folks singing your praise and trying to help you. There's one big problem with this case as I see it."

"And that would be?"

"Everyone who called, has unanimously stated, there is no way you committed this offense or, should I say, offenses. They all say you're totally innocent, that you aren't capable of such crimes. And yet you maintain you're guilty and that you acted alone. You still sticking with that story?"

"I am. I've got no reason to lie about it."

"Then, if you don't mind, would you be willing to come outside to our squad car and just prove to us that you can turn it on, reach the pedals and steer it down the street a little ways? Just to put our minds at rest that this whole thing you're admitting to is even possible."

"I really don't want to do anything like that. Look I'm not trying to be a pain or cause you any problems but the way I understand it, the facts are the facts and I can't be forced to testify against myself. Deputy Moeller called it my Miranda Rights. Am I correct on this?"

"You are. But you wouldn't be really testifying 'against' yourself. You'd be testifying 'for' yourself. That could prove you're innocent."

"How many times do I have to tell you that I am not innocent? This is an open and shut case. I'm guilty. I own up to it and I'm willing to accept my punishment. Case closed."

"Okay, you don't want to go out to the car with us. Will you answer just a couple of questions so that we can satisfy our minds that you're telling the truth."

"I'll try. What do you want to know?"

"To the best of your memory, where was the gear shift located in the Mercedes? Was it on the column or the console?"

"Let's see. I reached down and over to shift it so it had to be on the console. Am I correct? That's right, isn't it?"

"We haven't seen the car yet. We're just going to take your word on these things until we examine the vehicle later today. Can you show us with your hand about how far you had to reach to grab the shifter? Just pretend it's to your right side."

Jimmy made an effort to look to his right and realized he couldn't begin to move his right arm far enough away from his body to even touch a shifter on a console. He took his left arm, twisted his body around and could still reach less than six inches beyond his side. He understood they must know he wasn't capable of doing it.

"I'm having a little trouble with my right arm. More than usual. When I got beat up at the prison, I fell on that side and it's really affected what I'm able to do. What other questions do you have for me?"

"Just two more questions, Mr. Harrison. What color was the interior of the Mercedes? Can you tell us that?"

It was easy for the officers to see Jimmy was racing his mind trying to come up with the right color. He hesitated far too long before he guessed out loud.

"I'm thinking it was tan. Yeah, I wasn't really looking at the seat color. To tell you the truth, I could be wrong."

"Don't know yet, Jimmy. I'm just taking down your answers so we can corroborate them later today when we see the car. Now, last question. The car was off when the police arrived. Did you cut it off when you hit DeVaughn?"

"Hmm, I believe I did. Yes, I'm sure I did."

"Okay, in that case, can you tell us if it had a 'start' button or a key?"

"Funny how hard it is to remember all this stuff. You know, in the heat of the moment you don't notice a lot of these things. I remember being really upset and scared at the time. I just wasn't noticing a lot."

"I'm sure. Even a veteran rescue swimmer, such as your-self, would lose their train of thought at a scary moment like that. I can see it happening."

Jimmy knew he had done poorly and wanted the meet-ing to end.

"Are you done with me yet? Mr. Steinbeck said he didn't want me speaking to anyone without him present but I didn't see what it would hurt to talk with both of you. But I think I'm getting too worn out to think clearly so let's just pick this back up another time. I'm sure I must have remembered a couple of things wrong, so don't hold that against me. I was pretty shook up as you could imagine."

"I think we can see the picture quite clearly after speak-ing with you. We'll leave you now. Mr. Steinbeck has signed for your release so you'll be under his custody and as we understand it. Staying in his home until a trial date is set."

"If I were you, I'd stay tucked in here full-time. What-ever you do, don't go back to Trent Court. There's talk there about you killing the boy. I'm sure you know there's a lot of bad characters there and an excuse like this just gives them fuel for the fire. Most of them didn't even know DeVaughn, but that doesn't stop them from going after you. You were on their turf and you killed someone. You have to stay away from there. Then you can go plead your guilt to a Judge."

As the detectives stood and started walking toward the door, they hesitated and turned back to Jimmy.

"I don't know what you're trying to do here, Mr. Har-rison, but these are extremely serious charges and you can get yourself into a world of trouble by sticking to this story that neither one of us believes is true. But, good luck to you. We're still assigned to this case, so if you decide to change your plea give either one of us a call. Here's our cards."

"You can count on it. It was nice speaking with you both."

The two detectives could only shake their heads as they walked away. Pearson looked at Brown.

"Beats anything I've ever seen. Most of the time they're lying through their teeth swearing they're innocent. This guy is lying through his teeth swearing he's guilty."

❦

A trial date was set for June. The case generated a lot of talk in town and the Governor's direct interest in it assured that statewide newspapers and television stations were covering it. Jimmy refused all offers for an interview and had to give up his job at Mitchell's because of the press camping out there waiting to get a shot of him and maybe an off-guard sound bite. He didn't want to put Greg or the rest of the store's employees through a circus at work.

He laid low at Steve and Elaine's as the trial approached. They'd gotten to know Jimmy even better. He didn't discuss the case with them even though Steve was going to represent him in court pro bono. A week before the trial he approached the issue with him at dinner.

"Jimmy, let's sit here for a while so I can ask you a few questions."

"Okay. I'll answer what I can."

"With me representing you in court, I have to know what really happened that night. You understand there is attorney-client privilege involved here? I can't and won't reveal anything you tell me to another living soul, not even Elaine. It's just between you, me and God."

"I understand."

"My first question is this. Were you by yourself the entire evening on New Year's eve?"

"No. I agreed to close up the store at six so Greg could get away early to go see the fireworks. Later in the day, I was with my neighbors, Joyce and Beatrice. They gave me a sandwich and a glass of orange juice. I stayed with them until about eight. After that, I stayed home by myself till I could hear the fireworks starting. I just wanted to see a few minutes of them and check out the crowd."

"If you were going to the fireworks, why didn't you ride with Greg Smith and his family? He said they asked you and you said you weren't even going. You were tired and you were going to turn in early."

"I was tired and I did intend to go to bed early."

"What made you change your mind?"

"I don't know. I was just curious how many people went to see the fireworks. You know, I got caught up in all the excitement."

"So, you walked down by yourself. Why didn't you use your cart?"

"Too many cars. One of my tail lights burned out and I hadn't fixed it. I was afraid somebody would run over me."

"Everybody who knows you says there's no way you walked over a half a mile in all that traffic and as cold as it was."

"You're proving my point, Steve. I knew I couldn't walk all the way home. I saw this car just sitting there with the motor running. I was only borrowing it just to go half a mile. I would park it on Eden Street about a half a block from my place and nobody would be the wiser. I never intended to hurt anybody in any way but I didn't want to freeze to death. How much simpler can I make it?"

"At that time, you didn't realize the car belonged to your old rival, Morrison Brooks?"

"I wasn't thinking about anything like that. In fact, I didn't even remember Brooks had a Mercedes. I'm not impressed with that sort of car. Give me a Vette any day."

"Jimmy, if that's the story you are sticking to, that's what I'll do. I don't believe it myself, but you wouldn't be the first client to lie to me. I've been doing this a long time. It's totally apparent to me that you're covering for someone. There are times when a person pleads guilty to a crime that everyone knows they didn't commit. They know a few facts from the newspaper and just spit them back out when they're questioned. The facts come out and it's readily apparent they were never at the scene of the crime and perhaps they have some sort of mental problem. The court won't look at you that way. You were there when the police arrived, only moments after the wreck. No one else was there. You say it was you and, other than lots of people saying they don't believe you would or could do it, there's nothing to say it wasn't you. Other than common sense, of course. Look, I'm not going to push you on this anymore but as your attorney, I have to warn you that a guilty plea will most certainly guarantee you will be going to prison for a very long time. The minimum sentence I could probably get you for grand theft and involuntary manslaughter will have you doing at least five years. Are you really willing to do that? You've seen what prison is like."

"I'll just have to get used to it. They did have cable TV, a library and a rec yard. Not to mention a pretty good cafeteria. Three squares and ESPN. I don't see a whole lot to fuss about."

"You are one tough nut to crack."

"I'll consider that a compliment. Is there any more iced tea? Elaine makes it just like my mother did. Only women who grew up in the south know how it's done proper."

Morrison Brooks buried his head in his hands as he sat in his plush office. It was late in the day and the rest of the staff had already left the building. His drinking had taken one life and ruined another. He never saw how far off course his own life had gotten until it was too late. He didn't like where he was, but he couldn't see any choice left to him other than keep his mouth shut and try to stay away from the bottle. He had no urge to go home or even see Kay that evening. If there was a feeling that summed him up right then, it would be defeated. He was depressed too, but determined to try and correct the destructive path he was on. His reflections were interrupted with a phone call.

"Morrison?"

"Yes, who's this?"

"Jim Harrison."

"What do you want? I'm not in much of a frame of mind to talk right now."

"I'm sure you're not. But, that's your problem. I want you to drive over to the parking lot behind Mitchell Hardware. The store's closed now and we can meet without anyone seeing us."

"What do you want to talk about?"

"Just meet me there in thirty minutes."

"Okay, I'll be there."

Morrison realized he'd have to defer to whatever Jimmy asked of him. His choices were almost nonexistent at this point.

It was dark by the time Morrison pulled into the otherwise empty lot. Lights flashed on and off twice from a golf cart parked on the loading pad behind the store. It was pulled up tight against the building. Jimmy walked over to Morrison's car.

"Thanks for coming over, Brooks. We need to have a serious conversation."

"I'm listening. I don't know why. The last time I listened to you, it ruined my life."

"At that moment, you'd already ruined your own life, not me. Truth is, Morrison, you're not someone that I could even grow to like. You're an alcoholic and it's really taken a toll on your character and everyone around you."

"Yes, I'm an alcoholic. I admit it. I'm not proud about what I am. But I haven't had a drop since the accident. If I can hold things together, I'm not going to ever have another."

"That's a good start, but if history means anything, alcoholics don't have a good track record when it comes to quitting and staying quit. I'd like to think you'll be able to stay dry, but I have my doubts. I'm sure you've been a real shit to a lot of people, not just me. I wouldn't care what happened to you if it weren't for Kay. I want her to have a decent shot at life and I've taken some steps to make certain you stay clean, for her sake."

"What kind of steps are you talking about?"

"There's someone else besides us who knows every detail of what happened to Dee. It's someone who is completely trustworthy. This person will be watching you from here on out. If you go back to the bottle or hurt anyone else while you're chasing your own demons, it's over. You'll be outed and you can join the rest of the drunks with failed lives who are dead or in prison. It doesn't have to happen that way. All you have to do is stay sober and be good to Kay. You'll have a good career, a great marriage and a solid homelife. That's an excellent return on your efforts I'd say."

"It's going to happen. I don't want to go back to how things were. It was ruining my life and I know it."

"I see you've gotten a new car. A Beemer? Nice."

"I couldn't bear to look at the Mercedes even after it was repaired. I got this one to replace it."

"Pretty nice replacement package."

"If an attorney doesn't look successful, nobody will want to do business with them. I know it's shallow, but that's just how it is."

"Hey, I'm glad you've got the money to do it. That's another reason why I'm here."

"You're going to shake me down? Tell the court what happened if I don't pay you?"

"I'm sorry you think that way about me, Morrison. Your money is something that doesn't mean anything to me. It couldn't solve any of my problems. But it can help solve a few for a person I know. So, here's what I want you to do. No is not an option."

Virginia and Norah absorbed every small detail of Jimmy's situation they could obtain from every source, except Jimmy. He hadn't called since his release and it was upsetting Norah dramatically. Several times Virginia went to Mitchell's to see what Greg Smith knew. The only news was the fact that Jimmy was sticking to his story and would be pleading guilty. No one who'd ever known him believed Jimmy had stolen a car and struck Dee. That is, no one but the court. They dealt in facts and the fact was Jimmy had signed documents asserting that he, and he alone, stole the car and ran over the boy.

About a week before the trial was to begin, Virginia had gone to the grocery store leaving Norah at home. It was a safe neighborhood in a section of town that was heavily patrolled. Many of the city's most prominent citizens lived there. Norah never worried about staying there alone.

It was somewhat surprising to her when the antique bell on the front door rang. The sun was going down and it was close to dinner time. Not the time when people normally come to visit. She wheeled over to the door.

"Hello. Who is it?"

"It's Jimmy, Norah. Can I come in?"

She quickly unlatched the door and let him in.

"Jimmy! Oh, I'm crying. I'm so sorry. It's just that I'm so glad to see you. I've been worried constantly since all this happened. Tell me you didn't steal that car and hit that young boy. I know you didn't do it. You couldn't have. Without the special controls on the dash, you couldn't even drive the golf cart. What's going on? Why are you doing this?"

"That's why I'm here. I'm probably going away for a long time. I don't want to leave you with all these questions. I know how you are and you'll never stop being concerned unless you know what really happened. And besides, you're someone I know I can trust."

"You really think you're going to jail for this?"

"I don't think so. No one knows what's going to happen.

I'm not making any predictions. You do understand that there is no way under the sun I'd ever do anything to hurt anyone."

"I never considered it for a minute. Tell me what happened, please!"

"You'll find out soon. You'll know exactly what happened. More than anyone else. But I can't tell you tonight. It's nothing bad or that will upset you. I know you have faith in me and understand I would never mislead you."

Jimmy reached in his back pocket and pulled out a small stationery envelope. He'd written 'Norah' with a pen on the front.

"This explains every detail. From my motives to my actions. Everything is in here. But you have to promise me you won't open this for thirty days. Promise me that."

"Why do I have to wait? I'm worried sick about you."

"You'll understand when you read it."

"It feels like there's something inside besides a note. And why thirty days?"

"Everything will be settled by then. The trial will be over and justice will have been served. Things will be back to normal and I will have settled everything. But if I'm in prison, I won't be able to get this to you. They censor inmate mail. So, I'm hand delivering it to you now. I just need your word you won't open it till then. No matter what happens."

"I'm not happy about this, but if that's what you want me to do, then you know I'll do what you've asked of me."

"I knew I could count on you. Now give me a hug and

let me get out of here before it gets any darker outside. The cart has lights, but the way everyone drives so fast, I worry they'll run me over before they see me."

Jimmy gave her a one-armed hug and she replied with a kiss on his cheek.

"Be careful, Jimmy. I don't think I could take it if anything happened to you."

"Trust me, it's all going to be better soon."

Virginia came back about thirty minutes after Jimmy left. Norah wanted to tell her what had occurred, but she knew her sister would plead with her to open the envelope right away so Norah kept it to herself.

There was one other monumental task Jimmy felt he must complete before the trial started. He'd been warned not to venture back to Trent Court, but there was unfinished business that had to be done. He needed to see Joyce and Beatrice. As hard as he knew it would be, he felt he had to face Dee's mother, Cecille. Without telling her the entire story, he needed to give her some assurance that he would never hurt Dee.

He couldn't drive his recognizable cart to Trent Court so he called Greg and asked if he would take him to his old apartment for about an hour. Greg readily agreed and came by the Steinbecks' around 7 p.m. Jimmy thought Cecille would surely be home from work by then and there'd be no chance of missing her.

He had to be careful as he exited the car and walked across the lawn to Joyce's apartment. Handicapped white man limping across Trent Court would be too easily recognized and the situation would ignite into immediate mayhem if anyone detected him there. Greg agreed to come back to the drop off spot in exactly one hour. Jimmy knocked on Joyce's door.

"Lordy, Beatrice, come see who is at the door. Come on in, darlin'. I tell you what, Jimmy; we have worried about you and prayed for you nonstop ever since you made up that story about you stealing that car. You might fool some of the people, but we didn't fall for it, not one bit. We know you better than that."

"What about Cecille? She must hate me."

"She's angry and upset more than words can say. Trust me, she knows you didn't steal the car or drive into Dee. She just wants to know who did what. She's trying to deal with it, but I know she wants to hear it from you. Let me go get her."

"Please. That's one of the reasons I'm here. I wanted to see you, Beatrice and her. I only have an hour."

"I'm on it, darlin'. I'll be right back with her."

In less than two minutes, Joyce brought Cecille back into the apartment. Jimmy stood up to speak with her but, before he could utter a word, she came over to him and burst out crying. She hugged him so hard he could barely breathe.

"Tell me, Jimmy. Tell me just what happened that night. Who was it that killed Dee? I've got to know."

"I want to tell you all exactly what happened, but there are a few things I can't tell anyone."

"What do you mean? The truth is the truth. My Dee is gone and in the ground. I had to go to the welfare people to get the money to bury him. This has been the worst thing I've ever lived through. I wish I was walking beside Dee when he got hit and it took me with him. I don't think I'll ever get over it. Who was it that did it? You've got to tell me. This can't go unanswered. I can't go on if I don't know what happened. You know, Jimmy. You know everything. Why won't you tell me?"

"Cecille, come sit over here by Beatrice and I'll tell you what I can and explain why I can't tell you everything."

Jimmy took a long pause and a deep breath.

"You're right. It wasn't me who stole the car."

Joyce interrupted.

"We knew you didn't do it. We knew right off it wasn't you. We want to know who it was."

"There is a person I have loved all my life. She's someone I'd give my life for in a heartbeat. We can't be together because of my physical problems. You know I will be handicapped for the rest of my life. It was something I didn't want to burden anybody with. My problems would only bring her down. I would never do that to her. She deserved better. After we split up, there was a person who came into her life that seemed to make her happy again. At least I thought this person could. That person was driving the car that night and fell asleep at the wheel."

Joyce could sense they weren't getting it all. She spoke up.

"And can we assume this person had been drinking?"

"Perhaps, but I really don't know how much. It was late and most everybody would have been tired by then. Either way, I want so much for the woman I love to have a chance at a good life that I felt I took the blame for this, it would still work out for her. No one else was close to the scene. I ran him off and when the cops came and I told them I did it. It would do no good to ruin his life and hers. My life is already ruined. No one, except for you, Cecille, misses Dee more than I do. He was the high spot in my day, every day. I wanted so badly for him to make something out of his life and help you. I know he would have lived a great life and looked out for his mother. I can't replace that. I would if I could. But I do have something that I hope will ease some of your burden. I told this person he had to do this for you and he willingly agreed. He understands the hurt his actions have caused. He's not a mean person. He would have totally taken the blame for this if I hadn't forced him not to. He did what I asked to protect this woman we both love. He'll live with this guilt the rest of his life. He knows that. There won't be a day when he wakes up that he won't think about this, all the hurt he's caused by his actions. He wanted to do this. This is a cashier's check. There's no name on it but yours. It's enough to help you get a new start. That's what Dee wanted more than anything, to help his mother get away from two jobs and no way to pay all the bills. This check will, hopefully, help you with that. It's for one hundred thousand dollars. It cannot and will not replace Dee. But, in a way, he's responsible for you having it."

"Oh my word…I just don't know what to think. What about you? Aren't they trying to put you in prison? I don't want that happening to you. That would be just one more thing about this whole nightmare that ain't right."

"Not going to happen. I have the best attorney in the city working on it and he promises me that I'll wind up getting probation. He says the last thing the State wants is having to take care of somebody with all the health problems I've got for the rest of my natural life. I'll keep you all in the loop with what's going on but you gotta promise me that what I've just told you all is just between us, no matter what. Let me say that again, 'no matter what happens'."

Joyce responded.

"I promise that no one will ever hear about this from me or Beatrice. And you, Cecille?"

Cecille considered her words for a moment and answered.

"Jimmy, you were the only man in Dee's life and I always thought you were wonderful to him. You were a good example of how a person should live and how they should treat other people. There's no way I could do anything that would hurt you. You can count on me to keep this our secret. And, I don't know how you got me all this money, but every bit will be going to a good purpose and I thank you from the bottom of my heart for coming over here to tell me these things. I know this has to be terrible for you. I love you just like Dee did."

"And I love all three of you. It was a great day when I found myself living near you all here at Trent Court. Who would've thought this place could bring us together? No matter what happens to me in the future, I want you all to know how special you are to me. Well, I guess that's about enough tears and confessions for one evening. I think I see my ride out front. Please, you all be good to each other."

"We will darlin', we will."

✍

The trial date approached quickly. The day before was ominous with a dark threatening sky and the forecast of a coastal storm approaching by noon. There was already a light mist in the air and clouds overhead appeared to be on a mission moving in a west to east fashion at a fast pace. Steve, Elaine and Jimmy sat at the breakfast table.

"Pretty rough looking outside. I've got to go into town for a couple hours this morning. I need to go through the mail, make a deposit, and go speak with the D.A. about your case. You're still set on the same course?"

"Yes, sir."

"I just need to be sure because he's already called me this morning. He says to make absolutely sure you weren't willing to change your mind and you know you're looking down the barrel of several years in jail. I'm going to try and get you put on supervised probation. I can't guarantee you anything. I'm going to use your Coast Guard service record and the fact that you've never had a prior conviction for anything. Not even a traffic ticket. And God help the person who has to tell Governor Pollard if this doesn't go our way today. She's not going to be happy."

"Steve, Elaine, I can't tell you how much I think of you both. This isn't half as scary as sitting in the door of a chopper looking down about eighty feet as forty-foot waves roll underneath you and there's folks in the water waiting for you to come get them. Now, that will get your heart racing."

"I'll never understand how you did that or why you're doing this, but I'm heading to the office. Elaine, take care of him and try to talk some sense into him, would you?"

"You're the salesman in the family, Steve. I can make him comfortable and let him know we love him. The rest is up to you."

Steve walked into the District Attorney's office. The D.A. was a tall and striking man. He had the polished look of a politician which was an asset in his profession. The job was political and he handled it well.

"Steve, good morning! Coffee? Tea? Bourbon?"

"It's good I know you're kidding. With this Jim Harrison case, a bourbon would probably help."

"This is a conundrum, isn't it? I've never seen a situation quite like this. And to complicate matters even more, when you leave, we've got to have an answer as to what we're going to do with this young man and call both the Attorney General and Governor Pollard. Please tell me you have some thoughts on how we can handle this. If he goes to court and pleads guilty, the judge is not going to have any choice but to give him the minimum time under standard sentencing guidelines. Then I'm going to have to make those unpleasant calls. It will be like I'm the one pleading guilty. So, what do we do?"

"There is one overriding fact that the court can't ignore."

"And that is?"

"He doesn't have the physical ability to drive any car. He's almost totally paralyzed on his right side. How can somebody who can't lift his right arm start and drive a car that's not specially set up for a handicapped person? He's lying to protect somebody. It's right there for anyone to see."

"Okay, if they can order a defendant to take a blood test to check his DNA, then the Judge should be able to demand that the defendant sit in the car, start it, put it in gear and at least turn it around in the courthouse parking lot. We'll ask the judge to demand he do it."

"And if he refuses?"

"You and I will pick up the contrary, stubborn man and put him in the seat of the car ourselves."

"Hey, if that's all we've got, then that's what we're going to do. Are you on board?"

"Absolutely! Can you tell me again why we became lawyers?"

"I'm not certain anymore. See you in the morning around nine."

"I'll be there when you get there."

It was around one p.m. The weather was deteriorating with each passing hour. Elaine had just fixed a second cup of coffee for Jimmy.

"If I lived here, I'd put on a ton of weight. You've been spoiling me with your cooking."

"I love to cook. Having someone new to try out my

favorites on is fun. You certainly seem to be in a good mood this morning. Seems a little hard to believe really, considering your trial starts tomorrow. Aren't you nervous?"

"Not a bit. I'm thrilled to be getting this all over with."

"Even if you're not worried, I'm worried for you. You've just got to speak up in your own defense. Nobody believes you stole that car. You have to tell them what happened, Jimmy, and then get on with your life."

"I'll do what's right. I'm in a good place about it. I am a little concerned about my sailboat, *Sugarcane*, though. There's a big blow coming this afternoon and I haven't checked her lines in a month. The marina isn't far from here. I don't even have to cross the river. I can just stay on Madam Moore's Lane and be down there in ten minutes on my cart. I think I'll run down there and check on her. I'll be back in a couple of hours, hopefully for that dinner you're cooking. Can't wait."

"Ok, but you be careful on that road. People come flying through here like it's a racetrack."

"I always act like every car is going to hit me. Pays to drive defensively, even on a golf cart. See you in a little while."

"Listen, it really looks like the bottom is going to fall out any minute. If it starts to rain, you pull your cart off the road and call me. I'll come get you and we can go back and get it later."

"Will do. I think I've got the time to do what I need to do."

15

JIMMY PUT ON a rain jacket with a hood, opened up the side curtain on his cart and took off. Elaine's warning about watching out for cars on this stretch of road was on target. It was a winding road and most of the cars were speeding. He drove on the same side of the road as if he was in a car. They'd come up behind him at a high rate of speed and hit the brakes at the last minute. If they had to wait more than thirty seconds to pull around him, they'd either flash their lights or tap the horn to make their impatience clear. He'd just smile as they flew by him. He'd think to himself…'they shoulda left a little sooner if it's that important'.

He arrived at the marina around two in the afternoon and went directly into the office to speak with Edgar.

"Hey, Jimmy. Didn't I read in the paper this morning that your trial starts tomorrow?"

"You may have. I don't read the paper. I don't need to

look further than my own backyard to find bad news. That's all the news brings you, more things to depress you. But the trial is the reason I'm here."

"How's that?"

"There's a good chance, with these charges, that I might have to do some time."

"You've got to be kidding me."

"No. I did something stupid and I'm going to have to pay the price."

"I truly hate to hear that. If that's the case, don't worry about your boat. I'll pull it out of the water and store it here in the yard for you. No charge."

"That's awful nice of you to offer, but I already have a plan. I have a buddy with a place a little further up the river. He's got a dock but no boat. He said if he could use the boat some, he'd let me keep it there and he'd look out for it. You know, they're always better off being used. Sitting up neglected in a marina is the death of many a good boat."

"That's true."

"I feel bad that I've kept it here for so long and not paid my slip rent."

"You know I'm not worried about it."

"But, I am. Look, I've got a little money here that I brought you."

Jimmy reached in the bib pocket of his overalls and took out a small wad of bills."

"Here's three hundred and sixty-two dollars. I wish it was more, but it's all I have."

"There's no way I'm taking it."

"I want you to. It will hurt my pride if you don't. Besides, I won't be needing money for quite a while. Here, take it."

Edgar took the bills and reluctantly put them in his pocket.

"Consider us even. Your bill here is paid in full."

"I just want you to know, I've kept my boat here for almost ten years. You've always been good to me, a great friend and I'm appreciative."

"Thanks, Jimmy. Please let me know what happens tomorrow."

"I will. Now, I have one last favor to ask you."

"You name it."

"I'm going to go ahead and motor *Sugarcane* to her new home. It's only a mile up river. Won't take me long to get there, but I'll need some help untying the lines. Can you give me a hand?"

"Sure will, but have you seen the weather report? It's gonna be a rough ride even just a short ways upriver today."

"A little wind and waves never stopped me before. I'll go down and get her ready to go. Give me about fifteen minutes and I'll be ready for you."

"Alright, see you at the boat."

Jimmy looked out over the marina as he walked down the rickety pier to *Sugarcane*. This was not a place where people kept million-dollar yachts. This was for people who otherwise couldn't afford to keep a boat and not go broke in the process. He hated to be taking *Sugarcane* away from such a familiar dock, but it was time.

He started the old Atomic Four engine and checked the stern to make sure the water pump was cooling the engine and discharging a stream out the stern of the boat. He gave her a thorough once-over and waited for Edgar. By the time he got to the boat, the engine was warm.

"You ready to go, Jimmy?"

"I am. I want you to just keep the lines on the dock."

"Won't you need them at the new dock?"

"No. My buddy says he's already put new lines on for me. Just give these to somebody who needs an extra line. Some of these boats look like they're tied up with rotten clothesline."

"Tell me about it. I hope this all works out for you, the new dock and the trial."

"Either way, I'm going to a better place."

"Well, that's certainly a good attitude considering that place might be jail."

"It's what you make of it, Edgar. Thanks for everything over the years."

"No problem, my friend. Remember to call me after the trial and tell me how it went. I don't want to just read about it in the paper."

"I will."

Edgar untied the lines that held *Sugarcane* to the dock and pulled them back to the pier. It was blowing pretty hard and a light rain was falling. He watched as Jimmy headed out to the middle of the Trent river. He was surprised to see that *Sugarcane* turned right and headed under the Trent River Bridge instead of upriver. He figured Jimmy just wanted to run her a little bit since he'd probably not be able to use it for quite some time if his prediction of jail time was correct. *Sugarcane* disappeared downriver.

Jimmy steered the small sloop toward the Cunningham Bridge. He turned his VHF radio to channel 13 and called the bridgetender.

"Cunningham Bridge, Cunningham Bridge, this is *Sugarcane*."

"Cunningham Bridge back to *Sugarcane*."

"Yes sir. I'm approaching you from the Trent river. I'd like an opening at your convenience."

"Ok. I'll close traffic down in just a minute."

"Roger. I'll stand by on 13."

Jimmy idled the boat in the turning basin in front of the New Bern Grand Marina just inside the bridge. The siren started to blare and the crossbars dropped on the bridge. The old turnstile bridge had been replaced in recent years with a new drawbridge. The center of the structure would open up vertically with two sections of the road pointing almost straight up. Both spans started to lift up so *Sugarcane* could pass through. Jimmy called to the bridgetender on the VHF.

"Thank you, Cunningham Bridge. *Sugarcane* is clear."

"Okay, *Sugarcane*. By the way, have you heard the weather forecast?"

"I think I have the most recent. Going to be a little rough, right?"

"They're calling for wind steady at twenty-five knots with gusts up to forty. There's a small craft advisory for the Neuse. None of my business what you do, I just wanted to make sure you were aware."

"That's pretty much what I heard. I just got a new storm sail and wanted to try it out for a bit. I won't be out here too long. I'll call you to reopen for me in about an hour."

"Sounds good. Have a safe sail."

"Will do, *Sugarcane* switching back to 16."

Jimmy steered *Sugarcane* into the channel. It was starting to blow hard and the rain was now falling on a sharp angle to the ground. He went under the high-rise bridge that didn't require opening since it had a sixty-five-foot clearance. He continued motoring as he went under and then proceeded another quarter mile down river. He turned the small boat into the wind and idled it. He loosened the jib halyard which he'd secured to the winch in the cockpit. He wrapped it three times around the winch. The winch was self-tending which meant he didn't need to hold onto the loose end of the line that was held by a slot on top. He placed a winch handle into a socket on the top and started turning it with his left hand. Even his left hand had grown considerably weaker over the past year. It was all he could do to turn it. The boat was pointed directly into the wind and there was no tension on the sail other than its own weight. It took almost five minutes to get the sail up and in position to use. In the past that entire operation would have taken less than half that amount of time. He pulled in the jib sheet on the port side of the boat and turned downriver so the wind could fill the sail. The sail quickly grew taut and *Sugarcane* heeled to port. He bent down and hit the kill switch for the motor and turned the ignition key to the off position. He sat back up, held the tiller tight with his left hand and looked out in front of the boat.

There were parallel streaks all over the surface of the river indicating the wind direction and its strength. They only appeared when the wind speed exceeded twelve knots. There was almost double that amount of wind now.

With only the working jib in place to catch it, the boat was racing ahead and was on the edge of having up too much sail for the conditions. Jimmy tightened the collar of his thin rain jacket. The chill factor had to be in the low fifties with this much wind. It was unusually cold for June. The sky was dark and more black clouds filled the horizon further down river.

No one knew what weather conditions on the Neuse could be like better than Jimmy. He'd experienced the best and absolute worst it had to offer more times than any prudent sailor would ever claim. There was a good reason there were no other boats on the river this afternoon. It was only going to get worse.

He passed the last narrow spot in the river where the green marker indicated the entrance channel to New Bern. The waves continued to build. *Sugarcane* groaned as she put her shoulder into the waves striking her from the starboard side of her bow. The wind was slightly in front of amidships as she beat into it. The bow rose up and down with each wave and generated a loud slapping sound after each rise when she dropped back down into the next wave. Strong spray washed over the entire cockpit hitting his face with water that was actually warmer than the air temperature. There was no fear on his face. He smiled as his little ship continued to hold a straight course down the middle of the river. Over the next two hours, the conditions continued to deteriorate. As he approached the Minnesott Beach Ferry crossing, the seas began to worsen. He'd always called this section of the river, Little Cape Horn, because it took a turn to the north and was pinched in, making it considerably narrower. This caused the waves to speed up and grow steeper. He was startled to see a boat pounding toward him. It was about twenty-five feet long and moving at a rapid pace. It would jump off the top of one wave and into the next one generating a huge mass of white bow spray that virtually hid the boat each time. He noticed from the lettering on its side it was a commercial tow boat. With a red light spinning on the center console, it had apparently been called to help a boat in distress. It wasn't hard to believe that any boat out in these conditions that wasn't over fifty feet long would be in distress. Dangerously rough was the best description of what was occurring. The tow boat called him on the radio.

"White sloop headed downriver at Minnesott Ferry

crossing. This is the tow boat off your port bow. Do you copy?"

"This is the white sloop, *Sugarcane*. Go ahead."

"*Sugarcane*, let's switch to 14."

"*Sugarcane* switching to 14"

"*Sugarcane*, you copy?"

"Roger that, *Sugarcane* here."

"I just want to let you know, it's far worse down river. I just came out of Oriental. It's blowing a steady thirty-five knots and seas are close to five feet and breaking. It's no place to be sailing right now. You might want to turn around or put in at the marina by the ferry landing."

"Roger that, tow boat. I appreciate your concern. I'll take it under advisement and make a decision soon. You take care yourself."

"I will. Please heed my advice. It's dangerous out here."

"Consider me warned. *Sugarcane* out"

The tow boat quickly disappeared behind *Sugarcane*. Jimmy never altered course. He continued straight down the middle of the river. He'd been here in awful conditions before to help boats in distress, but never on *Sugarcane* and certainly not for pleasure.

Sea water was building up in the cockpit floor. There was a drain on each side of the cockpit floor but water was coming over the rail and inside quicker than the scuppers could remove it. His grip on the tiller was weakening and the pain in his arm was becoming more than he could deal with. He raised the tiller up into the air a little higher and held it between the side of his chest and the underside of his arm. This gave his wrist some relief but meant he had to stand up in the cockpit as he steered. It was a struggle just to remain on his feet in the violently rocking boat. The waves were burying the bow constantly as it pounded through them. Even though the boat was exceeding its hull speed in the high winds, it would shudder and almost come to a dead stop as it drove into sheer walls of water. It was not only growing darker by the moment from the storm clouds that were choking out any light, it was almost seven p.m. and dusk was turning into night. The wind howled. The waves were as big as Jimmy had ever seen on the Neuse.

He was nearing the mouth of the river where it emptied into the Pamlico Sound. The Sound was a large inland sea notorious for the rough conditions it could generate in conditions such as it was experiencing at the moment. Jimmy understood what he was heading into. Wave heights would increase dramatically as he entered the Pamlico. The wind was moving further toward the bow of the boat and Jimmy had to veer another twenty-five degrees to port to keep the boat from heading into the wind. That would cause him to lose steerage and the boat would be left to the mercy of the waves and in danger of broaching as it stopped between them. This turn to port brought another concern to *Sugarcane*. It meant she would have to sail close to the wind and that placed her in danger of running aground at Maw Point.

Many a vessel had met an inglorious ending on this shoal. The shallow bar caused the waves breaking over it to become towering waterfalls crashing with tons of weight onto any boat unfortunate enough to wind up over its sandy bottom. When a boat couldn't maintain safe distance from shore because of the wind, it was called a lee shore. It had been a danger since the first sailors took small wooden ships to sea. The terror caused when sailors saw breakers hitting bottom directly off their side as they were blown toward them was legendary.

Jimmy tried to hold the tiller firmly as the ferocious storm winds kept pushing the bow toward the shoal. He didn't know if he could make it to the deeper water just on the other side. It would be a close call. He watched as the breakers drew ever closer. The sound of waves hitting bottom was unmistakable. It was like being on shore as breakers hit the beach. He kept one eye on the waves and the other on the depth sounder mounted just in front of the cockpit. The water depth kept decreasing, slowly at first and then speeding up as *Sugarcane* began to feel the first breakers hitting her on her starboard side. Eight feet, seven, six and then the entire boat shuddered. She lurched, bounced and then leaned dramatically onto her port side as she ran out of enough water to float. All forward progress stopped immediately. Breaking seas exceeding ten feet began taking their turns crashing completely over *Sugarcane's* side. He understood fully what was happening. He released the tiller and sat down on the high side of the cockpit. Two or three waves pounded him as he sat there. Finally, a vertical wall of water hit *Sugarcane*, lifted her up and then dropped her hard on her side. As she struck bottom Jimmy went airborne and then over the side. He'd never put on a life jacket. He watched from several yards out as the seas pulled him away from his beloved boat. Their lives both ended on the same day.

16

Steinbeck Home – Later that night

THE STEINBECK HOME had become an emergency control center. Everyone who knew Jimmy and was concerned about him gathered there. Steve was on the phone. He hung up and turned toward them.

"The Coast Guard hasn't had any distress calls from Jimmy. They were as shocked as we were that he'd go out in these conditions. They all know him and say this isn't something he'd do. He's smarter than this."

The situation was becoming clearer to Elaine.

"No question Jimmy wouldn't do something this foolish by accident. He was in a great mood this morning. Said he had everything figured out; not to worry about him. He took his small sailboat and headed out into a violent storm. He knew the conditions. There's no accident here. He knew exactly what he was doing. There won't be any trial tomorrow. The trial has already been held. Jimmy won. He went out his way, on his own terms. Even as crippled as he was, he took that little boat out into the storm. He was one incredible young man."

⁊

Three days passed with no word on Jimmy. Along the banks of the Neuse, a waterman was checking his crab pots just inside Maw Point. The water was smooth and flat with no indication of the nightmare that had occurred there just two days prior. He noticed a white hull lying a few yards from shore about a quarter of a mile away. He put his motor in gear and took the flat-bottomed work boat over the shallow water to see what happened to this boat. Sometimes rough storm waters breaking on the sand would uncover old shipwrecks buried for many years.

He pulled alongside and could see the name *Sugarcane* on its stern. It was half buried in sand. The cockpit and cabin were completely full of water. A closer look revealed a huge hole in the bottom where seawater gushed in freely. The inside was a total wreck with settees broken free from the interior and all the ports pushed through. There were no barnacles or growth on the hull, so the crabber figured it was a recent wreck. He called the Coast Guard at nearby Morehead City.

"Yes, Coast Guard, this is Sam Pritkin. I was over here at Maw Point checking my crab pots and found a wrecked sailboat. Nobody on board. About thirty feet long I'd say. Got a name on the back. It says *Sugarcane*."

"That's a boat we've been looking for. No one near it?"

"Not that I can see."

"We're going to send out a cutter. Can you hold your position until it gets there?"

"If you don't take too long. I'm trying to make a living here."

"They're on the way. Should be there in about an hour."

"I'll work some traps close by and keep an eye out for 'em. Be sure to bring along a dinghy or something that'll float in a foot of water. This thing's almost on the beach."

"Affirmative. Coast Guard Morehead City, out."

∽

Union Point Park – Sunday, June 23, 2013

A large crowd sat in chairs placed in rows under the gazebo. The day was beautiful. The sun was out; a light breeze filled the air. Children could be heard playing on the swings across the park. The Cunningham Bridge, just a few hundred yards away, opened now and again letting sailboats and large powerboats pass through.

Greg Smith and the staff of Mitchell's took almost an entire row. There were numerous people Jimmy befriended during his time at the store and a few old family friends who had known him and his mother for many years. There was also a contingent from the media covering the memorial due to all the publicity the New Year's Eve incident had received. The Steinbecks, Joyce, Elaine, Cecille and other friends filled the third row.

Several rows behind them, wearing dark glasses to hide a virtual waterfall of tears, Kay sat next to Morrison. He, above all others, knew everything that led up to the service unfolding in front of him. He was the custodian of a secret he would carry to his grave. If he could do it all over, he would have gladly revealed the truth and his involvement in the wreck. If he did, there would certainly be a huge penalty to face. Now, if he revealed what he knew, it would make Jimmy's sacrifice unnecessary and futile since it was done for Kay, not himself. If that's what Jimmy wanted him to do, he'd have to live up to his promise. It was a burden to carry for the rest of his life.

Kay listened intently to every word as she wrapped her fingers around the diamond hanging on the end of a gold chain around her neck. Only she knew the origin of the tiny jewel. She gripped it tightly as her face became streaked with tears that only someone dealing with such a profound loss could ever feel.

Virginia and Norah sat at the end of the front row. Virginia was in the last chair and Norah beside her in her wheelchair. Norah showed her strength and smiled as she heard the tributes for Jimmy. Throughout the service she held the small white, unopened envelope in her lap. She would wait to read it just as she'd promised.

Paul Canady from Christ Church stood behind a podium and spoke into a microphone.

"I know all of you here today knew and loved James Robert Harrison, or Jimmy as his friends called him. He led quite a remarkable life. He thought of these waters surrounding us as his home. He lived on them, flew above them and eventually died in them. He was born here in New Bern. He went on to become one of the Coast Guard's most decorated rescue swimmers. I don't believe there's a more dangerous job in the world; to go out into the eye of the storm and retrieve people facing a certain watery grave. Who here today could jump into those turbulent waters? The Coast Guard rescue swimmer's motto sums it all up from my point of view. 'So others may live.'

I told Jimmy, not too long ago, that the Bible speaks of this in John 15:13. It says simply that 'Greater love hath no man than this, that a man lay down his life for his friends.' And now he's gone, taken by the sea that he loved so much. We'll miss him, but we need to learn from his life that no matter how far down our problems may bring us, there is a much higher calling that some of us choose to answer. Jimmy was always there to answer that call."

There wasn't a dry eye in the crowd. Governor Pollard was the next to speak.

"I knew Jimmy and his mother. I knew him most of his life. He was always what I would call a "yes ma'am, no ma'am" type of young man. He had respect for everyone. He valued every life. And I would hope that in his passing, he leaves a lesson for other young people about serving others and going all the way in for what you believe. He taught me the value of life and how a life can be changed profoundly in an instant as it happened for him. But, for Jimmy, only his exterior was changed. Inside, he was always the same person who was willing to lay down his life for others and he held firm to all he believed. I've thought about his passing a lot this week. It's helped me make the decision to leave Raleigh and not run for another term. I'm coming home to the place I love, New Bern. We never know how many sands are in our hourglass. We don't want to run out of time before we run out of life. On behalf of New Bern and North Carolina, I want to thank Jimmy for all he meant to us. You will be remembered in our hearts always."

As the Governor stepped away from the podium, a distant rumble became a loud roar overhead. Coast Guard Helicopter 2 from Coast Guard Station Elizabeth City maneuvered directly off Union Point and hovered overhead. The side door was open. As it remained stationary about thirty feet off the dark waters of the Neuse, Bill Flynn lifted up a wreath. He paused for a moment before respectfully dropping it over the side and into the river. Bill looked down as it drifted on the surface of the water.

"Goodbye, old friend. You lived the good life. We'll miss you and do our best to make you proud."

The chopper grew louder as its engines increased power. It moved forward, banked to the left and headed back down the Neuse. It was the final act of respect to remember a fellow Coast Guardsman and friend.

⤳

EPILOGUE

DESPITE AN EXTENSIVE search, Jimmy's body was never found. Even a strong healthy swimmer couldn't survive the conditions on Maw Point on the evening *Sugarcane* went aground.

Bill Flynn had his own ideas about what occurred. He knew Jimmy well enough to know that he'd never have been in the mouth of the Neuse River in those conditions without a life jacket on. Jimmy had preached about the importance of always wearing a life jacket to everyone for years. If he had been wearing one, his body would most likely have been found. To Bill, that left only the possibility that Jimmy didn't want to survive the grounding.

Having seen the life Jimmy was living first hand, he was satisfied that this was not an accident. He would most certainly have known what the conditions were around Maw Point in a severe storm. Bill thought the most remarkable part of the entire episode was the fact that Jimmy, as handicapped as he was, could sail *Sugarcane* the forty or so miles from New Bern to Maw Point in such horrendous conditions. Just knowing Jimmy, he had to smile when he thought about it. He surmised, that even though he was crippled, he was a tough character to the end.

When Hurricane Irene came ashore in August 2011, it set the 500-year flood record in New Bern. Being only a Category One storm by the time it got to the city, the winds weren't that severe. However, it brought flood waters with it not seen in the area for centuries. Everyone said it was the worst in history and would never be topped. That prediction proved dramatically incorrect less than ten years later as Hurricane Florence exceeded Irene's flood waters by several feet in September 2018. Damage was extensive throughout New Bern and surrounding areas. Again, everyone said "this could never happen again".

Greg Smith continued to run Mitchell Hardware. He still greeted everyone who entered the store with his trademark smile. One morning in January 2018, he suffered a massive heart attack while unloading a delivery truck on Craven Street in front of the store. He died instantly. His passing made the front page of the Sun Journal. The entire town mourned his passing and the crowd was so large for his memorial service that it had to be held in the Convention Center where there was standing room only. His two daughters, Lindsay and Winnie, took over the store after he died and manage it to this day.

True to her word, Becky Pollard served only one term as North Carolina's first female governor. She retired to her home on the Trent River just outside of New Bern city limits. She still attends Christ Church most Sundays and often reminisces with friends about Jimmy Harrison.

Paul Canady continued to be the presiding priest at Christ Church. He had many discussions with those who knew Jimmy and was often reassured by the statements Jimmy made leading up to his death. He felt that, in his final gesture, he truly believed he was going to a better place. If he had any thoughts as to who Jimmy was willing to sacrifice everything for, he kept them to himself.

Perhaps the most remarkable turn of events after Jimmy's passing involved Earl Watson who was elected Sherriff of Jones County, twice. Apparently, Earl was considered by most of the county's residents, the most qualified for the position after his many years of dealing with the law. By all accounts, he was one of the most loved and effective law enforcement officers the county ever produced.

Kay and Morrison Brooks were married the spring after Jimmy was lost. To those who knew them both, it didn't seem like a marriage with a 'meant to be' foundation. They both had their careers. Morrison became a senior partner in a law firm and Kay went on to become a well-respected District Court Judge. They had two children; the oldest a girl named Anne and a boy, they named Jimmy. Kay never brought up the issues surrounding the theft of Morrison's Mercedes that evening. Undoubtedly, with her legal intellect and reasoning, she would carry with her, doubts about what occurred that night. She wore her small diamond necklace every day for the rest of her life.

Steve and Elaine Steinbeck retired to a home in Fair-field Harbour, a short distance from downtown and across the Neuse River Bridge. With no other surviving family, Jimmy's folded American flag was given to them at his memorial service. They kept it in a place of honor in their home and many nights they'd sit together on their porch talking about Jimmy and the heartbreaking turns his life had taken. They were forever grateful for the unselfish sac-rifice he made to save them and yet always sad that such a tragedy started him down a path that ended on a shoal at the mouth of the Neuse River.

Bill Flynn went on to become one of the most respected Coast Guard Rescue Swimmers of his day. He served for roughly a decade after Jimmy was lost. Not surprisingly, after his retirement, he moved to New Bern. He married a retired school teacher named Roberta and established a second career as a building contractor.

Buddy Jewell remained on the West Coast after two tours at Kodiak, Alaska. Every couple of years, he, Bill, Chuck Hutaff, Phil Hewett and a couple of other guys who served with Jimmy, would have a reunion back in New Bern. Over a few beers, the re-telling of Jimmy's rescues would grow ever more dramatic. His escapades had become those of legend in the Coast Guard.

One month to the day that Jimmy disappeared, Norah opened the envelope Jimmy had given her. It had been difficult to leave it sealed but she made a vow to him and she kept it. Her bent hands struggled to open it. Inside, she found a small handwritten note and Jimmy's Lifesaving Gold Medal. The writing, like the front of the envelope was shaky with blue ink. It read:

"Dearest Norah. By the time you ready this, I have passed on. I gave you this note because you're the person I trusted the most of anyone I've ever known. I felt as though we had a special bond with all we had in common. Only someone who has also been confined inside a body that no longer functions could ever understand what you've suffered with for your entire life. I dealt with my infirmities only a short while compared to you. I have a deep admiration for you never letting your disabilities define you. You couldn't walk, but you smiled constantly. You couldn't sing or dance, but you still loved music more than all those around you. Your positive energy and devotion to those you love is an inspiration. If there is any justice in the universe, we'll one day have that long awaited waltz together."

Norah finished reading the letter and kept her vow to never reveal its contents. She passed away in Lakeview nursing home in February of 2016. As she requested, she was cremated wearing a white linen dress, blue ballerina slippers and holding a small, worn envelope tucked between her hands. The gold medal remained inside. Her sister was on the boat that carried her to her final resting place. As she wished, her ashes were spread over the waters of Maw Point on a beautiful Sunday afternoon.

ABOUT THE AUTHOR

Les Pendleton lives in historic New Bern, North Carolina. His writing style conveys the influence of his career in motion pictures. Many people share their impression that reading his novels feels as if you are watching the characters come to life on the silver screen. Actual locations in coastal North Carolina are featured in many of his books. His writing spans a wide array of genres from action adventure, romance, historical fiction, suspense-filled mysteries and autobiographies. Les spends every free moment with his family and friends sailing in Pamlico Sound and the Atlantic Coast.

For more about the author, visit **www.LesPendleton.com**

❧

Thank you for reading this novel. We invite you to share your thoughts and post a review by going to Amazon.com/author/lespendleton

Essie Press

Made in the USA
Middletown, DE
24 October 2022

13405152R00210